Just One Pucking Night

UNI Lions, Volume 4

Sofia M Kay

Published by Sofia M Kay, 2024.

JUST ONE PUCKING NIGHT

First edition. December 1, 2024.

Copyright © 2024 Sofia M Kay.

ISBN: 979-8230573104

Written by Sofia M Kay.

Chapter 1 – The morning after

Faye Angelica Emmerson

I've always been the good girl. I get good grades; I got into a good university, and I hardly ever lie to my parents. There are very few things about my life my parents would be shocked or appalled by. They know I've had boyfriends. We've had the talk and I know that they trust me.

But if they saw me right this moment, I'm pretty sure they would have some things to say. I have a few things to say to myself.

For the last five minutes, I've tried to understand what happened and where I am. I woke up in a strange bed. As far as I can tell, I'm only wearing my bra and panties. And there's a muscular arm draped over my waist. Not my proudest moment.

My head spins with pain, and my mouth is dry. It's taken me a while to get to this stage of waking up, and part of me wants to just close my eyes and pretend I'm in my own bed. But as I slowly inhale, the scent of the man next to me fills me and distracts me from my fantasy. It's a woodsy vanilla scent that makes it hard to think.

I'm in a room I've never seen before with a man I must have met last night. And I can't remember how I got here. The blanket is only pulled up to our waists, and his muscular back is on full display. I'm itching to run my fingers over it. But instead, I lift my head and try to get a good look at the guy.

His face is turned away from me and I can't make out any features to clue me in on his identity.

Last night was wild. Another thing my parents wouldn't approve of. I should not have been drinking.

But I was celebrating. I reached a milestone well before I thought I would, and my cousin Cora convinced me to take one night and let loose. One night to just have fun. There was drinking and dancing and more drinking. A lot more drinking than I'm used to. I remember having fun and feeling like I was on top of the world.

Then I met a guy. It's all blurry, but it had to be the guy whose bed I'm in right now. And we danced and flirted. His eyes mesmerized me and before I knew it, I was lost.

Ignoring the headache, I hold my breath and try to slide out from under his arm. There's a light snore, and he turns onto his back, freeing me. I wait for a few seconds until I'm sure he's still sleeping. Then I carefully get out from under the blanket.

As I get up and look back at him, my heart stops.

I fucked up.

Oh, fuck did I fuck up. I try to breathe through the panic that's growing inside me and blink a few times. There is no way I'm seeing what I think I am.

The man in bed with me is Liam Greenfield, defender for the UNI Lions, and sexy as fuck. His dirty blond hair is all messed up, and he looks peaceful.

"Fuck." I rub my forehead.

There is no fucking way that I already broke the rules. No fucking way. I start to breathe again and realize I'm in my underwear. I'm in my fucking underwear in Liam Greenfield's bedroom.

How the fuck did I let that happen? Even drunk, I should have known better.

I spin around and look for my clothes. The spinning is bad and I stop and breathe as nausea rises. No sudden movements.

I was all over him in the back of a car. Pressing my fingertips to my temples, I focus on the fragments of memories from the night before. I must have been wasted. I squeeze my eyes shut. We left the club. He ordered a car for us. My cheeks flush. It was impossible for me not to touch him, kiss him. I was all over him. And the way he kissed me back. I remember that clear as day, but I have no idea how I convinced Cora to let me go home with someone. She always looks out for me when we go out.

Slowly shaking my head, I quickly skip over the highly inappropriate touching in the backseat before we stopped.

He must have taken me to his place. There were stairs. Did I take off my shirt on the stairs? That can't be right. What if other people live here?

He was drunk. He struggled to take off his shoes. I laughed at that. And he lifted me up, and we almost tumbled over.

My stomach plummets and I open my eyes again. I need clothes. Scanning the floor, I soon see a familiar pile. Thank god. My pants and shirt are next to the door. I must have had the sense to bring them into the room.

As I quietly get dressed, I'm not sure I want to know what happened after we got into the room. I really wanted him. There's no doubt in my mind that I wanted him. But then, it's blurry. Disappointment.

I pull on my shirt and look at the sleeping man. The attraction was intense, and then there was nothing.

I find my phone and wonder if I should wake him up or leave a note. But that's Liam fucking Greenfield. And I threw myself at him last night. And woke up disappointed. Maybe it's best to forget this ever happened.

No note. And I don't think he ever asked for my number. Not that it's going to be hard for him to contact me.

Nausea rises at the thought, and I make my way out of his room and down the stairs.

Any illusions I might have had about hockey players have been shattered. I've worked with them for years, and when I finally sleep with one, it's not even good.

There's a noise from another room and my heart about stops. He doesn't live alone. And if they find me here, everything I've worked for would be ruined. Liam might forget me if he was drunk enough, but running into someone here and now would be bad.

Feeling like a burglar on a walk of shame, I hurry to the front door, where I find my jacket and shoes. Never have I ever snuck out of a house like this before. I don't do one-night stands. That's not me. I've only ever been with three guys before this and two of those were long-term relationships. Even the third one was a serious relationship. It just didn't last long.

I check that I have all my stuff and step out of the house and into the early morning air. If I'm at all lucky, he won't remember this. Maybe he'll forget he ever saw me and I won't lose the job that I've barely started.

Chapter 2 – No more relationships

Liam Greenfield

A door closes and the sound slams into my head as I squeeze my eyes shut.

Fuck. I drank too much last night.

Again.

Did I bring someone home? Am I home? I open one eye and close it as soon as I've established I'm in my own bed. Was it worth it? I can't even remember.

I turn to my side to get some more sleep, and it hits me.

The scent of roses is faint, but powerful enough to take over every part of my mind. There's something familiar about the scent. And something new.

I've inhaled this scent from someone's neck. Long wavy brown hair covered the neck. She laughed. She was drinking. I took another shot.

My recollection of the events fades away, and the pounding in my head intensifies. I'm pretty sure I hooked up with her. Why else would her scent be on my sheets?

Forcing my eyes open again, I sit up and take a look around the room. My clothes are strewn about the floor, but other than that, nothing seems out of place.

Curiosity gets a hold of me and I crawl over the bed to reach my pants and hopefully my phone. Grabbing it, I settle back under the covers and hope for some clue to this mysterious woman.

Contacts give me nothing. There's no missed call or new message. On a whim, I check my photos.

And there it is. A photo I took of her and me. She looks happy, cute. Like she doesn't have a care in the world. I'm staring at the camera with slightly hooded eyes. I must have been drunk when I took it. My arm is around her shoulders and she's holding a drink, looking at someone out of frame.

Her name? I have no idea. She must have told me. But all I remember is how she smells.

Not that it matters. I don't do relationships anymore. It was one night, and no matter how much I want to see that smile again, I'm not chasing after her. I've learned that lesson the hard way.

Thoughts of Kaitlynn make me wonder if there's any more alcohol in the house. Maybe I can drink away the regret and disappointment if I just keep going.

I look at the photo again and my finger hovers over the delete button. It was just one night.

The scent of roses reminds me of a garden.

I leave the photo and get out of bed.

As I enter the bathroom, I catch a glimpse of myself in the mirror. My eyes are red and I look like hell. I grab some painkillers and down them before hopping in the shower.

What the fuck has my life become?

It's like I'm watching myself spiral out of control and have no power to stop it. It's been a month and a half since I found out what Kaitlynn was like and during that time, all I can think is how fucking bad I am at relationships. If I even get that far. I'm the fucking worst at choosing women.

So I no longer pick and choose. Whatever puck bunny is willing to share my bed, I take home for a night. No feelings or talk of relationships. Just sex.

I carefully shake my head as the water eases the headache. That's all last night was. Another puck bunny that wanted sex. I should be grateful she didn't leave a note or her number somewhere. Hopefully, she's on the same page as me and that's why she left without waking me up.

I get dressed and head downstairs to get some food.

JD is sitting at the kitchen island and I groan a little and hope he's not in captain mode right now. There's only so much I can deal with while hungover.

"Hey," JD says and nods at me over his cereal bowl.

"Hey." I open the fridge and immediately spot some orange juice. The carton is almost empty, so I don't bother with a glass.

"You know we have a game today, right?"

I groan internally. This isn't JD, my friend. This is JD, captain of the UNI Lions, talking.

"I know," I say and toss the empty carton.

"And you still thought it was a good idea to go out drinking last night?"

"I'm playing just fine." I'm in no mood for this bullshit. There's more to life than hockey.

JD scoffs. "No. You're slow and sloppy on the ice, and it's starting to affect the team. Get your shit together, Liam. Before you hurt the rest of us."

He grabs his empty bowl and puts it in the sink.

"Relax, man. I'm better than most on the ice. And it's not like it's going to be hard to win tonight."

I ignore his scowl and walk over to the couch.

"You won't be for long if you keep this up. I get that you had a bad breakup, but you can't let it interfere with hockey. Not like this."

"I'm fine," I say and grab the controller to pick a game. Hoping he'll leave me alone.

The door down the hallway opens and Ethan appears.

"Maybe you can talk to him," JD says and gestures to me.

"What?" Ethan blinks and looks from JD to me.

Bitterness coats my throat and I fight to push it down. I can't be upset with my best friend for finding happiness. Lily is a good woman and they're perfect for each other. But seeing him happy while my life is going down the drain sucks.

"Just talk to him."

JD stomps back upstairs, and Ethan sits next to me and grabs the other controller. He clears his throat.

"So... Did you hook up with another puck bunny last night?"

I shrug. "What if I did?"

"It's not like you, man. I've never seen you like this. With the drinking and fuckboy attitude. You don't usually sleep around like this."

"Does it matter? It's not like the women I fall for are any better."

"That's not true." The hesitation is obvious. And the lie in his voice makes me want to laugh out loud.

"Really? May I remind you of the two women I've gotten somewhat serious with here at UNI. Eve, who basically treated your girlfriend as a slave, and was, overall, a horrible person. And Kaitlynn, who actually thought it was ok for her to hit me because she's a woman. Do either of those sound like good choices? Which one would you want me to end up with?"

"So you made two bad choices. Maybe the third will be better."

"Or she'll be a serial killer who kicks puppies. You got lucky, dude. But not everyone finds that one person. And I'm starting to accept that love isn't for me."

"Listen, Eve was really good at hiding who she was. I had no idea. Without Lily, I still might not know. And Kaitlynn was fucked up. What she did to you was not ok, but that's no reason to give up."

I sink into the couch and focus on the screen. "It is to me."

Ethan sighs. "Fine, then give up on women. But don't give up on your friends and teammates. You're a UNI Lion, and we need you.

We have a real shot at reaching the Frozen Four this year, but only if you stop with the excessive drinking and late nights."

"You know I'm good on the ice."

"Yeah, not as good as me." He elbows me playfully, and I take the opportunity to end the conversation and focus on the video game.

Deep down, I know they're right. I'm jeopardizing the team. But at the same time, it's not like I chose this. My life is fucked up and I'm doing what I can to survive.

Chapter 3 - Girlcode

Faye

After a quick walk back to my apartment, I stop at the door and take a deep breath. Cora is going to have questions. And I'm not sure I have any answers.

Moving in with my cousin was one of the best decisions I made when she came to UNI. She's two years younger than me, but that never stopped her from taking charge and asserting her place. In the six months she's been here, she seems to have gotten a better grip on life at UNI than I've gotten for two and a half years.

The apartment is small with a living room, a kitchen and two bedrooms. As I enter the living room, Cora stops the show she's watching and spins up from the couch. She plants her hands on her hips.

"Faye, we have a girlcode for a reason. You're supposed to message me. What happened to you? I was just about to call the cops or something."

I glance at the spaceship on the screen as I take off my jacket. "Are you watching Firefly again?"

"Yes. But do not distract me. I got back from the bathroom and saw you leaving with some guy. I tried to chase after you, but you just vanished."

Rubbing my temples, I head for the kitchen. "I know. I'm sorry. It was a crazy night." She turns off the TV and follows me eagerly.

"Luckily for you, I managed to find out who the guy was and everyone seems to think he's decent enough, so I figured you went willingly. Especially considering how you were all over each other on the dancefloor."

She smiles broadly at me, no doubt expecting details.

I grab some water from the fridge and find the painkillers. "Yeah, I went willingly," I say when she doesn't stop staring at me.

"So, tell me everything. How was it?"

"Are you sure you're old enough to hear this?" I tease her and swallow the pills.

She rolls her eyes. "Which one of us has more experience?"

I clear my throat and drink some more water. "Did you wait up for me?" She's in sweats and a t-shirt, but it's early for her to be up.

Shrugging, she sits at the kitchen table. "I stayed out pretty late and then I got back and you weren't here."

"You didn't have to do that."

She huffs. "Oh, please. Like my parents would ever forgive me if anything happened to you. Our moms would kill me and lock me up in a basement somewhere. Maybe marry me off to a dentist."

"A dentist? Really?" I smirk and she shrugs.

"And you didn't have to take off without telling me." She crosses her arms and stares at me. "You owe me details, Faye. How was it?"

I grimace. "Honestly, I can't remember much."

"Did he take advantage of you?" The steel in her voice matches the fire in her eyes, and I know she's ready to go to bat for me.

"No, of course not. I'm pretty sure we were both wasted."

"Even so, I'm surprised you even made it to a bed. You did make it to a bed, right?" She gasps. "Faye Angelica Emmerson, did you have sex in the back of a car?"

"What? No. Of course not."

"Oh." Her shoulders slump as if I robbed her of an amusing anecdote.

Honestly, I'm surprised we made it to a bed, too. What I remember from the car ride is feeling the absolute need to be closer to him, to be naked next to him and have his hands all over me. I'm

11

pretty sure his hand was under my shirt while the driver giggled at us.

Liam Greenfield felt me up in a car. The name starts all the alarms ringing in my head again.

"Cora, I fucked up so badly." I bury my head in my hands as I sink into the chair opposite her.

"Why? What's wrong?"

"The guy was Liam Greenfield."

"So?"

"So, he's a hockey player. For the UNI Lions."

Realization dawns on her. "Oh. Yeah, I can see that being awkward with your new job and everything."

"Not just awkward, Cora. It's against the rules. I signed a contract where it specifically said I'm not allowed to fuck any of the players."

"That's the word they used in the contract?" Cora raises an amused eyebrow.

"No. It was way more lawyer-y. It doesn't matter. If they find out about this, I could lose my job."

"Do you think he'll tell them?"

I close my eyes and rub my temples. "I don't know."

"So call him and tell him not to."

"I don't have his number."

She rolls her eyes again. "A number isn't hard to get. You want me to talk to him?"

Carefully, I shake my head. "No. I just... I don't think he knew who I was, so maybe he won't say anything." Tiredness takes over and I roll my shoulders. "I'll just talk to him on Monday."

The thought of going to work on Monday and facing my mistake makes me want to throw up.

"What if he tells someone?" Cora asks quietly.

I try to shrug it off. "Then I guess I need to look for another job."

"This isn't just a job, Faye. This is your dream job." She reaches out and holds my hand. "Maybe nobody will care. And technically, you haven't started the job yet, so it's not like you've really broken any rules."

I laugh mirthlessly. "It would be so typical if I fucked it all up before I even start."

"There's a first for everything." She shrugs with a smile. Then she leans in. "Now, stop avoiding the question. I want details."

I sigh. "There's not much to say. We went to his place, made out in the car. Next thing I know, I'm waking up practically naked with the hangover from hell."

"But was the sex any good?" Her eyes are twinkling, and I want to curse her out for looking so fresh with no sleep. Then again, she didn't drink last night, so she does have that advantage over me.

"All I know is I woke up feeling disappointed." I still can't remember what happened. But maybe that's for the best.

"Aww, man. I thought the hockey boys would at least have some stamina." She looks so genuinely disillusioned I almost feel sorry for her.

"I'm sure some of them do. But for now, I need to sleep. And so do you. Just don't tell anyone about this. With any luck, I can talk to Liam and make him keep quiet." And if I can't, all I have to do is reevaluate my entire life.

"You can always threaten to expose his subpar lovemaking if he talks."

Rolling my eyes, I keep the laugh from bursting out. "I'm not going to blackmail him."

"Then let me. I have no qualms about that."

Cora has no issues being the villain. If it's about protecting me, or any of her friends or family, she will happily burn down the world and face the consequences. But this isn't her fight. Hopefully, it won't be a fight at all.

"No, Cora. I'll talk to him. I'm sure he can be reasoned with."

"The offer stands if you change your mind."

"Thanks."

She heads into her room and closes the door, and I do the same. I still feel like shit when I crawl into bed, but hopefully, a few more hours of sleep will get rid of that gloomy feeling. I put my phone in the charger and let myself drift off to sleep, dreaming of a heavy arm over my waist.

Chapter 4 – Starting a new job

Faye

I'm a professional. Nerves threaten to take over as I view my reflection in the bathroom mirror. I'm at the Den, about to start my new job and meet the hockey players.

Whatever happened this weekend was a one-time thing and is all over and done with. I had too much to drink and made a mistake. But with all the research I did yesterday and the plans I already have, I'm sure I'll be an asset to the team. I'm good at what I do, and the Lions need me.

I check my teeth for lipstick and fix a strand of my hair. With a smile on my lips, I take a deep breath.

I'm ready.

I leave the bathroom and walk across the lobby to where I see JD waiting. He's a familiar face and takes the edge off my nerves.

"JD," I say and he puts away his phone.

"Faye. Good to see you again."

"Thank you so much again for putting in a good word for me. I really appreciate it, and I won't let you down."

"Yeah, no problem." He clears his throat. "Listen, before we go in there. There's something I wanted to ask you?"

"Ok." He looks nervous and for a moment, I wonder if he somehow found out about the one-night stand. Would Liam have told him? Oh, fuck. I should have called him straight away. I need to stop trying to avoid confrontations.

"So, the guys on the team don't know about my photography."

I raise an eyebrow. That's not what I was expecting. I first met JD in a photography class some time ago. We worked on a project together and his girlfriend Morgan modeled for us.

I wouldn't call us close friends or anything, but we occasionally run into each other or let each other know about photography events and things like that.

"They don't? Why not?"

He shrugs. "I just haven't told them. So if you could keep that between us."

"Yeah, sure. Not a problem. By the way, I saw that Morgan's mom is putting on a new exhibit. I was thinking of going sometime this week."

"I think it opens on Wednesday, but you could call Morgan about it."

"Will do."

We start walking towards the parts of the arena the public doesn't get to see.

"Nervous?" He asks when I rub my hands on my pants.

"Yeah. A bit."

"You'll do fine. I've seen your posts, and I know you'll be a lot better than the previous social media manager."

"I hope so."

He shakes his head. "I don't know who thought it would be a good idea to hire a boomer with shaky hands and no concept of what a meme is to run social media for a college team."

A small laugh escapes me and I feel slightly more at ease as we stop by Coach's door.

"Ready?" JD asks and raises his hand to knock.

I nod. He gives the door a few quick knocks before opening it.

Coach Harrison is standing behind his desk and looks up from a tablet as we enter.

"Ah, Ms. Emmerson. Right on time."

"Coach Harrison."

My eyes glance over at the rest of the room. There's a small conference table off to one side surrounded by people.

"I thought we'd just have a quick introduction before we let you get to work." Coach gestures for me to sit and I put on a polite smile as I do.

"I think you've met Will already."

"Yes, at the interview. It's nice seeing you again, Mr. Travis." I reach into my mental notes. William Travis is the assistant coach who leads the defensemen during games.

"This is our equipment manager, Mickey Gordon. Our director of operations, Lloyd McGuire, and one of our trainers, Pat York."

I greet the men and try not to be overwhelmed.

"It's nice to meet you all."

"Welcome to the team," Lloyd McGuire says. "I'm sure you'll be a great asset."

"I will do my best."

JD sits down next to me and I'm glad to have his support.

Coach takes control of the meeting. "Let me quickly go over what everyone does before we talk more about what we expect of you."

He tells me more about each of the people at the table and the ones not able to make it. I know most of the stuff already from the website, but I make sure to ask questions and get clarifications on what exactly it is that they do.

After I briefly introduce myself, the conversation moves on to strategies and goals. Overall, they're ready to give me my freedom and trust that I know what I'm doing. But even so, the discussion takes a while.

"So, what I need for now," I say, referring to my notes, "is access to the team so I can take photos and footage to use. Individual and as a team. Candid photos are great, but they don't really have good, recent professional photos. I think if they could all be available for a photo session sometime this week, that would be a good start."

Lloyd McGuire laughs. "You move fast."

"It's a good idea," Coach says. "The Frozen Four is coming up, and if we get there, all eyes are going to be on us. It won't hurt to have everything look professional."

The rest of the men nod.

"How about Wednesday?" JD suggests. "For the photo session."

Coach nods. "Sounds good. We'll let the guys know to be presentable."

"There is one more thing," Lloyd McGuire says and places his forearms on the table.

My heart jumps to my throat and I'm certain my career is over. "Oh?" I try to sound calm, but my palms are sweaty.

"It's one of the players, Liam Greenfield."

Next to me, JD squirms, and I struggle to keep my breathing even. They can't know. There's no fucking way they know.

I clear my throat. "What about him?"

"Well..." McGuire looks around the table, clearly hoping for support. "There have been some concerns lately."

"What kind of concerns?"

"It's just bad press, you know." McGuire looks uncomfortable. "We don't tell our players how to live their lives, but even Dean Mckinney brought it up to me."

"What exactly did he say?" I ask, my heart beating a million miles an hour.

"Just that he's noticed some students talking about his drinking and... hooking up. It's become a public issue. A PR issue."

"Liam is fine," JD says defensively. "He's just been going out partying a bit more lately."

"I noticed him slacking on the ice," Coach says. "And with everything at stake this year, I think we should consider doing something about it."

"I'll talk to him," JD grumbles.

"Great," Coach says. "And Faye, you can consider this your first challenge. Fix his image."

"There's a rumor that he's flunking out," McGuire says. "Those are not the kind of headlines we want."

I nod and relax. They don't know.

"Great, we all agree that Faye will handle this. I'm sure you know how important it is to look good for the sponsors and future recruits. Now, I think it's time we introduce you to the team."

He gathers his things, and as he gets up, everyone follows suit.

While we walk to the locker room, Coach comes up next to me. "I don't think I have to remind you to keep your relationship with the guys professional. We had a bad experience a few years ago that we are not eager to relive."

"What happened?"

"Let's just say mixing personal issues with business was not a good idea."

With that, he walks ahead of me and I'm left wondering. I've heard rumors of a social media manager that flipped when she was fired and published some things she never should have had access to, but it was all hushed down very quickly.

Chapter 5 – Locker room

Faye

The locker room is modern and, surprisingly, not smelly. Most of the players are already there and my eyes fly across their faces, desperate to find the one person I don't want to see.

But he's not here. My stomach is churning with anxiety as I wait for Coach to introduce me.

"Alright." His voice booms out and every eye turns to him. "Before you hit the ice today, I want you all to meet Faye Emmerson, our new social media manager. I expect you all to behave and make her feel welcome. If she asks you for something, you comply. Is that understood?"

There are some nods and murmurs of agreement across the room.

"Great, I'll let you get acquainted." With that, he leaves and for a moment, I feel like a sheep in a wolf's den. Or a lamb among lions. I swallow hard, then JD steps up next to me.

"You all know that Faye is off limits."

My cheeks flush as he speaks to the room. Someone boos and I shift from one foot to the other.

"I'm not kidding," JD continues. "It's in her contract. Mess with her and you risk her getting fired. Not to mention what Coach will do to you. You treat her like a sister. Got it? You should also know she's a friend to me and Morgan, so I better not hear her complain about any of you."

"Or what?" someone says jokingly.

"Or I'll tell Morgan," JD says, and there's nervous laughter from a few players.

"Fair enough," the first guy says and I notice it's Cayden Marsh, an aggressive forward who spends much too much time in the penalty box.

There are some nods and smirks, but nothing sinister.

JD turns to me. "Do you know everyone's names?"

I study the faces once again. "I think so. Most of them."

"Well, this is Ethan, he lives in the hockey house with me, Jonathan, Dustin and..." he points to each player in turn before looking around. "Liam. But he's not here yet."

My heart skips a beat.

"The hockey house?"

"Yeah, it's become somewhat of a tradition that five players live there every year."

That must have been where I woke up then. In a house filled with hockey players. Hockey players that I'm not allowed to wake up with. Fuck, that was a close call.

"Hi, I'm Pan." A young, blond guy holds out a hand.

"Pan?" I run through the roster in my head.

"Peter Green. They call me Pan." His cheeks redden a bit.

"Why?"

"Peter Pan? The boy who never grows up?"

I look him over again. He undoubtedly looks young.

"Ok."

"It's because I look like a kid. You can call me Pan, too. I don't mind."

"It's nice to meet you. You can call me Faye."

"So what exactly will you need from us?"

"Oh, just some photos and stuff. I'm going to try increasing your social media presence and letting everyone get to know you. I might ask questions or film you when you do everyday things."

Pan nods deeply and I can tell he's absorbing every word I say. "I see. And would you say that's all part of hockey?"

I'm a bit taken aback by his question, but he seems so serious I don't know what to think.

"I mean... Yeah. You're public figures, and if you want to move on to the NHL, then you will need more media training so you're comfortable representing yourself and your team."

He nods and hums.

"Leave her alone, Pan," a deep voice says and I turn to face Cole, a bearded forward that's been known to smile on occasion when he scores a goal. Sometimes. Mostly, he just looks as if he'd rather be somewhere else. "You're not in media training right now."

"Well, excuse me for wanting to learn," Pan mutters and slinks back to his place.

"I don't mind," I say. "I'm here to help you guys out."

The door opens and I hold my breath as I slowly turn to see who it is.

Disappointment and relief mingle as goalie Hudson Ward steps inside.

I keep chatting with the guys and am quickly feeling at ease. Most of them seem to be happy to have a new social media manager, and I don't blame them.

"Please tell me you'll post more interesting things that season stats," Enzo, one of the defensemen, says with a half smile.

"I think I'll manage that." I smile back at him. Apparently, the previous social media manager loved posting boring columns of numbers. Stats are good and all, but not fifteen times in a row with absolutely nothing to spice them up. "How about we take a quick selfie right now?" I might as well get started now that I have access to the accounts.

"Sure." The players all fall in line behind me and I raise the camera and smile.

The door opens again. My entire body freezes. I don't have to look to know who it is.

JUST ONE PUCKING NIGHT

"Liam, get in the picture," JD says, and I quickly lower the phone and pretend to adjust some settings. "This is Faye Emmerson. She's the new social media manager."

I glance up and my stomach flips. It's him. I don't know what I was expecting, but it's really him. That's Liam Greenfield. The man whose bed I woke up in.

"What picture?" he asks and moves to join the others. His eyes look me up and down and... Nothing. His expression doesn't change. Does he not remember me?

I put my smile back on and raise the camera again, trying to get all of them into the frame.

How the fuck can he not remember me? I'm a memorable person. Who slept with one of the players I'm supposed to keep a distance from.

I take a few pictures and pretend that I don't care if he remembers me or not.

"Great. Got it. Thanks, guys. I'll see you on the ice." Before anyone can say anything else, I hurry out of the locker room and make my way to the rink. There are two rinks here at the Den and I take a few pictures of the practice rink in case I need them.

I've never been to a hockey practice before, so I stand by the ice and follow along, trying to memorize everything they do.

The players hit the ice hard. They're fast and strong, and it's a bit intimidating watching them. But as I see more and more of what they can do, I start to notice how Liam is lagging behind. He's still very good at what he does, but he's not putting in as much energy as the others.

Throughout the session, he never even looks in my direction. He is making it ridiculously clear that if he even remembers me, it's as just one more woman in a long line of hook-ups.

It shouldn't bother me. I should be overjoyed with relief. I should be celebrating. But I can't seem to get my thoughts straight. Or my feelings.

Nobody wants to be insignificant. But it's more than that. He's making me feel used and dirty. And I don't like it.

Chapter 6 – The first confrontation

Liam

Practice is torture. My legs feel heavy and my movements are too slow. It's all starting to catch up to me. The late nights, the poor sleep. The drinking. I feel sluggish and weak.

I miss another simple pass and Cole squints at me as I try to shake it off.

"What's up with you, man?"

Shaking my head, I line up to do the exercise again. "Nothing. Just need to get my head in the game."

Cole returns to his starting position, and I take a deep breath. I hate to admit it, but JD was right. I'm messing this up for everyone.

As I take control of the puck again, my eyes stay far away from the woman watching us, taking pictures. She's not supposed to be here. It was a one-night thing.

Determined not to make more of a fool of myself, I adjust my grip on the stick and line up for the next exercise. All around me, my teammates are putting in effort I can barely imagine at this point. And it scares me. I used to care. I used to live for hockey, and now it's just one more thing to get through.

When I walked into the locker room earlier, it wasn't the familiar smells that made me excited. It wasn't the thought of pulling on the skates and getting to spend time on the ice that made my heart beat fast.

It was the faint scent of roses.

Hidden under all the usual smells, it was the one that called out to me, the one that told me what was about to happen, before I even saw her. It made my stomach churn and heart race.

Thank god, JD introduced her before I fucked up in more ways than one.

All weekend, I tried to not think about her, to not care. She was a notch on the bedpost. One of many. And I'll make sure the notches keep increasing. So what if I wondered what her name was? Or who she was. Or what exactly we did before we passed out.

It doesn't matter. Whatever we did, it's over now.

Now that I know who she is, I'm almost glad I can't remember. For the last few weeks, Coach has spoken to us several times, stressing that we are not allowed to get too familiar with the new hire. Not after what happened.

We all know the story. A few years back, the social media manager started dating one of the players. They were hot and heavy for a while. Which brought up smaller issues, such as her posting mostly about her boyfriend.

But when they broke up, all hell broke loose. She became a vindictive bitch and did everything she could to hurt the guy. She posted private pictures, shared information she was not supposed to, and almost destroyed the team.

The boyfriend ended up having to quit hockey because of some of the things she revealed. Which, granted, was not her fault. But it should have been dealt with more discreetly.

It was a complete and utter mess that took weeks to sort out. And none of it reflected well on UNI or the Lions. So now, there's a very strict no dating the social media manager rule.

Which doesn't matter. Because it was a one-time thing. And it's not like she looked happy to see me. If anything, she seemed slightly shocked and mostly disinterested.

Which is fine. I don't care. It's for the best.

They must have told her about the rule. That's probably why she seemed so cold.

My mind struggles against the haze of alcohol from that night. She couldn't have been dissatisfied, could she? Fuck. What if it wasn't good for her? I was pretty drunk.

I spend the rest of the session trying to focus on what I'm doing. The displeasure is growing on Coach's face every time he looks in my direction, and I have a feeling he's going to blow soon.

When he finally tells us it's enough, Ethan comes up to me.

"You ok, man?"

"Fine. Why wouldn't I be?" I glance across the area where she is. Making sure she doesn't notice me watching. She's studying the pictures she's taken, oblivious to everyone clearing out.

He shrugs. "Don't know. You seem quiet."

"Just trying to focus."

I slow down and let the others go on ahead.

"Ok. Let me know if you need anything."

"Sure."

I take my time, pretending to adjust my gear until I'm the last one on the ice.

Too late, Faye notices that she's going to have to walk past me. She hesitates for a second, then she takes a deep breath. Her shoulders straighten as if she's going into battle.

Every step she takes toward me has my heart beating faster.

She stops right in front of me and raises her chin. "I'm surprised you don't remember me." Her eyes lock onto mine and I'm lost.

I raise one shoulder. "Why should I?"

Her face darkens, and her eyes smolder in a way that makes my dick crave her.

"Right, because I was just someone new for you to sleep with."

"Maybe you're not that memorable?" My brain is screaming at me to stop being an ass, but the sucky practice and her confrontational mood have me all worked up.

There's a slight gasp before she recovers. "Well, considering how disappointed I felt when I woke up, I'd say that goes both ways."

Ouch. Low blow.

I move closer so I can tower over her. "I'll have you know I'm excellent in bed. You can ask any of the puckbunnies."

I know I'm rattling her and I love how her breathing picks up.

"How you've managed to pull any of them, I'll never know."

"And yet, I got you into bed." I raise an eyebrow at her.

"That was a mistake. But don't worry, I've learned my lesson and it won't happen again."

"Too scared?"

"Of being disappointed? It's not like there's much to remember, anyway. I could ask a hundred puck bunnies, and it still wouldn't make me any less dissatisfied."

"That tells me I wasn't the problem." Her cheeks have red dots from the anger. "I'm good in bed."

"I'll believe that when I see it." She tries to walk past me, and I follow.

"You want me to show you?"

She stops in her tracks, and her mouth opens in confusion. "Wha... It.... You... No."

She walks away from me, but as I watch her ass sway in the jeans, I can't stop smiling.

Chapter 7 – Debrief

Faye

With my first day finally over, I heave a sigh of relief as I enter the apartment and drop my bag on the floor. I'm excited to get started with everything I have planned and I think I'm going to love this job. But my interaction with Liam almost ruined it all.

I still can't believe he doesn't remember me. He must have been joking. God, that man is arrogant.

"How was it?" Cora asks from the living room.

I blink and realize she's asking about the job, not Liam.

"Good." I kick off my shoes and take off the jacket before I join her on the couch. She's still watching Firefly while doing homework. "Work was really good. It's everything I had hoped for. They're giving me guidelines, but lots of freedom. And I think they liked my ideas."

"Did you see any naked hockey players?" She wiggles an eyebrow.

I laugh. "What? No. Of course not."

"So you didn't get to go to the locker room?"

"I did, but it's not like they walk around naked."

"Hm. Well, maybe next time."

I toss a small pillow at her.

"No. Not next time. There will be no naked hockey players."

She puts her book aside and pulls her feet under her as she turns toward me.

"Speaking of naked hockey players, did you talk to Liam?"

I close my eyes and lean my head back, sinking into the couch. "Yes."

"And?"

"And he barely remembered me."

29

"What? What an asshole."

I shrug and ignore the blow to my ego. "He was drunk. And apparently, I'm not memorable."

"I will kick his ass. Of course you're memorable."

"It's fine. At least he didn't seem to care, so I doubt he'll cause any trouble."

"So he promised not to say anything?"

The blood slowly drains from my face.

"I forgot to ask." My voice is almost just a squeak.

"Faye. What the hell? That's the one thing you were supposed to do."

"I know. But he kind of insulted me, and I forgot."

She crosses her arms and stares at me. "You forgot?"

I give her a sheepish shrug. "It slipped my mind?"

"You've been freaking out over this all weekend. Are you telling me that one word with this guy had you so disoriented that you forgot that your career is on the line?"

I grimace. "He caught me off guard, and then we started arguing..."

She shakes her head. "Should you really be arguing with the one guy that can get you fired?"

Sighing, I rub my temples. "I'll take care of it. Ok? I'll make sure it isn't an issue."

"So, next time you see him..."

"I'll ask him not to tell anyone about our hook up."

"Good. Now tell me more about the job."

"I got the first few posts up."

"Oh, let me see." She grabs her phone and starts searching. "Oh, that's a cute selfie of you. And the twenty gorgeous guys in the background don't hurt."

"They're really nice guys."

Cora scrutinizes the posts I made while we move to the kitchen so I can prepare some veggie wraps for us.

"It's insane how boring these accounts used to be," she says as she leans against the counter.

I take out a container of ready cut vegetables and start loading the wraps. "It wasn't that bad."

She frowns at the phone. "I mean, nobody cares how many passes someone made. Did you see all these posts that are just walls of text? Who did they even have doing this before you?"

"I'm pretty sure there are people that care about stats." I cut up some zucchini and add it to the wraps. "But yeah, there are other sites for that. I think I can really turn these accounts around."

Cora sighs and scrolls back to my selfie from the locker room. "It should be illegal to have access to all these gorgeous men and never post any pictures of them."

"You need to stop objectifying them. Not everyone is comfortable being so public."

"They're hockey players. Doesn't it kind of come with the territory?"

"To an extent, but it's still their choice how much they want to be featured."

"Speaking of..." She searches for something on her phone. "What if they objectify themselves?"

I glance at the screen. It's a dance video. And it takes me about half a second to recognize Liam and Ethan.

Forgetting about the hummus, I grab her phone and watch their moves as they flirt with the camera.

"What is this?" I ask and check out their profile. "Shit, that's a lot of followers."

"Seems like your man has some hidden talents."

"Not my man." I scroll through the posts. Ethan definitely seems to be the front man of the duo. He's the one talking, answering comments and posting little snippets in between the dance videos.

"Did you not know about this?" Cora asks and loads hummus on one of the wraps.

"No." I shake my head. "I was going to check out their personal profiles, but I haven't had time yet."

"You should definitely do something with that."

"No, I shouldn't. I can't."

"You need a face for the team, and it's right there. Two faces even."

I watch one of their videos again. Ethan is a natural in front of the camera. It would make sense to do some kind of collaboration with him. And I do need to work on Liam's social media presence.

"Maybe."

I hand the phone back to her and finish the other wrap.

Cora shakes her head. "God. I can't believe he's bad in bed." She's staring at her phone. "He moves so... Well, I guess one skill doesn't necessarily translate to another."

"Yeah." It's baffling to me, too. All I can remember is how hot and heavy we were in the car. There was definitely nothing wrong with his moves there. But maybe the alcohol affected his performance? Maybe it affected my performance? What if I'm the problem?

I grab the wrap and head back to the living room with Cora. She unpauses Firefly and I barely follow along as we eat our dinner. Luckily, she's watched the show enough times that I know the gist of each episode.

Surely, Liam won't be a problem. We had one night, and it's over now. That's it. Just one night.

Chapter 8 – Confession

Liam

"Hey, it's been a while." I pause the game and look up at Ethan, who is standing in front of me.

"What?" My mind is all over the place and I'm barely able to focus on the shooter game.

"We should do another dance. It's been way too long."

He's not wrong. Lately, dancing hasn't been much of a priority.

"I guess." It's hard to muster up the enthusiasm for it right now.

"Come on, I found one we can do." He shoves his phone in my face and I sigh and grab it.

I watch the video a few times and can feel that spark growing inside me. The urge to move. How long has it been? A couple of weeks? More?

I sit up straighter and watch the video again while Ethan waits.

"Yeah, we can do this," I say when I've watched it thoroughly.

"Great. Get up." He gestures for me to get off the couch.

"Right now?" I put the controller down.

"Why not? You've been moping around here for way too long."

"I have not been moping." I get up and we move the couch forward to make some room.

"You've been moping."

We place the phone where we can watch it and start repeating the movements.

We're pretty good at learning new moves, so it only takes us a few minutes to pick up on the dance. The music is good and ideas soon start flowing for how we can make this our own thing.

We practise the dance a few more times with different variations.

"I've been thinking," I say when we're taking a break.

"Shocker. I didn't know you were capable of that."

Glaring at him, I make a mental note to send his girlfriend Lily a photo I have of Ethan passed out with drawings on his face.

"I'm done with relationships."

I'm not sure what reaction I was expecting, but Ethan laughs. I raise an eyebrow at him.

"What's so funny?"

"For as long as I've known you, you've always been in or been looking for a relationship. And now you're saying that's all over?"

"I'm serious. Kaitlynn and Eve proved to me that I suck at relationships and from now on, I've decided I just won't get involved."

"And what does that mean? Are you becoming celibate?"

"No way. But you don't need feelings to have sex."

"Is that what you've been trying to do lately? With all the puck bunnies? I'll give it another month, then you'll be sick and tired of it."

"What's that supposed to mean?" I glare at him.

"It means you're not that kind of person. There is no way you can do that."

"I have been doing it."

Ethan looks condescendingly amused. "It's not going to last. You're boyfriend material. Not a fuckboy. No matter how hard you try."

"I tried being a boyfriend. It came back and bit me in the ass. From now on, it's just sex. And hockey. And chemistry."

"Oh, speaking of, we should do a dance video in lab coats. In a lab." He nods at me as if it's the best idea ever.

"Not in any lab I have to work in. The others already don't take me seriously. If I do that, they'll never let me live it down."

"Are you serious? What do you mean they don't take you seriously? You're one of the most serious people I know. Do they know how hard it is to keep up with any subject, let alone chemistry, while playing hockey?"

"Yeah, they don't see it like that."

"Well, fuck them, then."

We're about to run through the moves one more time when I turn off the music.

I clear my throat. "There's something I should tell you." I've been debating keeping it to myself, but Ethan is my best friend, and I need to tell someone.

"Ok?"

Fuck, am I doing this? Part of me is screaming to keep my mouth shut. But I don't like keeping things from him.

"I slept with the social media manager."

"What?" He blinks at me in confusion.

"Faye. We had a thing. Last Friday."

"You slept with Faye?"

"Yes."

"The new social media manager?"

"Yes."

"Faye, who is the new social media manager for the UNI Lions?"

"Yes."

"The one woman you're not allowed to sleep with?"

"Listen, I didn't know who she was. We met at a club on Friday. We danced and drank and made out and then we drank some more. We were both pretty wasted. One thing led to another, and she came home with me."

"Were you not listening at all to the lecture Coach gave us? He's been on about this for weeks."

"It really doesn't seem fair that we get punished for something that happened before our time."

"It's not about punishment. It's about how work relationships fuck everything up."

"It's not a relationship. It was one night. And it's not like she's going to tell anyone. She'd be in just as much trouble if she did. More even. Besides, it happened before she got hired. I think."

Ethan shakes his head. "This is going to end badly. I mean, I won't say anything, but you can't believe this will end in any sort of good way, right?"

I shrug. "It's over now."

"It better be. And you need to get a grip and stop fucking around."

"You're starting to sound like JD." I grimace at him. "When did you become so responsible? Aren't you the one who spent a summer partying all over Europe and Asia?"

"I've got a new view of the world." He blushes slightly, and I know this is Lily's doing. She's finally been able to knock some sense into him.

Right. He has Lily. Everyone has someone. They're all capable of finding partners that aren't horrible people. It's just me that's fucking incapable. "Just forget I told you anything. It's not going to be an issue."

"If you say so..."

"I am saying so. Now, do you want to film this dance or not?"

Faye isn't going to be an issue. And I'm not going back to being boyfriend-material. What even is that? I'll be back to picking up more women soon. As soon as my pillow stops smelling of roses.

Chapter 9 – An indecent suggestion

Faye

One of the things I love about my new job is the flexible hours. I don't have to worry about missing classes or stressing about getting to an office I'd never use. Most of what I do, I can do from my phone. Which means I can work whenever and wherever.

The only obligations I have are certain games and meetings with Coach and the others. We agreed to a certain number of posts per week and set up some goals they'd like me to hit when it comes to engagement.

Mostly, they have no idea what I'm supposed to be doing and are very interested in listening to my feedback and opinions.

It's the perfect job.

I've already cleared my schedule so I can be there at most of the home games and some practises, and I've set up a photo shoot with the guys tomorrow during their practise. I'm not sure how long Coach will give in to my requests, so I'm taking full advantage of his current goodwill.

But right now, I can do what I need to without being at the Den.

I'm eating the last of my lunch in a quiet corner of the dining hall, planning out the posts for the rest of the week, when a shadow falls over me. My entire body tingles, and I make sure to take a moment before I look up.

Liam is studying me.

"Oh, it's you. I've been meaning to talk to you." I do my best to sound professional and disinterested.

"Really?" He raises an eyebrow.

"Yes, a friend of mine found your dance videos."

"A friend?" His smirk tells me he doesn't believe me.

"Yes. My cousin, in fact. Anyway, I was thinking, if you're interested, we could do something similar with the team."

He walks around the table and sits down opposite me.

"You want them to dance?" He furrows his brow as he leans back in the chair.

"Yeah. I want to have regular fun posts. Posts that show off what the players can do, or give some insight into their personality. And I think having some of them do a dance video could be a good start."

He blinks at me a couple of times and I swallow as I wait for an answer. Why does it matter to me what he thinks about my idea? It shouldn't I don't even know the guy.

"Sure," he finally says. "We could do that."

"Great." I bring out my tablet and find my notes on the dance. "I have a few suggestions for music, but I'll, of course, need your input. And your help with the choreography."

He clears his throat. "Yeah, I can do that."

"Good." I make a few notes, mostly to have something to do besides stare at the way the muscles in his forearms tense and relax as he moves. "I'm not sure who would want to be involved, but I'm hoping at least five or six of the players."

He places his forearms on the table and leans in. "I'm not bad in bed."

"What?" My eyes fly from his arms to his face.

The change in topic is jarring, and my mind is instantly back in his bed with his arm over my waist.

He lowers his voice almost to a whisper. "I'm good at sex."

"You could have fooled me," I whisper back, leaning in just a bit too close.

His eyes narrow and I can't look away. "I can prove it."

Scoffing, I shake my head. "I'm not watching whatever porno you've made with the puck bunnies."

"What? No. I haven't made any pornos."

My relief is immediate. "Good. That's one less PR disaster I have to worry about."

"That's not what I meant." The blue in his eyes darken and I'm sucked in.

"I'm not going to ask them about your sexual escapades, either."

"Worried you might get jealous?" The smirk on his face is annoying as hell.

"Hardly."

"Don't worry, I came up with a different plan."

Every syllable is a challenge, and my entire body wants to take it on. So I lean in closer and hope he won't notice how fast my heart is beating.

"And what plan might that be?"

"I want a do-over."

For a moment, I'm sure my brain has stopped working. There is no way he just said the words my ears picked up on.

"What?"

"I want a do-over."

"On a one-night stand?"

"Yes."

"That's not a thing."

"Why not?"

"It was a one-time thing."

"A do-over won't change that."

Worried my body will set on fire, I grab my things and start packing them up. "You're insane for even suggesting this."

"It's the only way I can prove to you that it's not my fault you woke up disappointed."

"I'm not sleeping with you."

"Give me one good reason why we shouldn't."

"I can give you a million. We don't like each other. We already tried it. And what's that last thing.... Oh, right, I'll get fired. Because it's against the rules."

"Let me guess, you never break the rules."

There's a glimmer in his eyes, promising much more than I'm ready to accept.

"Rules are there for a reason."

"Rules are overrated. They haven't done me any good. Besides, no one would know."

The way his voice caresses my spine makes me want to give in. The memory of his hands under my shirt is making me excited.

Someone drops a plate in the distance and I shake my head. "No. This is not happening. I'm not risking my career to sleep with you."

"It would be worth it."

"Not to me."

His eyes dip down to my chest, and I silently curse my body for making my nipples hard.

"Come on, you're dying to know, aren't you?"

I shake my head. My mouth is dry and I can't get my breathing under control.

He smirks at me. That crooked, infuriating, adorable smirk.

As he gets up and leaves, I'm left feeling confused and flustered.

He did not just suggest we sleep together again.

There is no way he thinks that would be a good idea.

I mean, I am curious. But no. No. I can't risk my job just to satisfy an urge. There's no way.

Chapter 10 – Photo shoot

Faye

"Looking great," I say to Pan as he assumes a typical goalie pose in front of me. I struggle to keep my balance on the ice as I take his photo from different angles. "How about something more relaxed? Without the helmet?"

I move up closer as he takes off the helmet and gloves and gives me a smile. "Great." I snap a few more photos before I flick back through them to see what I've got. Stumbling, I shuffle over to him.

"What do you think about this one?" I show him one of the more serious ones where he's reaching for an imaginary puck.

"Yeah, sure. That looks good."

"I think I'll use that one and... this one." The second photo is of him smiling at the camera with his blond hair falling onto his forehead. His clean-shaven face, soft eyes, and dimples make him look like the perfect boy next door.

"Ugh."

"You don't like it?" I take another look. It's a good photo.

"I look like a kid."

"You look good. I promise you, women will swoon over this picture."

"Are you sure?"

"Oh, yes."

"Then I guess it's fine."

"Great, thanks. Could you tell Dustin to come on over?"

I glance back at the other half of the ice where the rest of the team is practicing. I have a small area set up to take photos of the guys, and I'm trying to get through them all during this practice. It's

41

also a good way for me to figure out who's who and start to get to know them. You can learn a surprising amount about people just by the way they act in front of a camera.

Pan skates back to the others and relays my request and I mark him off on the list of players I have on my phone.

Coach was very adamant that we need to finish the photos today and everyone needs to cooperate, so I'm not surprised when Dustin stops in front of me before I can even put my phone away.

"How do you want me, Ms. Emmerson?" he asks, and I raise an eyebrow. Which causes him to immediately turn bright red. Well, shit. I guess no joking around with Dustin.

"What's a pose you're comfortable with?" I ask instead and hope his face will regain normal color soon. "And you can call me Faye."

He clears his throat. "Well, I guess... Maybe this?"

He stands in front of me, holding the stick horizontal with both hands, almost as if it's a shield.

"Great." I move around him to include the other players as background. "Could you look off in that direction?"

He does as he's told and I even manage to get some pictures of him looking more comfortable and not red-faced. Once we're both happy with his photos, I move on to the other goalie, Hudson Ward, and coax him into smiling for the camera.

The one person who never seems to smile is Cole Langley. His stone face remains the same no matter what prompts I give him, so I have no choice but to play into it and make him look even surlier.

"Some of your guys don't seem to be able to crack a smile," I say when JD comes up to me.

"Let me guess. Cole and Hudson?"

"Pretty much. And Enzo. Do they have some kind of aversion to looking happy?"

"Hey, not everyone can be as charismatic as me?" He takes a pose as if he's about to receive a pass, while smiling and winking. I take the picture. He's instantly comfortable in front of the camera and takes direction easily.

"You're almost as good at this as Ethan," I tease him. "Are you sure you shouldn't be in front of the camera instead of behind it?"

"Fuck off. By the way, Morgan is headed over to the exhibit later today if you want to join her."

"Yeah, I'd love to. I'll call her later. I think I'm almost done here."

"We good?" He gestures to the camera.

"Yup. I have enough photos of you." I take a deep breath. It's almost over. Just one player left. Fuck. Why did I leave him for last?

"Who do you want next? Or has everyone been?"

"Just one more. Liam."

I try not to put any emotion in his name. Maybe I should have gotten his shoot out of the way first. Stupid me for trying to put it off.

"I'll send him over. Make sure you call Morgan about tonight."

"Will do."

He skates off and I bring out my phone and double check that I haven't forgotten anyone. I almost hope that I have.

I take a breath as Liam comes over and stops in front of me.

"I was starting to think you forgot about me." He raises an eyebrow.

"No, just a busy day. Do you want to look like you're skating straight at me?"

I back away from him a little and he moves to where I'm pointing.

"Like this?" He poses and I clear my throat.

"Yeah, that's good." I start taking photos and his eyes never leave me.

"You want me to actually skate?"

He moves in a circle, and I shake my head. "Not today." I do a quick check of the photos I have of him. He slowly moves in closer and I hold my breath.

"Did you change your mind yet?"

With wide eyes, I glance over at the others. They're gathering up the equipment they've been using and heading off the ice.

"What?"

One by one, the other players are leaving.

"Are you ready to find out what it could be like?"

My cheeks flush.

"It's against the rules."

He's standing way too close to me and with his skates on, he's towering over me. I crane my neck and meet his eyes, refusing to back down.

"Are you always such a good girl?"

The last two words don't sound right coming from him.

"I... I don't get into trouble like that."

"Like what?" His eyes are firmly on my lips.

"I'm a straight-A student." My voice is too high pitched. "I've never broken curfew. Well, once, but the car broke down and I called my parents straight away. Whenever my friends planned to do something bad, I'd leave. I don't break rules. I mean, I've broken rules sometimes, but not like this. Not rules that could get me fired."

Fuck, I'm babbling. Since when do I babble? What is this effect he has on me?

"And yet, you hooked up with a guy you didn't know. A guy you met at a club."

"I was drunk." I almost add: and horny. But stop myself in time.

"You were more than drunk." He bites his lip and his gaze slowly moves down my body and back up again. "You were wild."

"I was not. Even if I was, it doesn't matter. I don't want to sleep with you again."

"I don't believe you."

"Well, it's not up to you."

His smile is enervating and fucking hot. I glance around the rink, but it's only the two of us left now.

His voice is low and husky. "No. It's not. It's up to you. And one of these days, you're going to agree."

I shake my head. "No, I won't." I won't, I tell myself, but I can feel the pull from my lower abdomen. The urge to give in.

He just smiles. "What else do you need from me?"

It takes me a while to realise he means in terms of the photo shoot.

"No-nothing. I'm good."

Fuck, I hope I have what I need. Because if I don't get away from him, I might just give in to the urge.

"Fantastic." He skates past me, much too close, and I could swear he pauses to take a deep breath next to me. Is he smelling me?

He glides across the ice and I take a moment to gather myself before I slowly shuffle across the ice.

Why is he so fascinating? It has to be because he's off limits. I've been a rule follower all my life. Maybe this is my rebel phase?

I groan. Why couldn't I just have dyed my hair green like Morgan? Or gotten a nose piercing? Both of those would have been way less destructive. And so much safer.

Chapter 11 – Rumors and revelations

Faye

"That sounds great." I kick off my shoes as I enter the apartment. "I'll see you there." Ending the call, I head for my room to get ready. I haven't hung out a lot with Morgan, but it's nice to have someone to talk to about photography. She's been a model for her mom for years, so she's a lot more knowledgeable than she thinks.

While I check my closet for something to wear, Cora emerges from her room.

"I hate math," she growls and throws herself face down on my bed.

"Then don't study math."

"I have to pick a major."

"Yeah, but not one you hate."

She sits up. "True. What are you doing?"

I grab a sweater and hold it up in front of me. Cora makes a face, and I put it back.

"I'm going to a photography exhibit with Morgan."

"Sounds boring."

"Well, you don't have to come." I find another shirt and Cora gives me a so-so motion of her hand.

"Did you talk to Liam? Because I have information."

"What kind of information?" I dismiss a couple of shirts before sighing and moving on to pants.

"Well, I did some research. I wasn't going to let you go in blind."

"Go in where?" I pull out a pair of black jeans and hold them up with the so-so shirt. "I'm not going in anywhere."

"You say that, but I think you will. Anyway, some light stalking of some people, a few compliments to some friends of friends, and I have the whole story."

Shaking my head, I try not to think about what she could possibly have found out. "Maybe you should become a private investigator."

"Oh, you think you're joking, but it's on my list."

"Really?" I shake my head and change into the new outfit. Cora has been struggling to figure out what she wants in life and the main reason she's at UNI is to placate her parents.

"Stop trying to distract me. I figured out what happened to your man."

"Not my man."

She ignores me. "He used to date this woman named Eve. So I found her and made contact, and just so you know, she's a bitch. Like a genuine evil bitch. I followed her to a restaurant and the way she talked to the server..." She shakes her head. "I almost strangled her there and then."

"I guess he has poor taste in women. That's not a crime." I take a step back to study my reflection in the mirror on the door.

"Not that top," Cora says. "Try the red one. Yeah, I had no idea what he saw in her. I mean, she's pretty. But that's about it. So I did some more digging, and the general consensus is that she somehow manipulated and blinded him in order to hook him. I guess she can pretend to be decent when she sets her mind to it. Then, after they broke up, she tried to get with his best friend."

"How do you know all of this?" I pull on the other shirt. Cora was right. It's much better.

"Oh, I know a lot more. After their lunch, I stalked her for a bit until I had the perfect opportunity to talk to her, and you know what she did?"

"No." I hold my hair up to see if I should change it.

"She flipped her hair while looking at me like something the cat dragged in. Then she walked away. Didn't even answer my question or anything."

"Up or down?" I turn to Cora.

"Ummm, down."

"Ok."

"Everyone agrees that Liam is a good guy and Eve was just a phase for him."

"That's good."

"But." She holds up a finger. "After Eve there was Kaitlynn. Now, for this, I had to go to Rivers, but it was worth it."

"You went to Rivers today?" I blink at her.

"Yeah. So?"

"When did you have time for all of this?"

Cora shrugs. "I drove my bike really, really fast."

"No wonder you can't get your math homework done."

"I was bored. Now let me tell you what else I found out."

"Go ahead." It's pointless to argue with her. Once Cora decides she's doing something, there is very little that can stop her.

"Kaitlynn should come with her own set of warning labels. And I can tell you, Liam really dodged a bullet there. He was chasing after her for a couple of months before Christmas, then during the holidays, they apparently got together, but he immediately broke it off. Like within a few days."

I swallow and pretend to look for a pair of boots. "Do you know why?"

"Yes, I do. Well, I can imagine. Because two weeks ago she was suspended from Rivers equestrian program for hitting a horse."

"Oh, my god." My eyes go wide as I gape at Cora. I stumble back and sit down on the desk chair.

"Yeah, fucking insane. The horse is fine, by the way. I made sure. Kaitlynn thought she was alone at the stable, and the horse shied away from her, so she... overreacted. Luckily, one of the teachers was there and saw everything. There are a lot of rumors about her, and I don't want to believe all the things I heard, but a former friend came out of the woodwork and said Kaitlynn used to raise her hands against her as well."

"That's..." What do you even say to that? "How could someone treat an animal like that?"

"Beats me, but oh, I met a group of the horse-girls when I was there and they're all determined to fuck her life up and make sure she never studies or works with animals. They've written like every college with an equestrian program and all the stables they could find and they're keeping tabs on her."

"Wow, they really don't like her."

"No, they do not."

I take a moment to sort through everything Cora just told me. "So, you think maybe she was abusive to Liam, too?"

"Yes."

It's such a straightforward answer, but Cora doesn't sugarcoat.

"I don't know about this," I say. "I feel like a lot of this is stuff that we shouldn't be talking about."

Cora shrugs. "It's all public knowledge."

"I know, but doesn't it feel like we're invading his privacy?"

"Not really. I mean, I can see how you would think that, but at the same time, you keep telling me there's nothing going on between the two of you, so why do you care?"

My mouth opens and closes. "Well, I still have to work with him."

"So you want me to look into all the players?" She wiggles her eyebrows.

"No. Oh my god, I can't even imagine what you might uncover. And I think plausible deniability might be my friend."

"As you wish." She gets up off the bed. "One more thing, though."

"What?"

"After breaking up with Kaitlynn, he started sleeping around more. I met several puck bunnies who were all too eager to tell me about the nights they spent with him."

"I don't want to hear this." I resist the urge to cover my ears with my hands.

"Ok, but you might want to know that there are people saying his hockey days are over. That he's out of control."

"Yeah, I know. I have plans to remedy that."

"Good. You look nice, by the way. Have fun at the exhibit."

"Thanks." I still haven't put any plans in motion when it comes to Liam's reputation, but Coach called us to a meeting tomorrow to see what I've come up with. Maybe it'll be easier for him to hear it from someone who isn't me? Then again, he might feel ganged up on, or ambushed.

I freshen up my make-up and can't stop wondering what exactly happened with Kaitlynn. I'm having a hard time imagining how someone becomes so evil. Or why you would want to be with them. But maybe she was good at hiding it?

I grab my purse and head out to meet Morgan. It doesn't matter. Because Liam is just someone I work with.

Chapter 12 – Plans put in motion

Liam

"So, what's this about?" I ask as I sit down in Coach's office. I try to not focus on the fact that Faye is sitting next to me. She's pulled her chair as far away as she can without seeming weird, and I have this intense urge to grab it and pull her closer. I want to lean in and inhale her scent. Hell, I want to rub her all over me so I can smell like her. But that probably wouldn't be appropriate.

Aside from Faye, Coach and JD are both there, and for a moment, I think maybe she said something, or they found out some other way. I'm preparing to defend myself and give them the spiel about how we were drunk and didn't know who the other one was. But they look more nervous than angry, so I wait.

"Well," Coach says and avoids looking at me. "I guess we can just get everything out in the open."

"Sure." My eyes go from JD to Faye. Neither of them is looking at me.

"There have been a lot of rumors lately," Coach says. "About you and your commitment to hockey."

"What's that supposed to mean?" I turn to JD. "Did you put him up to this?" He's been going on about stuff like this for a while now.

"No, he didn't," Coach says. "This has come from several sources, including the dean's office. It's become public knowledge that you are out drinking too much and... meeting up with a lot of women."

My eyes flicker to Faye, but she just calmly looks up and meets my eyes before looking back down.

"That's not against any rules," I say.

"It's not." Coach looks uncomfortable. "But we have a real shot at making the Frozen Four this year and we have more eyes on us than usual. Going forward, that pressure is going to increase. It's very important that we show our sponsors our best sides. And right now, what you're doing is a problem."

"I'm a problem?" I stare at him, unable to close my mouth. "Me?" I've never been the problem. Sure, I've been having a bit more fun lately, but nothing extreme.

"We want the sponsors to see the best the Lions have to offer. When they open social media, they need to see players that are committed to hockey. Not an endless parade of women." He gestures to Faye. "Show him."

She grabs her phone and clears her throat. I turn to her and watch as she opens a photo. The mild scent of roses wafts over me and I indulge in it.

"These are just the latest posts I've found," she says and scrolls through some unflattering pictures of me with different women, or clearly drunk.

I see the photos through her eyes and for the first time; I realize how fucked up it all is.

"I've seen the photos," Coach says. "And I'm not impressed."

I hold my breath as each photo appears. What if there's one of her? What if someone saw us at the club, or in the car? She would have done something about that, right? She wouldn't let Coach see it.

When there are no more images for me to see, all I can feel is relief that our secret is safe. She puts away the phone and I can breathe again.

"This is where Faye comes in," Coach says, and my heart stops.

"What?"

"She will be working with you to improve your image."

"Faye?" I'm so confused.

"She's good at what she does," JD says. "All you have to do is work with her to get the sponsors off our backs."

Her cheeks are flushed and her jaw tense.

"I know she's good," I say. "I just didn't know this would fall on her plate."

"I think we're lucky she joined us when she did," Coach smiles at her in a fatherly way and I instantly narrow my eyes at him. "She's in charge of cleaning up your reputation, and I think she already has some plans."

"You have got to be kidding me?" The implication of what they are saying is starting to sink in and I'm not sure what to think. "I don't need someone to tell me how to behave."

"Your behavior is affecting the entire team, Liam." Coach brings out his stern voice. "You may think it's all just fun and games, but we are talking about people's lives here. What you're doing could impact your teammates' future. I've known you for a long time, and I can't imagine you'd be ok with that."

Fuck. He's right. "I'll do better. I don't need anyone to tell me what to do."

"This has gone too far for that. Faye will help you."

"She's talented, Liam," JD says. "She'll know how to fix this. And she's like the ultimate good girl."

"What's that supposed to mean?" I ask at the same time as Faye.

I glance over at her. "How is she a good girl? And how do you know?"

JD shrugs. "I recommended her for the position."

I didn't know that they knew each other and I'm instantly annoyed at the fact.

"You're friends?"

"I know Morgan," Faye says quietly in a voice that soothes.

"Faye does photography and Morgan's mom has a gallery." JD squirms in his seat and I get the feeling he's holding something back.

I'm just about to ask more about this and why he hasn't said anything before when Coach interrupts.

"She wouldn't have gotten the job if we didn't trust her. Now, you boys need to get ready for practice. Afterwards, Liam, you and Faye can get together and do what you need to."

"Sounds good," Faye says.

"Yeah, sure."

I get up and walk out of the office with JD. Coach and Faye follow close behind.

All of a sudden, JD laughs.

"What's so funny?"

"Nothing. Just this thing Morgan said. She's been reading one of Kat's books, and there was this situation that reminded me of this."

"What are you talking about?" I glare at him. "Why is that funny?"

"Because in the book, they solve it with a fake relationship, and I just had the idea in my head of you and Faye dating." He laughs, but my stomach flips.

"I don't do relationships." I clench my fists.

Behind us, Coach laughs. "Maybe that's the problem?"

"What?" We stop and JD is still laughing.

"Well, most of the complaints are about you hooking up with puck bunnies. Maybe a relationship would solve that."

"Faye would be the perfect candidate," JD chuckles.

"Well, no," Coach says as my eyes meet Faye's. "Faye is off limits. But maybe this is an idea she can use? A relationship would put a stop to the rumors."

"I'll think about it," Faye says with not a care in the world, as if she's actually going to set me up with someone.

I know I shouldn't. I know it's a bad idea. And yet, I turn to Faye. "So you wouldn't want to pretend to date me?"

Her breathing hitches and I can feel her reaction. She's thinking about the question I asked her earlier. I'm still holding out for an answer to that, and she knows it.

"It's not appropriate," she finally says.

"Let's move on." Coach gestures for us to keep walking. "Faye will be following practice today and taking some more photos. So you better behave."

"Yes, Coach," me and JD answer as we head to the locker room. This time Faye doesn't join us, and I try to keep her scent with me for as long as possible.

Chapter 13 – Soft and perfect

Faye

It was such a stupid idea, and I wish JD hadn't said anything at all. As I watch them finish up practice, I try to ignore the strange pang that came over me at the thought of Liam being in a fake relationship.

Of course, Coach is right. I'm not a good candidate for that. Because everyone knows it's against the terms of my contract. But I don't like how ready Coach was to see that as a viable option. As if setting Liam up with someone would solve all the issues.

It wouldn't solve anything.

I grab a few more photos of the guys as they leave the ice and head to get showered and changed.

"I swear they're performing better when you're here," Coach says as we watch them leave.

"It's the camera." I smile back at him and hold it up. "It makes people want to show me their good side."

"I take it you have time to talk to Liam?"

I nod. "Yes, as soon as he's changed."

"Good. I have to head out for a meeting, but you can use my office if you want." He gestures toward the office and we start walking.

"That would be great. I'm not sure Liam really likes what's happening, so I think if we could talk in private, that would help."

"I've been keeping an eye on the things you post. And how people are reacting to it."

My stomach clenches. "Oh?"

"It's looking good so far. I even got a call from one alumnus about it. He said some photos brought him right back to how it was when he was on the team."

"I'm glad. I'm trying to capture their everyday life, so I'm glad it's working."

We stop outside of his office, and he unlocks the door.

"Let me grab some stuff and I'll go tell Liam to meet you here once he's done."

"Thanks." I sit down at the conference table and go through the photos from today.

"Just make sure you lock the door when you leave." Coach grabs his jacket.

"Will do."

"Oh, and don't let Liam push you around. You're in charge of this."

"Thanks."

As he leaves, I relax. I like Coach. He can be tough and intimidating with the players, but he seems to always treat people fairly.

With every minute that passes, I get more and more nervous. The office feels secluded and I haven't been alone in a room with Liam since that morning I woke up in his bed.

When there's a knock at the door, I almost jump out of my seat. I take a minute to compose myself before I let him in.

"Hi," I say and stare at his damp hair. He smells fresh and woodsy and as he pushes back his sleeves to show his forearms, I forget why we're here.

"What do you think you're doing?" He steps closer to me so he can close the door and I take a step back.

"What do you mean?"

"What's this about Faye?" His voice is calm, but there's an edge to it. He moves closer, and I have to force myself to stand my ground.

"You've been drawing a lot of attention to yourself lately. People are talking." I stare at his collarbone.

"What I do is nobody's business. Neither is who I do."

"The photos are all over the place." Why is it so hard to breathe around him?

"So what now? You take some pictures of me and tell people I'm good?"

I clear my throat and move away from him. Before I turn back to face him, I make sure there's a chair between us.

"It's a bit more complicated than that. The biggest concern is the team and the sponsors. Not to mention your reputation and chance to get onto an NHL team."

"And you can fix this?"

I nod. "I can. But you have to work with me."

A sudden smirk makes my stomach roil. "And what do I get out of it?"

"Wh-what do you mean?"

"I'm not bothered by my reputation."

"You'll be helping your teammates."

"I'm going to need more than that."

I swallow as his eyes land on my lips. "What do you want?"

"I want to make you come."

My entire body shuts down. For a few seconds, I don't breathe. I can't think. All I can do is stare at him with my mouth open. Then warmth floods to my core and my cheeks.

"What?"

"I'll do whatever it is you want me to do, if you let me make you come."

"That's not... What?"

"Don't pretend you don't want me to. I can easily prove it."

I manage to blink a few times as I struggle to suppress the urge that's growing inside me.

"How?" Why am I entertaining this? I should walk out the door. Or tell him to shut up and sit down. This is not how I envisioned this talk going.

"It's easy." He takes a couple of steps around the chair, and we're too close again. "Let me kiss you."

His lips look soft and inviting. "That won't prove anything."

"Then what are you afraid of?"

"I'm not afraid."

He takes another step and we're so close I can feel the heat from his body. "So you'll kiss me?"

"And if I don't like it?" There's a chance I won't like it. Right? It might be awful.

He smiles. "You will."

"But if I don't?"

"If you honestly don't like it, I'll do whatever you want."

I suck in a breath. "And... if I do?"

"If you do like it, all you have to do is tell me you want me to make you come and I will listen to whatever plans you come up with."

I bite my lip. This should feel inappropriate. I should be pushing him away and filing a complaint. But I know I won't.

"What's the matter? Too much of a good girl to do something against the rules?"

Fuck, I don't even care that it's against the rules.

I tilt my head back and look up at him. He's so close.

"When I don't like it, you'll do what I say?"

"If." He nods.

I nod back and steel myself for a moment. Then I raise myself up and brush my lips against his.

It was supposed to be a quick kiss. Lips touching, nothing more.

But that's not what happens.

I brush my lips ever so gently against his and electricity shoots through me. His lips are soft and perfect, and I gently taste his bottom lip. His hands land on my waist and a moan escapes me.

When his tongue flickers across the seam of my lips, I'm ready to melt into him. I let him in and clutch his shirt in my fists.

The kiss is intense and deep, and my head is spinning.

Then it stops. He pulls away from me and I slowly open my eyes.

He looks far too unaffected, but all I can do is try to get my breathing under control and release the death grip I have on his shirt.

Leaning in, his breath tickles my ear. "I'll make you come, then I'll listen to your plan."

Before I know what's happening, he's walking away from me as if nothing happened. I slump back against the desk as the door closes after him.

My chest is heaving and my lips feel swollen. I gently touch them.

Fuck.

Fuck.

Oh, fuck, what did I just get myself into?

I wait until my hands stop shaking, then I gather my things and leave the room. This is going to be an interesting job.

Chapter 14 – Setting it up

Faye

The kiss will not leave my mind.

His hands on my waist, the taste of him. His heartbeat under my fingers. It all stays with me. But most of all, I remember the way he made me feel. The way my stomach filled with butterflies and caused a cascade of lust to course through me.

It makes it difficult to sleep. Or pay attention in class. Or think.

By the time the game starts on Friday night, I'm ready to combust. My camera searches for Liam and I struggle to get good pictures of the other players.

It doesn't help that he, every so often, looks in my direction with a knowing smirk.

Once the game is over, I make sure to get a picture of the Lions celebrating so I can post it. I take some time to reply to comments as the guys head back to get changed and the Den slowly empties.

"Faye, I hope you're planning on posting about the victory." Coach is smiling happily.

"I already did. You're getting loads of congratulations."

"Good. We're one step closer to the Frozen Four."

"Looks like you'll have a great season this year."

"It really does. By the way, how did your talk with Liam go? Did you get things sorted?"

Well, fuck. How do I answer that without lying too much? "I think we'll be able to work something out."

"Just make sure he doesn't give you any trouble."

"I will."

"If any of them misbehave, you just tell me and I'll take care of it."

I nod. "They've all been very respectful."

"Good."

"But thank you."

He waves a hand at me. "I have a daughter a couple of years younger than you."

"Does she go to UNI?"

"Not yet. She's trying to decide if it's worth going to the same school her old man works at." He laughs. "I need to go meet the guys. You have a good evening."

"You too."

I watch him leave and wander the Den for a bit, soaking in the atmosphere of people still lingering. I should go home. If I was the good girl everyone seems to think I am, I'd go straight home and take a cold shower. I'd put Liam out of my mind and find another way to deal with him.

I keep telling myself I shouldn't, but my feet are already leading me towards the locker room.

The camera is an excellent excuse to greet the players as they emerge one by one, and I smile and make them pose for me.

Some of them do so happily, others look embarrassed. I post a picture of Ethan and include his stats for the game. With his smiling face, I'm sure the stats won't appear too boring.

Every time the door opens, my heart skips a beat. I do my best not to show my disappointment as the players come out, but for some obscure reason, it's there.

The door opens again, and I hold my breath.

Liam laughs at someone behind him as they both step out into the hallway.

He spots me and raises an eyebrow.

I want to sink through the floor. He knows why I'm here. My cheeks turn red and I pretend to look at my phone.

"Did you want to share your ideas?" Liam asks as he stops by me.

"See you later," Jonathan says and keeps on walking.

I swallow. "Yes, if you don't mind."

I keep looking around, wondering who might overhear us.

He tilts his head, and my eyes are glued to the rapid pulse on his throat. Is it too fast? Probably from the game.

"Say it."

My eyes flicker to his.

"What?"

"Say it, Faye. I need the words."

I'm drowning in his dark brown eyes. The hallway is empty, but I still take a step closer so I can lower my voice.

"I want you to make me come."

Sparks fly between us and time stops. Neither of us is breathing.

The door to the locker room opens and Liam coughs and takes a step back.

"Hey, good game," Dustin says and punches Liam in the shoulder as he passes by.

We wait until we're alone again.

"My place?" Liam asks.

I shake my head. "No. You live with how many other players? If any of them find out, I'll be fired."

"Right. So where?"

I swallow hard. This is it. I should not be doing this. I should tell him I was joking and leave. If I go through with this, I'm putting my career at stake.

But I want this. Whatever he is doing to me, I need more.

"My place." I grab my phone and unlock it. "Here, give me your number."

He grabs the phone, and I wait nervously.

"You have your own place?"

"I live with my cousin. She won't tell anyone."

He hands my phone back and raises an eyebrow. "You've told her about me?"

My cheeks flush. "If anyone asks, we're working on your reputation. That's it."

He nods and I text him the address.

"In about an hour?" I'm desperately trying to remember what state my room is in and if I need to shave my legs.

"I'll see you soon," he says and saunters off down the hallway.

Fuck, he looks good. I ogle him for a bit before I shake it off and head in the opposite direction.

Chapter 15 – Home

Faye

"I can't believe you're doing this," Cora says but she can't stop smiling.

"I know." I bury my face in my hands. "I don't know what I was thinking. Maybe I should tell him not to come."

"Don't you dare." She grabs her keys and jacket. "I will want details when I get back. How long do you think you'll need?"

My mouth falls open, and I blink at her. "I..."

She laughs. "For your sake, I hope you need at least a couple of hours. Don't worry, I'll be careful coming back in case you need more."

"Cora!" My face is red from embarrassment, but she just laughs.

"If you need more condoms, I have some in my nightstand. Just ignore the other stuff in there." She winks and I make a mental note never to look in her nightstand. There are certain things I don't want to know about my cousin.

"I'm sorry for kicking you out."

"It's not a big deal. I have places to be, people to see." She grabs her helmet and waves at me before opening the door, and revealing a broad-shouldered man about to ring the doorbell.

"Oh, hi."

My stomach flips.

"Well, well, well," Cora says and runs her eyes up and down his body. "Not too shabby."

"Liam, this is my roommate and cousin, Cora. Cora, Liam." I swallow as she narrows her eyes and try to send her stern thoughts about not embarrassing me.

"It's nice to meet you." Liam looks unsure of what to think.

"Bye, Cora," I say.

"See you later." She slides past him and turns to walk backward and look from him to me. "Way later."

Liam clears his throat.

"Ignore her. Come on in."

I scowl at Cora as I close the door behind him.

"Nice place." He takes off his jacket and looks around. It's a small apartment with a tiny, windowless kitchen to the left and a decent living room straight ahead with a view of the street. The bedrooms, one to either side of the living room, each have their own bathroom. That was one of the main selling points when we got this place.

I've never noticed before how much space just one person can take up. As Liam hangs up his jacket, I don't know what to do with myself. I don't know where to put my hands. What do I normally do with them? Do I just let my arms hang at my sides? Do I cross them in front of me? Fuck, why does he make me so nervous?

"So," he says, and makes it sound like an open-ended question.

He turns to face me and I'm hit by how good he looks. His dark blonde hair is styled shorter at the sides and even under his t-shirt, I can make out his muscles.

I straighten my back and pretend I have some sort of confidence. "This way." I lead him into my bedroom. We're going to end up in here anyway, so we might as well cut to the chase.

I know we're alone, but I still close the door.

"You're eager." He smirks at me.

"I have a feeling you won't make this good for me, so I'd like to get it over with." That's a lie. The thought of his hands on my skin is already turning me on.

He raises an eyebrow. "And you think you'll be able to make it good for me?"

I'm taken aback at his question. Then I realize it's only fair.

"I don't remember you saying you woke up disappointed."

He grabs his t-shirt and pulls it off in one smooth motion.

"You know, I'm getting sick and tired of hearing that word."

I'd like to give him some witty response, but the lines of his muscles are mesmerizing. There are a few bruises on his arms and chest, some of them more faded than the others, and I want to reach out and touch him.

He steps closer, breaking the spell he has me under, and I raise my eyes to his.

"What?" He asks with a smile. "You're not feeling disappointed right now, are you?"

I shake my head. "No," I croak out.

I desperately want to wipe that smug smirk off his face, so without thinking, I grab my own shirt and pull it off. I'm wearing a red lacy bra and his eyes immediately dip to my chest.

Taking a few deep breaths, I let him look. "Are you?" I ask.

He keeps staring, and just slowly shakes his head. Two pink spots appear on his cheeks and I feel victorious.

I wait for him to make a move, but he doesn't.

"Well?"

Our eyes meet. "What?"

My stomach contracts. "You said you were going to make me come. Did you change your mind?"

I want to be as brave as my words. I want to be confident and secure, but the words have barely left my lips before I regret them. And this whole situation. "Because," I continue like a fool, "I have the plan I made for you in the living room, and we could just go over that."

He shakes his head and stands as close as he possibly can without touching me. My chest is heaving, but his eyes are on my face now.

"If you don't want to do this, we don't have to." He's giving me a way out. Just like I gave him one.

I inhale his woodsy vanilla scent and my knees go weak. Electricity shoots through my body as our eyes lock.

My hands shake as I unbutton my jeans and pull them down. Eyes still locked, his breathing is rapid. I step out of the pants.

"If you don't make me come, I will be very upset. I haven't had a good orgasm in a long time."

He swallows visibly before his eyes trail down my body to the red panties. He reaches out a hand and cups my hip. I shiver.

I reach up and place my hand on his shoulder. His face moves closer. I lean my head back and slide my hand up to his neck.

"You won't be able to walk tomorrow," he growls before his lips crash into mine and lust and desire becomes my world.

I give in to the kiss and taste him just as he tastes me. My other hand lands on his back to pull him closer. He squeezes my hip with one hand and the other is in my hair.

My core is aching with need and I give in and rub against him to alleviate some of the agony. His pants are rough against my skin and I whimper when I can't get any closer.

Before I know what I'm doing, my hands are struggling to get rid of the fabric between us.

Liam takes my face in both hands and devours my mouth. My head is spinning and I finally manage to get his pants off.

"Fuck," he moans as I pull them down. He pulls away from me. His eyes are darker than I've ever seen them before and his lips are swollen.

As much as I love seeing his face filled with lust for me, curiosity wins, and I lower my gaze. He's naked. His cock erect. And it's big. Not scarily big, but bigger than any I've had before.

I bite my lower lip. I want it inside me.

When I look back up at him, he reaches behind me and undoes my bra. As I help him get it off, I know there's no turning back. This is happening. We both want this.

He takes one breast in each hand. "Fucking perfect size." I glance down. His hands are large, and barely cover each breast. My boobs aren't massive, but they're a good size. When Liam squeezes them, I couldn't care less if they were grapes or melons. All I want is for him to keep touching them.

He leans in and takes a nipple in his mouth. I fist his hair and arch my back to give him better access.

He sucks hard, then he licks the hard bud.

I'm practically hanging on to his hair as he moves to the other nipple.

"Liam."

"Don't worry, Faye. I'm going to make you feel so good you won't be able to say anything but my name."

"Prove it." He looks up at me, and I know he's accepted the challenge.

I almost regret it when I see the wildness in his eyes. Then he lifts me up in one smooth movement and tosses me on the bed.

I let out a surprised yelp, but he's already pulling down my panties and pushing my legs open.

"You're playing with fire, Roses."

"What?" I want to ask what he just called me, but before I get to it, he's buried his face between my legs and takes a long lick and my question turns to a moan.

His tongue misses no spot as he starts licking my pussy. I've never experienced anything like it. It's been my experience that men don't like to eat women out. Whenever it's happened before, it's been half assed and over way too quickly.

But Liam is taking his time. And I know he's just warming up as he explores every part of me. His tongue makes me vibrate as he works his way to my clit.

When he finally reaches it, he teases me, circling around it and softly grazing over it. He barely touches it at first and I squirm under him, trying to get him to lick me in all the right places. But he just laughs, sending bursts of hot air over my sensitive parts and making me want more.

"Please," I say, and close my eyes.

"Not yet."

I groan in frustration as he softly circles my clit. Then I feel a finger at my entrance, and a new desire erupts in my body.

"Yes," I moan.

He pushes his finger inside me, and I'm desperate for relief. But it's not enough. As he plays with me and fucks me slowly with one finger, I can feel myself losing my mind.

"Please. More. Give me more, Liam."

The finger leaves me and he lines two fingers up. I'm so ready for it. I want it.

His lips close over my clit and he sucks, just as he pushes his fingers inside me and I scream.

"Oh, fuck. Fuck. Yes."

He pumps his fingers in and out and starts flicking my clit with his tongue.

He alternates between sucking and using his tongue and drives me closer and closer to an orgasm.

Then he stops.

"Please." I beg, not caring how desperate I sound.

"You're going to come around my cock. I want to feel it."

He's pulled away from me and the air cools me down as I'm naked with my legs spread in front of him.

Somehow, he's got a condom, and he's putting it on.

"Fuck me," I whisper and watch as he grabs his hard cock and pushes into my entrance.

My back arches, and I lean my head back as he fills me up.

"Fuck, you're tight. You feel so fucking good, Roses."

"More. Give me more. I want it all."

"Beg for it. Beg for my cock in your pussy."

"Please, Liam. Please give me your cock."

He pushes into me with one long stroke and I finally feel at home. He leans over me, supporting himself on one arm. Our eyes meet and he licks his thumb. I shiver in anticipation as his hand slides between us. His thumb finds my clit, and he starts rubbing.

"You're so wet for me. So ready to be fucked."

All I can do is nod. His thumb finds the perfect pressure and rhythm and he pulls his cock out, agonizingly slowly.

"Liam." I grab his shoulders and hold on.

"Yes?" He slams into me. Hard. And I'm done for.

"Liam." I tremble and shake as the orgasm takes over. He pushes deeper into me as I spasm around his cock and all I can do is scream his name.

He doesn't let me catch my breath. As soon as the orgasm subsides, he starts fucking me. He lies on top of me, pushing into me, over and over.

I open my eyes and he's right there. His face is so close, our breaths become one.

"Kiss me," I breathe out and his lips take mine. It's a tender kiss, and he's fucking me slowly, gently.

I hang onto him and give myself to the moment. To him.

When he starts moving faster, he pulls back, and we lock eyes. It's the most intimate experience I've ever had.

It's as if our souls connect and in unspoken harmony, we both climax at the same time. His lips silence my moans and a tear escapes my closed eyelid.

Afterward, he rolls off me and disposes of the condom into the trash can. We lie panting and sweating next to each other. I have an urge to reach out and hold his hand, but I stop myself in time. Instead, I clear my throat.

"So..."

"Yeah," he says, still breathing hard.

"Right."

He raises himself on his elbow and looks at me. "That wasn't too bad, was it?" And he smirks. That fucking adorable smirk.

"Not horrible," I admit. "You did make me come."

"Twice."

I nod.

Staring at the ceiling, I finally come clean. "I don't actually remember what happened that night."

"I don't either."

The silence lays over us like a blanket. I strain my satiated brain for something to say, but he speaks first.

"I should go."

"Yeah... Don't get caught."

He finds his clothes and I watch him get dressed. My body is heavy and satisfied as he looks me over once more before leaving.

Chapter 16 – A mix of emotions

Liam

Not horrible.

Not fucking horrible.

I run my fingers through my hair as I leave her apartment. That's what she said. Not horrible. When I get out of the elevator, I have to take a moment to remember where I parked.

What she thought was not horrible, has me all loopy and intrigued. Fuck, that was the best sex I've ever had and I know she liked it. She came for me. Twice. I got to feel just how good I made it for her.

I knew it would be great. There was never a doubt in my mind. Whatever happened that night we were drunk was an anomaly. Now, she knows.

I get in the car, and a sense of sadness comes over me. Now she knows what it was supposed to be like and we don't have to think about it anymore.

My actions are on autopilot as I navigate my way back to the hockey house.

I proved my point, and it's all over. Maybe it was a stupid thing to do because if we got caught, it's her job on the line. It was stupid of me to put my pride over her job. But it's done now.

It's over.

When I pull in at the hockey house, I have no idea how I got there. The house is dark and quiet. It's Friday night and everyone's out celebrating. I could meet up with them, but instead, I go to my room and lie on my bed, staring at the ceiling.

The way she felt when I slid between her legs... How she welcomed me. So hot and willing. I've never experienced anything like it.

But it's over now. It would be a shit move on my part to keep putting her job at risk, and I can't do that. Besides, I don't do relationships anymore.

What I should do is shower and wash the scent of her off me and then never think about her again. Until tomorrow. When she'll be at practice. Fuck, I'm going to have to see her and know what her pussy feels like, what she tastes like, sounds like. And I can't ever touch her again.

But it is what it is. We did it and now it's over. I'll just have to keep my distance.

I move, and the scent of roses fills my nostrils. Her scent is on my skin. The scent that surrounded me when she looked up at me while I was inside her...

Fuck, I'm hard again. How the fuck is she doing this to me? I grab my phone and find that one picture from the first night we met. I felt her up in the car. Had her in this bed.

My hand is in my pants. It's nowhere near as good as her, but she is driving me insane. I keep stroking myself, imagining her here with me.

Fuck.

But it's fine. I'll just jerk off to her this once, and then I'll be done. Completely over her.

***

I arrive late and get changed quickly. Then I hide out in the locker room like a coward until I know I'll have no time to stop and talk to anyone or even look in her direction.

Once I'm sure Coach will be just annoyed enough at my lateness, I book it for the ice. I can do this.

I keep my eyes straight ahead and focus on the instructions.

She's here, I can feel it. But I refuse to give in to the urge to look over at her. Even when I can feel her eyes on me.

I proved my point to her. And now, she's just like all the other puck bunnies. It's over and I can stop thinking about her.

My eyes flicker past her and take in every detail, her low ponytail, how she's on the ice, but with no skates on, the red jacket that's the same color as her bra and panties.

Fuck.

I glue my eyes to the puck and decide not to look at her anymore.

It almost works. Until I hear her laugh. It's a beautiful sound and I can't help myself. I have to know what made her happy.

My chest instantly constricts as I watch JD say something to her. She's smiling up at him and I want to murder him. The urge to skate over there and throw her over my shoulder so I can get her away from him is overwhelming. And it distracts me enough that I skate straight into someone and lose my balance.

Taken by surprise, I fall flat on my ass and have the wind knocked out of me. It's not a hard fall, but the guys closest to me all burst out laughing.

"What the fuck, Cayden?" I get to my feet.

"Dude, I barely touched you."

"Yeah?" Anger and embarrassment swirl inside me. "Maybe you should keep your head in the game."

"Me? Really?" He quirks one eyebrow and his eyes flicker to Faye.

"What the hell are you implying?" Fear joins the mix of emotions and I hold on stronger to the anger.

Cayden skates up to me and gets in my face. He's a freshman, but he spent a couple of years preparing for college hockey, so he's not only taller than me but also bigger and stronger.

"I'm implying that you should get your head out of your ass, old-timer."

"You need to show some respect." I shove him away from me.

"Or what?"

"Hey, hey, hey." JD pushes between us. "Break it up. What's going on here?"

"Nothing," I blurt. The way he glanced at Faye terrifies me. Even if he just implies something, it could be enough to get her in trouble.

"Just practicing trash talk," Cayden says and curves one side of his mouth.

"Well, don't." JD seems confused. I'm not sure he believes us, but the fact that Cayden isn't saying anything is enough for me to let it go.

We break it up and go back to the drills. I give it another minute before looking over at Faye. Her eyes are instantly drawn to me and I can see the concern on her face. I try to smile at her, but the cocktail of emotions makes it hard. So I go back to ignoring her.

"What the fuck was that earlier?" JD asks when we're heading off the ice.

"What?"

"Why are you picking a fight with Cayden?"

"I'm not. It was just an altercation. He knocked me over." I shrug and avoid looking at him.

"It looked like you were about to punch him."

"It's nothing, just let it go."

"No, this is what people are worried about. Liam," he grabs my arm and pulls me to the side, "you have to stop this bullshit and start thinking about the team."

"I am," I say and spot Faye putting away her camera and talking to Coach. "Don't worry about it."

"It doesn't look like you are."

The anger is still bubbling close to the surface. "I'm fucking thinking of the team. Everyone needs to stop worrying about stupid bullshit."

I walk away from him.

"Liam."

I ignore him and storm into the locker room. JD doesn't approach me again as I shower and change. He's probably giving me time to cool down, which I can appreciate.

Chapter 17 – The plan

Faye

I need to start working on my plan with Liam. But how am I supposed to talk to him after he gave me the best two orgasms of my life? And I can't stop thinking about all the things we didn't do?

I'm still trying to get more footage of the guys. It seems for every hundred pictures I take, I'm lucky to get one good one. It's taking me some time to figure out their movements and how to work with the sharp turns and sudden bursts.

So I decided to try some videos today. What else do I have to do on a Monday afternoon?

It's not that I want to see Liam, that's not it. But I do need to talk to him. Professionally. Not about what we did. That was a one-time thing.

It helps when they keep repeating the same maneuvers over and over. It gives me time to work on angles and makes it easier to follow along.

"Hey."

I almost jump out of my skin when Liam stops next to me.

"Oh. Hi." I turn off the recording, just in case he's about to say something unhinged.

"I have some time after practice if you want to meet up."

My heart skips a beat and my skin flushes.

"To talk about the PR campaign," he adds.

"Right. Yeah, sure." The PR campaign. That's what he meant. Why would he want anything else?

"You didn't think...?"

"What? No, of course not. That's all over now." I keep my eyes on the players in front of me as they go into a new drill.

"Good. Yeah. So, we can meet in the lobby after practice then."

I nod, but still don't look at him. "Sounds good."

"By the way, wouldn't this be easier if you wore skates?"

I look down at my feet. I've been shuffling around like a penguin, feeling very ungraceful while the guys swoosh about as if it's easier than walking.

"I don't know how to skate," I say

He shakes his head. "You work for a hockey team and you don't know how to skate?"

"So? It's not like I need to."

"It's just weird."

I want to give him some scathing reply, but in that moment, Coach calls him over and he sets off at a speed I could only dream of.

***

Once practice is over, I take a seat near the entrance. There are some low tables and couches there and I take out my notes about Liam and go over them.

"You're still here? Do you need a ride?" Coach stops by where I'm sitting.

"Oh, no thanks. I'm waiting for Liam. We're going to go over the plan."

"Good. I'm glad you're getting moving on that. Hopefully, people will forget all about his little tantrum soon enough."

"People are usually ready to move on to the next interesting thing in a heartbeat."

"That's true."

My eyes are drawn to the movement behind Coach. Liam is approaching and I suck in a breath. He's fresh out of the shower with glistening hair and looking good.

"Here I am," Liam says. "Ready to listen and obey." There's a glimmer in his eyes that makes my stomach feel funny.

"I'm glad you're taking this seriously," Coach says and turns to me. "If you have any problems with him, you just let me know."

"Will do." I glance from Coach to Liam and we both know I won't.

Coach leaves us to it and Liam sits down on the couch next to me. "So, what are we doing?"

I shuffle through some papers where I've brainstormed a bunch of ideas.

"Basically, there's two things. Hide the bad stuff and show some good stuff."

"Seems easy enough."

"Right." I feel out of breath sitting this close to him. He's leaning forward, with his forearms on his knees, studying the papers I have on the table. "Well, if you could hide the drinking and... the hooking up with puck bunnies, that would be a good start."

I can't look at him. I keep my eyes on a list of upcoming events I thought might be good to get him seen at.

His eyes burn into me and I feel myself blush.

"Just so the press doesn't get any more ammunition," I say when I really want to tell him not to hook up with anyone at all. But that's not my call to make.

"Sure," he agrees.

"Good. So, I have this list of events that it might be good for you to attend." I hand it over, still without looking at him. "Not all of them, but a few. It's mostly charity events and places where the alumni and sponsors might be. I'd also like to find an angle."

"Angle?" He wrinkles his brow and I want to smooth out the crease between his eyebrows.

"Yeah, something that they could associate with you instead of drinking and hooking up."

He nods and meets my eyes and I realize I've been staring at him, so I look away.

He clears his throat. "I'm majoring in chemistry."

"That could work. It's quite impressive."

"Yeah?"

"I'm surprised there isn't more about that on your profile."

He shrugs. "It seemed weird to bring it up, but if you think it will help..."

"Definitely. Do... do you ever wear a lab coat?" For some reason, the image of him in a white coat, doing science things, comes to mind. Just a white coat.

"Sure, when I'm in the lab."

"I think, if we could get some photos of that, it would help show everyone that you're serious."

Fuck. The thought of him mixing liquids and writing down results is hotter than I thought it would be. Just a scientist measuring things and being all serious. Maybe he could wear glasses and be shirtless. I'd walk in and try to distract him by sitting on the counter. He'd get up and grab my knees, opening them up...

"Faye?"

I snap back to reality. "What?"

"You ok?"

My cheeks burn. "Yeah, I just got... lost in thought."

"Did you now?" He sounds amused.

"The serious student angle is good. I think we should run with that."

He's smirking. "Good to know."

I squirm in my seat and notice I'm turned on. Fuck. Why does he do this to me?

"So, is that what you want to do? Chemistry? Or hockey?"

"Hockey is fun, and for a while, I thought that was my future. But lately, I'm more and more sure I don't have what it takes."

"What do you mean? You're great on the ice."

"I'm good, but not quite good enough. And I'm not sure I love it enough to fight for a spot on a team all the time. Not when I know there are other, better players who want it more."

"Oh."

"It's no big deal. I'll finish out the season and then find some low-level team that only plays for fun."

Nodding, I try to decipher if he's sad about that or not. I don't think he is. Maybe a little, but he seems to be fine with not having a future in the NHL.

"So, you'll be a chemist?"

"Yeah, I like figuring things out."

This is a new side to him I haven't really seen before. And it's a side I had no idea I'd like this much.

"So, photos," I say and try to get back on track. "If it's ok with you, I'd like to tag along to the lab some day and grab some. Then we'll come up with some appropriate captions and make the world see you for who you are."

"Sounds good."

I gather up my things. "I should go." I have to go. If I stay here any longer, I'm likely to jump him and make a fool of myself.

"Ok, what about these events?" He holds up the paper I gave him.

"Just look it over and check your availability. We'll go to a couple of them and I'll get photos. It might help if you have some of the other players come along, so it won't be too obvious."

"Sure."

I stand up and back away.

"Just let me know which ones you prefer."

He stands. "You need a ride?"

"Nope." Not a chance I can be in an enclosed space with him right now. "I'm good. See you later."

JUST ONE PUCKING NIGHT

I almost run outside.

Chapter 18 – More plans

Faye

Is it wrong that I want him again?

As he walks down the hallway to Coach's office, I bite my lip and try to ignore the heat he sends to my core.

It was hard enough walking away yesterday, but I'm starting to think it's going to take a while before I get over the sex. Seeing him every day might become my personal form of torture.

"I didn't know you'd be here," I say when he approaches.

"Coach asked me to." He stops half a step away from me and all I can think is that he's too close. And not close enough. "I think he wants to make sure I'm working with you."

I hate that my entire body goes hot as soon as he's around.

Clearing my throat, I desperately hope he doesn't notice the effect he has on me.

"I have a few more ideas we can try. Hopefully, you'll like them." My eyes are locked on the logo on his hoodie. It's a UNI hoodie in dark blue.

"What kind of ideas?" His voice is too dark. Too husky. Too slow. I inhale sharply. Why is he doing this to me?

"Well..." I can't think of a single one of them.

"Because I'm pretty sure I'd like most of your ideas." His hand is by my face, stroking my jawline.

My brain is overheating. His gentle fingers are sending pulses of electricity into my body.

He raises my face, so I have to look at him.

"I have some ideas of my own."

Oh, shit. Oh, fuck.

I part my lips, and his eyes immediately find them. My breathing is erratic, but just as I'm about to lean in, voices ring through my mind. JD and Coach are approaching.

I take a step back and turn away from Liam.

"Oh, good, you're both here." Coach unlocks his door while JD slaps Liam's back.

"I'm glad you're taking this seriously, man."

I avoid getting too close to Liam as I take a seat at the table.

"So," I say and try to keep my voice steady. "We talked about the situation and came up with some plans. First of all, Liam has agreed to keep his partying to a minimum and not be so public with his hook-ups." I have to stop and swallow away the annoyance at the thought of him still going after puck bunnies.

"Faye also gave me a list of events to attend," Liam says. "I've picked out a few that can get some good rumors started. There's one charity event for dogs. And I'll go to a few of the public skates."

"That's a good start," Coach says. "But the dean is still concerned about the photos. He feels you have a reputation for being unreliable. Especially when it comes to women."

"I don't think this no relationship-thing is working for you," JD says and I want to punch him. But I bite my tongue and stay quiet.

"It's fine," Liam says with clenched jaws.

"Can't you just get into a relationship with someone for a couple of months?"

"No." Liam sounds determined and I sink down in my chair a bit.

"But it's a good way to stop rumors," JD says. "Don't you think so, Faye?"

"Umm. Well, yeah, I suppose. But it's not really something we can force on him." Liam is sitting still, only his eyes move from JD to me.

"I'm not starting something with someone just for the cameras."

"It wouldn't have to be real," JD says. "Just something that shows you're over your outburst. Right?" JD looks at me again. And I hate him for it. I hate that Coach is also scrutinizing me.

"I think it's a great idea." I put on a fake smile. "Of course, we'd have to find someone trustworthy who is in on the whole thing."

"You think I should do this?" Liam asks and looks me straight in the eyes. There's more to the question, but what does he expect from me?

"Yes," I say.

"Too bad you can't do it," JD laughs at me.

"We do have rules about fraternization," Coach says. "If you're going to do this, everyone has to agree, and it has to be someone with no connections to the Lions." He sits up straighter. "My suggestions would be that Liam just stays away from women for a while."

JD laughs. "Nobody would believe he's all of a sudden gone celibate."

"I'll see what I can do," I say, to move the conversation along. "I'm sure I can set something up."

"Great," Coach slaps the table and stands up. "I'm glad everyone is ready to cooperate."

We all stand up and JD laughs to himself. "It really is a pity it can't be you," he says to me. "Because you are exactly Liam's type."

My stomach does a somersault as we leave the office.

"No, she isn't," Liam says angrily and my stomach flips for a different reason.

JD tilts his head. "You're both into social media, but in a serious way. Neither of you is likely to let it get to your head. You both work hard and, from what I can tell, you have a lot of the same values. Not to mention visually, she's exactly like you've described your dream girl."

I blink at Liam, but he just looks angry.

"When have I ever described my dream girl?"

"It was a couple of months ago, I think. You were drunk. Oh, you both like the same kind of shows. And you've both seen all the Fast and Furious movies."

We're slowly walking away from Coach's office now, but Liam stops.

"How do you know what Faye watches?"

Oh. Shit. JD knows because we discussed it during one of the photo shoots with Morgan, but Liam isn't supposed to know about JD's photography.

"Uhh." JD hesitates. Then he grabs his phone. "Oh, look. Morgan is calling. I should get this." He runs away pretending to answer the phone, leaving me to come up with a lie.

Liam turns to me. "How well do you know JD?"

I shrug. "I know Morgan. We probably discussed it in front of him."

He eyes me suspiciously. "Right."

He's mad at me? That's hardly fair. I get a better hold on my bag. "If you'll excuse me, I have to go find a woman for you to date." Without waiting for an answer, I turn on my heel and walk away from him. Not caring that I'm going the wrong way.

Chapter 19 – Is it worth it?

Faye

"Cora, I think I fucked up."

Cora turns off the tv and turns to me. "In what way?" I have her full attention as I join her on the couch.

"In the sleeping-with-Liam way."

"Oh. You still haven't given me any details, you know." She tilts her head.

"Yes, I did. I told you it was good."

"Right. But how good?"

"Very good." I close my eyes and sigh. "Very, very good."

"Ooh, I'm so happy for you," she squeals. "So what's the fuck up?"

"It was good."

She furrows her brow. "What?"

"Cora, it was amazing. But it was a one-time thing."

"Oh." Understanding comes over her. "And you want more?"

"I don't know how to act around him. I have to see him almost every day. I work with him."

Cora crosses her legs under her and sits sideways on the couch.

"You should probably be careful. For several reasons. First of all, I don't want to see you get hurt. So you need to figure out if it's only lust or something more."

"It's lust," I say quickly. "That's it. He doesn't do relationships."

"That doesn't mean you can't fall for him."

"I know. But I'm not. I'm not stupid enough to think I could change him."

"Ok. Well, second of all, does he feel anything for you? Did he like the sex?"

"I think so."

"But he hasn't approached you since?"

"Well, he did stroke my jaw."

"What?" She looks confused.

"Like this." I show her how his fingers caressed me.

"That's it?"

I nod. "But it meant something. You probably needed to be there. I think he was going to kiss me. But we got interrupted."

"Which leads me to the third thing. Your job. You know this could backfire."

"I know." I grimace at her.

"So, is it worth it?"

My mind goes back to the orgasms he gave me. Fuck, yes, it's worth it. It probably shouldn't be. The smart thing would be to say no. To put my job above some great sex. But the way I felt under him, when he kissed me, that's something I've never experienced before. So what if I have to find a new job? I can do that. But I have a hard time imagining ever experiencing that immense satisfaction ever again.

"Yes," I finally say, and Cora raises an eyebrow.

"I was so sure you were going to say no." She blinks a few times. "Wow. That must have been some really good sex. Does he have a magic dick or something?"

I blush. "No. He's just... really good."

"Well, then go for it. You should call him and find out if that weird jaw touch was what you think it was."

"I can't do that." I pick at the hem of my shirt and stare at my fingers.

Cora starts counting off on her fingers. "We already established that you're not falling in love with him, just lust, so no problem there.

You're willing to give up this job to experience some more naked Liam. So if things go really bad, you're perfectly aware of what you're getting yourself into. The only thing we don't know is if he feels the same. Which we can find out by you making a phone call."

"What do I even say?" I'm already reaching for my phone. "Won't I seem desperate?"

"Want to have sex? That always works for me." Cora shrugs.

"You don't really do that, do you?" I gape at her.

"Why not? I don't always have time to bullshit around."

"Right. Well, I'm not saying that." I find his name in my contacts and hover over it. Then, without thinking, I press the call button.

My stomach turns as it starts ringing. Maybe he won't answer. If he doesn't, then everything will be fine. If he doesn't answer, and doesn't call back, then I'll know...

"Hey, what's up?"

His voice comes out loud and clear and I forget everything I was about to say or do. My mouth opens, but no sound comes out. I try again, but I have no words. There's shuffling on his end and a door closing.

"Faye?"

"You touched me," I blurt out and slap a hand to my forehead. I can't even look at Cora. She's probably looking at me as if I'm crazy.

"What? What are you talking about?"

"Outside of Coach's office. You're not supposed to touch me in public. We could have gotten caught."

"But we weren't."

"I could lose my job, Liam."

"Relax, Faye. Nobody saw us. We didn't get caught and you're not losing your job." His voice soothes me and I hate that he can calm me down like that.

"This job is important to me. I don't want to lose it."

Cora's eyebrows are raised and she mouths, 'what are you doing' at me.

"It was a mistake. It won't happen again."

Fuck. I want it to happen again. Why is my brain so scrambled?

"Good. Thank you."

"Is that the only reason you called? To yell at me."

"I wasn't yelling," I say quietly.

"Debatable, but you can yell at me if you want."

Cora is gesturing for me to move on, and I know what she wants me to ask, but now that I'm talking to him, I don't know if I can do it.

"So," I say. "Did you think about the fake dating?" Cora is now utterly confused, but I press on. "I think it could be a good way to dispel any rumors."

"No."

"Why not? It's not like it matters to you."

"I don't do relationships."

"It wouldn't be a relationship. It's a public relations strategy."

"I hate this idea."

"What if I can make you change your mind?"

"How are you going to do that?"

I glance over at Cora, who is following the conversation intently. "We could talk about it. At my apartment?"

The line goes absolutely quiet.

"Liam?"

I check to make sure the call hasn't ended.

"Yeah?" He sounds... strange.

Fuck.

"You know what, never mind. We can just talk tomorrow at the Den."

"Faye?"

"Yeah?"

91

"I'm coming over."

"Ok." My voice is squeaky and I hurry to hang up.

"What the fuck was that? You just went completely off script." Cora stares at me.

"He's coming over."

She smiles. "I guess that answers that question. I'm not sure I would have started by yelling at him, but you got results."

"I wasn't yelling."

"Right. Well, I'm going to make sure my noise-canceling headphones work. I'm sorry, Faye, but I'm not going anywhere tonight. These cramps are killing me."

"I'm just going to talk to him. We probably won't do anything."

"Right. Because when a man drops everything to come over, they never want to have sex."

My cheeks flush and I bury my head in my hands. What have I done?

Chapter 20 – Just sex?

Faye

"Oh, my god." I stare at Cora. "He's coming over."

"I know. You invited him."

"What do I do?"

She shrugs. "Wait for him to get here?"

I nod. "I should change my shirt."

"I don't think he cares."

She's probably right, but I still get up and go to my room. I find another top and put it on. And take it off. It looks like I'm trying too hard. I rummage through my closet and try on top after top.

"Cora, help me." I shout when I'm ready to just greet him in my bra.

"Black t-shirt. The one with the cute fox," she shouts back from the living room.

I dive into the closet and find the one she's talking about.

It's perfect. It's fitted, but not revealing. Casual and cute without making me look like I just spent fifteen minutes ravaging my closet.

"Good?" I ask when I emerge into the living room.

The doorbell rings.

"It's going to have to be." She smiles and throws off the blanket she was under.

"He's here." I take a few deep breaths while Cora hurries to open the door for him.

"That was fast," Cora says and I want to kill her.

"Hi. Cora, was it?"

She looks over her shoulder at me. "He remembers."

"Let him in, Cora."

"Right, wouldn't want you to get caught." She gestures for him to come in and closes the door after him.

"Hey." He looks me up and down and my nipples immediately go hard.

"Hey."

"Fascinating," Cora says. "Well, as riveting as this is, I'm going to go to my room."

"Nice meeting you again," Liam says.

"You too." She stops in her doorway. "Happy fucking and don't worry about me. I have my headphones." Before I can throw something at her, she disappears and I'm not sure what to do or say.

"So?" Liam says. "Are we fucking?"

Shit. I'm going to kill Cora.

"I thought you wanted to talk about the fake dating?" I gesture to the couch and he takes off his jacket before sitting down.

"Not really, but you and JD seem obsessed with the idea."

"It's not a bad idea. People do it all the time." I carefully sit down next to him.

"That doesn't make it right for me."

"But it would help..." I vaguely gesture between the two of us.

He raises an eyebrow and leans in closer. "Are you telling me there will be more..." He does the same gesture between us.

I give him a small shrug. "Is that something you would want?"

"Is the fake dating a condition?"

I shake my head. He's so close, I can't think.

"I don't want a relationship, Faye."

"It wouldn't be like that."

He puts his hand on the back of the couch and leans over me. I instinctively lean back toward the arm of the couch.

"What would it be like?"

I have no idea what we're talking about. Us? Or the fake dating?

"Liam?"

94

He keeps moving in closer and I can't lean any further back. "Yeah?"

His eyes are on my lips.

"Why did you come?"

Our lips are almost touching.

"Isn't it obvious?"

I grab his neck with one hand. "Yeah, I guess it is." Then I kiss him.

His body covers mine and I open my mouth for him. His hand rests on my waist for a moment before it trails up. His lips claim mine and our tongues meet as his large hand covers my breast.

I let slip a small moan, and he takes it as encouragement.

He pinches my nipple through the fabric, and I let my fingers glide into his hair. The kiss deepens and intensifies, and I shift under him to get him closer. He grabs my waist and sits up, lifting me onto his lap. I place my legs on either side of his hips and grab his shoulders.

His tongue explores my mouth, and his hands grab my ass. I move my hips and feel his erection through the pants. Knowing he's turned on makes this so much hotter.

His hands leave my ass just long enough so he can slide them into my pants. As he squeezes me closer, I can't help but moan again.

Fuck, I love making out with him.

I pull at his shirt and place my palms against his chest. His muscles are hard and smooth.

I lose track of time as we slowly turn each other on more and more.

When Liam finally breaks the kiss, I'm dizzy and horny.

"Do..." He clears his throat. "Do you want to take this into your room?"

I nod. "I think we should."

I untangle myself from him and get up. My clothes are disheveled and I'm certain I look thoroughly kissed.

As I walk into my bedroom, I try to smooth out my hair.

He follows me and closes the door.

I face him and pull off my t-shirt. He's breathing hard as I take a step closer and sink down in front of him.

"Fuck," he says as I start undoing his pants. He pulls off his shirt and tosses it aside, keeping his eyes on me.

I pull down his pants and he eagerly steps out of them. Then he stands in front of me, his dick hard and eager right in front of my face.

Last time, I didn't get to play with it. I'm about to make up for that.

I gently slide my fingers over the tip and he shudders. A tiny bead of pre-cum glistens and I smear it out before I lean in and lick it.

"Fuck," Liam says again.

I run my tongue around the tip, enjoying the silky smoothness before I place my hand at the base and close my fingers around him. I take him in my mouth and swirl my tongue around the sensitive areas.

His body tenses and vibrates and every so often, a moan escapes him. I work his dick with my mouth and hand. I love the feel of his skin and lick and kiss him all over.

When I glance up at him, he has his hands locked behind his head, and I know it's to stop himself from grabbing my hair so he can facefuck me. Our eyes meet and I smile up at him as I close my mouth around him and guide him deeper.

I take him as deep as I'm comfortable with, and he groans. I start moving back and forth and try to find what rhythm he prefers. The noises he makes are clear indications and they're also turning me on.

"Faye, stop." I pull back and look at him. He reaches down and grabs my arms, pulling me up.

"Is something wrong?" I ask, wondering if I hurt him or made a mistake.

"You're going to fucking make me come too fast."

I can't hide the smile. "That was kind of the point."

He blinks at me. "At least let me eat you out first."

I nod and unbutton my pants.

He pulls them down in one swift movement and I'm about to lie down on the bed when he picks me up and spins me so my back is against the door. I want to ask what he's doing. But he reaches back to undo my bra. In an instant, he gets rid of it and pinches my nipples as he sinks to his knees.

I lean back and support myself against the door as he lifts one of my legs and puts it over his shoulder.

"I've had dreams about this," he says as he places a kiss near my opening.

"Really?" I'm breathless.

"Oh, yeah. I love the way you taste." He buries his tongue in me and I angle myself so he can go even deeper.

He licks and explores, and I can barely remember how to breathe.

His thumb finds my clit and this time he rubs gentle circles, almost like an afterthought, while he's feasting on my juices.

He's making me feel worshiped. It's as if he needs to taste me. And it's making me even wetter.

"Fuck me," I moan.

"Just say the word." His voice vibrates against me and I shiver.

My fingers are buried in his hair, pressing him closer. He rubs my clit harder, digs his tongue deeper, and moans. The moan sends me. The thought of him enjoying this hits me hard and releases the pent up orgasm and I scream as I come on his face.

He licks up every drop before slowly setting my leg down on the floor. When he stands up, his chin is glistening with my wetness. I take his face in my hands and kiss him, tasting myself. Tasting him.

I pull back just enough to whisper. "Fuck me."

He kisses me quickly before bending down and grabbing a condom from his pants. My chest heaves as I watch him put it on.

"Ask me again," he says when he grabs my hands and holds them above my head against the door.

"Fuck me, Liam." I meet his deep, dark eyes and see the lust I feel in them.

"Like you've never been fucked before," he says and kisses me.

I lift a leg and wrap it around his waist. He lets go of my hands and hooks one arm under my knee and uses his other hand to guide his cock to my wetness.

"Liam," I gasp as he sinks into me.

"Fuck, Roses, you feel so fucking good." He rests his head against my neck, and I lean my head back against the door.

He fills me up and I grab his shoulders and hold on when he starts to move.

My entire body welcomes him as he starts pumping into me. I love his skin against mine, the sweat on his forehead, the way he smells of himself and sex.

He reaches down and hooks his arm around my other leg. My foot leaves the floor and all I can do is hold on to his shoulders as he lifts me up and down on his cock.

"Liam." He's completely in control of my body, and I'm happy to surrender to him. I've never been fucked like this before. I lean my head against his neck and gasp as he slams into me. My mouth opens and I taste his skin. He moans and holds me still while pumping his cock into me. I bite lightly, nibbling his neck.

"Fuck, Roses. You have no idea what you do to me."

I suck on his neck, marking him. Relishing in the knowledge that any other woman he sleeps with after me will know I had him first.

He pushes me back against the door and pants as he studies my face. Dropping my legs, he moves his hands to my waist, holding me steady as he leans in and kisses me.

It's as if he couldn't wait another moment to taste my lips. It's a desperate, hungry kiss and I answer it just as passionately. Barely noticing that he's no longer inside me.

When he pulls away suddenly, something flashes across his face. "Turn around."

I do as he says and lean forward, palms against the door.

His fingers trail between my legs. "You're so fucking wet for me."

He replaces the fingers with his cock, and I arch back into him as he, once again, fills me up. The fucking is ferocious now, as if he has to make up for the lost time when he kissed me. As if he needs me so badly, he can't slow down.

I brace against the door with my palms as his fingers dig into my waist.

Gasping for air, I can do nothing but enjoy the ride.

Liam speeds up and hammers into me, bringing pleasure I've never known before.

When he slows down and brushes my hair to one side, I'm not ready for the tenderness. His lips touch my ear.

"Am I being too rough?" There's almost panic in his voice. Regret?

I shake my head. "No." I still can't breathe. "Please. More."

His teeth nip my ear and pull gently at my earlobe. "Hold on, Roses." His mouth trails down my neck and shoulder and I shiver. "I'm about to ravish you."

His hands grab my hips this time, and I brace myself again.

Fuck, I love hockey. I love the stamina and speed it gives its players.

Liam fucks me like there's no tomorrow. It's fast and furious and primal. What's happening between us is pure and utter enjoyment. How he can keep it up for so long, I have no idea.

When I think I won't be able to take it much longer, he pulls out and I'm immediately disappointed.

"Liam," I whine.

"On the bed," he says in a harsh voice.

I practically run to the bed and lie down. He's on top of me in an instant, pushing my knees up and out.

"I need you," I say, and he doesn't hesitate. He thrusts his cock inside me and looks down at me.

And now, I can't breathe for a different reason. As he drives into me with long, slow strokes, I know I'm fucked. Because this is more than sex.

"Liam?"

My voice seems to wake him from a slumber, and he leans in to kiss me.

Our lips lock and he reaches down to rub my clit as he speeds up. Whatever's been building between us comes to a crescendo and it's not long before we're both coming, silencing each other with our mouths.

The waves of pleasure seem to last forever. And then his tongue seeks entrance into my mouth. I greet it and open up. He pulls out of me and still keeps kissing. So I slide my fingers into his hair and grab his head, holding onto him.

I'm lost in the kiss until he rests his forehead against mine and takes a deep breath.

"Is that why you called?" he asks, in a sarcastic tone.

"Wh...what?"

He stands up and looks down at me for half a second before turning away.

"You asked me to come over. Did I deliver what you wanted?"

His words hurt. As if what just happened was nothing to him. As if he was just giving me what he thought I wanted.

I can't speak. I watch him get his clothes and pull a blanket around me. Feeling used.

He looks back at me with a crooked smile. "It's just sex, remember?"

I nod at him. My mind is racing.

"I still need to know what kind of woman you would want to date."

He stiffens for a bit, then he pulls on his shirt. "I'll think about it. But I won't date just anyone. Even if it is fake."

"Yeah, of course."

He puts on his shoes. "I'll see you tomorrow."

Before I can nod, he leans in and kisses me. When he retreats, he seems as surprised as I am about the kiss. He instantly turns and leaves the room.

I raise my fingers to my lips. Why was it so natural? Why did it feel like he was supposed to kiss me? And why was he trying to make it sound like he didn't enjoy the sex? I know he did.

Chapter 21 – Fucked

Liam

I'm so fucked.

How can I still want to kiss her again? What spell does she have over me?

I leave her apartment yet again. But this time, I'm not sure I'll ever be able to stay away from her.

Coming inside her was one of the most profound things I have ever experienced. Until I kissed her right after. Fuck, she reeled me in with that kiss. I lost myself completely. And I hated it.

I mean, I loved it, but I'm not supposed to. That kiss took things too far. And I had to find a way to bring it back. Fuck, I shouldn't have said what I did. But how else was I supposed to show her it didn't mean what it felt like?

And I was doing so good, being just mean enough to her. Even when she hit me with more of that fake dating bullshit. I was doing good. Until I kissed her goodbye.

Why did I do that? That wasn't supposed to happen. I was supposed to leave her without looking back. Without making things weird.

That kiss caught me by surprise.

It felt way too fucking easy.

I rub my forehead as I walk to my car. Fuck, I'm messing this up. If I had any sort of sense, I should stay away from her. She's trouble with a capital T. And I don't need that right now.

The sane thing to do is find another puck bunny to hook up with as soon as possible.

JUST ONE PUCKING NIGHT

I get into my car and lean my head back against the support. It's wild how good the sex was. But it's different from any I've had before. That's why I had to do it from behind. Because seeing her face had me melting. In that moment, I would have given her the world. And that scares the shit out of me.

She's nobody. Just another woman.

I glance at my reflection in the rearview mirror and gasp. As I pull on the neck of my shirt, there's a hickey. She fucking gave me a hickey.

I laugh as I start the car. She fucking marked me. And it makes me feel all warm and... happy?

Oh, I'm so fucked.

***

Every part of me is on edge as we approach the Den the following day. I'm with a few of the guys. We met up after the last class and drove over together. They're joking and talking as if it's just another day, just another practice. But my thoughts are on one thing, and one thing only: Will Faye be there?

Should I have texted her last night? Asked if she was ok?

I shake my head. No. That's what you do for a girlfriend, not someone you're hooking up with.

Fuck, I hope she's here. I want to see her.

I'm so occupied by my thoughts, I barely notice a thing when we head back toward the locker room.

"Hey, Faye. Will you be filming us again today?" Dustin asks. My head snaps up and I can't take my eyes off her.

"Hi guys. No, I won't be filming today. You can relax. I just have some things I'd like to bring up with you."

"What about?"

I love how quickly the guys have accepted her. They all treat her like a sister. Well, most of them. I do see some of the guys looking at her a bit too closely, but I'm keeping an eye on that. I adjust the scarf and wonder if she gave me the hickey on purpose, or if it was in the heat of the moment.

"I'll tell you when it's all of you." Her eyes meet mine and time stops. I want to look into her eyes when she's coming around my dick.

She breaks eye contact.

"I'll see you guys on the ice." She steps to the side to let us pass, and I pretend to look for something in my bag, letting the others walk ahead.

When she's about to walk past me, I reach out a hand and place it on her stomach, stopping her.

She inhales. "Liam." My name is soft and breathy, and the way she says it makes my cock twitch.

"Feeling ok, today?" I was pretty rough on her, and I'd hate to think I hurt her.

"Remembering you with every step." Her eyes are dark and there's a hint of a smile on her lips. My hand drops to my side and as she walks away, I desperately try not to get turned on by the way she said it. I have to get changed in front of a bunch of guys in a couple of minutes.

I turn to look after her, and she smiles at me over her shoulder.

Fucking hell.

I'm going to have to wait before I can show myself.

As soon as she disappears, I lean my forehead against the wall and try to calm myself down. She's not supposed to be spicy like that. But fuck if that doesn't make it even hotter.

And what exactly did she mean? Can she feel it? It didn't sound as if it's painful? Fuck, I want to know exactly how I affected her.

No. I can't think about that now. Ok. Unsexy thoughts. I start naming off the NHL teams in my head as I straighten up. I can do this.

When I open the door to the locker room, I've managed to compose myself.

I start changing and think nothing of it until I notice Ethan staring at me.

"What the fuck is that?" He points to my neck.

Shit. "What does it look like?"

"Looks like you fought with a vacuum cleaner."

"Fuck off."

I keep getting dressed, but Ethan isn't letting it go. Some of the other guys are watching us.

"Who did it? One of the puck bunnies?"

I grind my teeth. "She's not a puck bunny."

Ethan laughs. "I knew it. I knew you couldn't stay away from relationships."

"It's not a relationship."

"Come on, tell us who she is." Ethan looks around at the others, and they encourage me to spill the secret.

"She's none of your business."

"I'm sure we'll know soon enough," JD says, and raises an eyebrow at me. "When he's ready to tell us."

I can't tell if he thinks this is part of the fake dating scheme or not. Either way, it's not something I'm going to discuss with any of these guys.

I finish getting ready while ignoring more jokes and jabs.

There's a knock on the door and Coach comes in. He rarely knocks, so I'm not surprised when Faye steps in behind him.

"Listen up. Before we hit the ice, Faye has something she wants to ask you."

The room settles down, and we sit and wait.

Faye smiles and steps up beside Coach. Her eyes scan the room and I see her flinch slightly as she spots the hickey on my neck. She looks flustered for a second, but quickly recovers.

"There's a public skate coming up Wednesday, and I was hoping as many of you as possible could make it. It's a great opportunity to get some public relations going. I'll be there to get some photos and stuff, but this is more than just a photo op. I know you regularly do public skates and from what Coach has told me, some of you do show up occasionally to help out. Which is great. But I'd like all of you to think of this as a way to build your own fan bases."

"What do you mean?" Pan says and looks at her as if she's the sun imparting knowledge with every breath.

"Well, many of you hope for careers in the NHL. NHL players are public figures. People will talk about you. Good and bad. When it comes to public relations, having a loyal fanbase could be the difference between a rumor destroying your career, or just getting laughed at. People want to get to know you. I don't mean to make it sound so transactional, but that is part of it. Other parts include just being decent people who care about fans. And role models who inspire younger kids to play hockey."

"Do we have to... do something?" Dustin asks and turns red.

"Be kind." Faye looks over all of us. "Don't be assholes, is the main thing. The kid you help next week could be a future NHL player."

Fuck, she's hot when she takes control of a room like this. I barely hear the questions and answers that follow. All I can do is study her and hide my smile.

Until I see Coach looking at me. I quickly break eye contact and stare at the floor instead.

Chapter 22 – The phone call

Liam

I can't take another cold shower.

It's past ten at night and I'm ready for bed. But as soon as I no longer have things to focus on, my mind goes to her. To what we did.

Seeing her yesterday was torture. But not seeing her all day today was just horrible.

Sleep is not coming for me. I know that as I stare at the ceiling. What is coming to me is all sorts of thoughts. Uninvited thoughts of how she tastes and smells and feels.

I grab my phone and find the picture from that first night. I've stared at it way too much lately.

Her number is right there. I slowly find it and stare at it.

I could call her. Not for any reason. Maybe just talk about the fake dating? Or I could text her. See what she's up to.

No, that's stupid. It's late, and she's probably asleep. Like I should be. I have an early class tomorrow.

I shouldn't call.

But I could send her a text. See if she answers.

I open the empty conversation. What do I say?

I've never been good at writing. But there has to be something I can say...

I start typing. And delete it. Again. And again.

Fuck. Why is this so hard?

In a fit of frustration, I press the call button instead.

My stomach flips when I realize what I've done. The signal goes through and it's too late to hang up. So I swallow hard and put the phone to my ear.

"Hello?" She sounds sweet.

"Hi," I force out.

"Liam?"

"Yeah. Hey." I squeeze my eyes shut. Why the fuck did I call her? What do I say now?

"It's late." She sounds confused.

"Sorry, did I wake you?"

"No. I was just getting into bed."

Oh, fuck.

"Really?"

"Mhm. What are you doing?"

"I'm in bed." I glance down at myself. I'm in boxer shorts under the blanket. "What are you wearing?"

There's a moment of silence.

"A t-shirt."

"Nothing else?"

"Panties."

I smile to myself. Maybe calling her wasn't such a bad idea after all.

"What color?"

"Oh, they're black. Cotton."

"That sounds... nice."

"Why did you call me, Liam?"

Because I missed you. I can't say that, though.

"Same reason you called me the other night."

"I'm not coming over. I'm too comfy. And it's a bit late for a visit."

"That doesn't mean we can't talk," I say and hold my breath.

"You want to... talk? Like... have phone sex?"

I clear my throat. "Well, if you insist."

She laughs. "I didn't."

"We can talk about other things." God, I love her laugh.

"Like what you're wearing?"

I pretend to sigh. "You're so insistent. Fine, I'll tell you. I'm wearing a pair of black boxer shorts. Nothing else."

"Really? I don't know why I imagined you sleeping naked?"

The smile on my face is ridiculous. "You've been thinking about me naked?"

"I..."

"What exactly am I doing while naked in your imagination?"

I settle deeper in the bed, ready for whatever might come.

"I don't know if I want to tell you." Her voice is shy and quiet.

Now, I need her to tell me. "I promise it'll stay between the two of us."

"Well, you... came to my room."

"Naked?"

"No, but you went to sleep in my bed, naked. And I came home and found you there."

"Rest assured, If I'm in your bed, I'm not sleeping. What did you do?"

"I... this is silly."

"No, it's not. The thought of being naked in your bed is turning me on. Please, tell me more."

"In my imagination, I didn't notice you there. I got naked and slid under the covers. And then I fell asleep."

"Huh? I was expecting something more... active." I'm almost disappointed by the story.

"Well, a while later, I wake up to your... hands on my boobs."

"Now, we're talking. Did I pinch your nipples or just squeeze them?"

"You massaged them." I can almost hear her blush through the phone.

"Mmm. I like that idea. Then what?"

She hesitates. "Then you pressed your... dick against my ass."

Fuck, she's making me hard already. "Yeah?" I encourage her.

"Yes."

"Tell me there's more, Roses, because you're doing things to me now."

"You slid one hand between my legs."

"Can you do me a favor?" I'm in pain.

"What's that?"

"Can you take off your black panties while you tell the rest of the story?"

"Oh."

I hold my breath.

"I've never done this before."

"Taken off your panties?"

"Not while on the phone with someone."

"Will you do it for me?"

"Yes. Hold on."

My heart does a somersault as there's the sound of fabric and shuffling.

"Ok, they're off."

"Now, tell me. What did my hand do to you?"

"At first, you just pressed your palm against me, circling."

"Can you do that to yourself?"

"Liam."

"I want you to touch yourself." I move the blanket aside. The boxers are tented by my hard cock.

"Ok."

"Now, tell me more."

"Then you let one finger slide between my lips."

"Are you wet?"

"Yes." She's breathless and I'm full of triumph.

"Good girl. What happened next?"

I reach down and pull off my boxers, freeing my erection.

"You pushed a finger inside me." I almost drop the bottle of lube.

"Mmm, I'd love to do that now." I squeeze out a dollop and rub it on my cock.

"And then..."

"Then what?"

"Liam, I'm not sure I can..."

Shit, I pushed her too far.

"I had a fantasy about you the other day," I say as I lazily spread out the lube.

"You did?" I don't know why she sounds surprised.

"Yeah. You want me to tell you about it?" I start slowly stroking my cock.

There's a moment of silence, and I wonder if she has to think about it.

"Yes." The word is faint, but it fills my heart.

"I was alone in the locker room. Everybody else had gone. I was showering."

"Ok."

"You showed up. Somehow, you were just there. Looking gorgeous in a flowery dress. And as I came out of the shower, water running down my body, you looked at me like you wanted to devour me."

She moans and I desperately want to know what her hand is doing.

"I walked up to you and kissed you. You were wearing that dress, and nothing underneath. And when I bent you forward, and lifted up the dress, you were dripping for me."

"Just like that?"

"Oh, I was ready to work for it. I went down on my knees and tasted you, but you started begging me for cock. Just like the other night."

"I did do that, didn't I?"

"You did. And hearing you want me like that is enough to make me the hardest I've ever been."

I'm stroking myself faster now.

"Did you grant my wish?"

"Yes."

She whimpers so softly, I almost think I imagined it.

"Tell me."

"You were bent over, dress at the waist, and your ass in the air. So I grabbed your hips, placed my cock at your entrance and enjoyed every moment as I slowly entered you."

"Oh."

"Faye?"

"Mm?"

"Are you touching yourself?"

"Yes. Are you?"

"I'm about to explode from hearing you moan."

"Tell me more."

She sounds out of breath and I wonder, hope, pray that I can make her come.

"I buried myself deep inside you before I slowly pulled out. Your pussy is addictive, and I couldn't resist sliding back in again. And again. And again. Over and over. Just so I could feel you around me."

"Mmm."

"Then I reached around and found your clit. Tell me, are you rubbing your clit right now?"

"Yes."

"Are you wet for me?"

"Ah, yes."

"Fuck, I want to bury my tongue in your pussy again."

"Oh."

"Are you getting close?" I can tell by her heavy breathing that she must be.

"Yes."

I speed up my own strokes. "Fuck, I want to feel that pussy around me as you climax. I want to suck your nipples into my mouth and hear you scream as you come."

"Liam." She's about to lose it. I release my last restraint and listen to her panting and moaning as she comes. It's enough to make me follow her. I feel the hot, wet liquid as it squirts over my stomach and bliss takes over my body.

"Fuck, yes. Fuck me, Roses. You just made me come all over myself."

She's panting. "Oh, god."

"Was that good for you, Roses?"

"Uh-uh."

Fuck, I wish I could hold her. I want to wrap my arms around her and let the last of her shivers transfer to me as she comes down from her orgasm.

I clear my throat, not sure what to say now. "Did you...?"

"Yeah."

"Good."

"Oh, shit."

"What?" I sit up straight at the panic in her voice. There are some sounds in the background.

"I'm fine," Faye says. "Nothing's wrong."

There's a muffled voice. It has to be Cora.

"No, he's not here. I'm... I'm on the phone."

I think I hear laughter, but I can't be sure. I'm close to laughing myself.

"Did she hear you come?"

"It's not funny, Liam."

I do my best to not laugh at her. "I'm sorry. It really isn't." Pride fills my chest. I made her come so loudly that her roommate had to check on her.

"I should go," she says, and the pride is exchanged for disappointment.

"Oh, yeah, me too. I have to clean myself up." I look down at the mess I made.

"I'll see you around."

"Yeah. See you."

I wait for a moment to make sure she hangs up first. Then I sigh and sink back into the pillows. Fuck, that woman has some magical control over my body. I just hope that was half as good for her as it was for me.

Chapter 23 – The party

Liam

It's Friday night, and we just won another game. All my teammates are out celebrating, and what am I doing? I'm at home, scrolling on my phone. Being a good boy.

I take another sip of the water and sigh as I flicker past some photos from a party. It sucks sitting alone at home when everyone else is out having fun.

But it's not like I have a choice. Faye and Coach have seen to that.

I keep scrolling and glance at the photos. I should stop torturing myself. Since I can't be there, I should just do something else.

I'm just about to close the app when a familiar face catches my attention. Sitting up straighter, I zoom in to make sure I'm not mistaken.

Fuck. I'm sitting home here like some spinster and she's out there having fun, dancing with Cayden of all people.

Oh, hell no.

I change into a fresh shirt and make sure my hair is decent before I hurry downstairs and grab my car keys. The car I got has already paid for itself many times over. Like the other night, when I was able to make it to Faye's in just a few minutes.

And now. I try not to speed as I make my way to where the party is.

It's not hard to find. There are loads of cars out front and the music and smoke smell are clear indicators. I park and know I should take a moment to think before I storm in there, but all I can see in my mind's eyes is Faye dancing with Cayden.

People greet me as I arrive and I nod at them and push on deeper into the house. My eyes scan room after room, looking for the red shirt she was wearing in the photo. Red like the bra and panties she wore that first time.

Fuck. What is she doing to me?

I shake my head and spot Ethan and Morgan playing beer pong. Morgan seems to be winning.

Moving on, I find the dance floor. The music here is loud, and the room is warm. Even with the open window.

Faye is still dancing. But Cayden is nowhere around, which is good for him. She's dancing with Pan, laughing at something he said. He leans in to say something else and I see red.

Barging across the dancefloor, I ignore the people I push past and only stop when I'm next to them.

"Oh, hey, man," Pan says as the music reaches a semi-quiet part. "I didn't think you were coming."

"Well, I did." I glare at Faye. Her eyes flicker around the room, as if she's trying to look at anything but me.

"Join us," Pan shouts over the music and gestures for me to dance with them.

I shake my head. "I need to talk to you," I shout at Faye.

"What?" She shakes her head subtly.

"Talk," I say even louder and point to a door that leads outside.

She looks furious, but before she can say anything, Pan interrupts her. "Yeah, go ahead. I see someone I want to dance with." He's already abandoned her and has his eyes on a woman in a white skirt and hoodie.

I grab her hand to pull her along, but she immediately tugs it away from me.

"What are you doing?" she yells, but she follows me through the door and into the still snow-covered backyard.

"Me?" I can't believe her. "Me? What am I doing?"

"Yes, you." She glances back and moves further away from the open window. "What the hell is wrong with you?" She keeps her voice low. "You can't just appear out of nowhere and try to get me alone. Do you realize how suspicious that looks?" She looks around the backyard. There's a few people out there, but none close enough to overhear us.

"What are you doing here?" I cross my arms.

"What do you mean, what am I doing here? I'm at a party. Having fun. Celebrating the team winning."

"Dancing and drinking?"

"What's your problem? I'm allowed to go to a party."

"But I'm not?"

She blinks. "Is that what this is about? Are you mad because you can't drink and sleep around?"

I clench my jaw. "It's not fair."

"I'm not the one with the bad reputation," she says, and her eyes are on fire.

"You're going to get one if you keep this up."

It's her time to cross her arms. "What the hell is that supposed to mean?"

"I saw a photo of you dancing with Cayden."

She tilts her head. "Is that why you came here? The guys asked me to join them. I've danced with almost all of them."

"All of them but me."

"You weren't here."

"Because you told me not to."

"I never said you can't go out. I said you can't get caught on photos doing stupid shit like drinking or putting your hand down some puck bunny's pants."

She's mad. Why is she mad? I'm the one sitting at home, feeling like a fool.

I stare at her, not sure what to think.

"What's this about, Liam? You can't just storm in here and act all... weird."

"I'm not weird. I'm upset because everyone is here having fun except me."

"You can go to parties, Liam. Just avoid alcohol and any situation that might make the rumors worse."

I shake my head and take a step closer. She immediately steps back, away from me.

"Don't," she says softly. "There are people here taking photos."

"Right. And we don't want them getting the wrong idea."

She rubs her arms, and it dawns on me that we're standing outside in the cold. I take off my jacket and offer it to her. She takes it and puts it on. It's too big on her, but it looks good.

"So, I can't touch you?"

She pulls the jacket closed and buries her nose in it for a second.

"No, not here."

"Pity. Because I wouldn't mind lifting that red shirt up to see if you're wearing a red bra underneath."

"Liam," she admonishes softly, and I wonder if she's trying to keep up appearances for herself.

"I think you'd like it if I checked," I say. "Maybe if I played with your boobs? I need to get my hands on them again. And my mouth. I feel like I've woefully neglected them."

"I don't think we should talk like this here. It's not appropriate."

"It's not? So you won't beg me to fuck you? Again?"

Her cheeks turn red.

"Not here," she says so softly I almost miss it.

Her eyes flicker to the side and I could scream when I see JD walking up to us.

"Hey, what are you guys doing?" He's clearly a bit drunk.

"I was just giving Liam some guidelines if he wants to stay here." Faye doesn't miss a beat.

"Yeah, she's tough," I say. "I'm not allowed to drink or have sex in public. I might as well be a monk."

JD laughs and slaps a hand down on my shoulder. "Sorry dude, sex in public is the best."

Faye's eyebrows almost fly off her head, and I groan. "Dude, that's too much information. I really don't need to know what kinky stuff you and Morgan are into."

JD giggles. "Shit, don't tell her I said that. I should find her. Fuck, she's awesome."

"Sure, dude." I spin him around and aim him toward the door. "Go find Morgan."

He stumbles away, and I return my attention to Faye. She's taking off my jacket.

"I'm going back inside," she says. "I'm actually having fun."

I nod and take back the jacket. "Yeah, I'm going to leave. I shouldn't be here."

"You can still stay."

She sounds sincere, but I shake my head. "No. Not tonight." I put on the jacket and walk away. I can't stay, because if I see her dance with Cayden again, or any of the other guys, I might lose it.

Chapter 24 – Rejections

Faye

I don't understand Liam. One minute I think maybe he likes me. The next he seems to get mad at me or treat me like I'm just someone he's sleeping with.

He goes from sweet to mean in an instant, and I don't get it. And I never know what mood he'll be in.

So, Monday afternoon, I suck in a deep breath as I approach him after practice. It's time for him to give me some feedback on the candidates I've found. But I have no idea if he's even onboard with the idea yet, much less will accept any of the women.

"Oh, hey, Faye," Pan says as he comes out with Liam and a couple of the other guys. "You missed practice."

"I'm sure you managed to get by without me."

Pan laughs. He's a good guy, and I could see us becoming friends. He gives little brother vibes.

"I did, but I'm not sure what crawled up Liam's ass and died." He glances over at him, as if he's worried he overstepped.

My eyebrows rise as I glance at the man I'm sleeping with. He's not looking at me.

"In a bad mood today?" I ask.

Our eyes meet, and my skin tingles. Fuck, why does he do that to me?

"Not really."

He seems calm enough to me, so I don't get what Pan was talking about.

"Liam said you wanted to some kind of dance number?" Ethan says.

"Yeah. I think that would be fun. And I saw your videos. You're really good."

"I don't know who will want to do it with us, but we can set something up."

"That would be great."

"I'll do it," Pan says.

"Do you know how to dance?" Liam asks.

"I'm sure I can learn."

"Nobody is expecting it to be prefect," I say.

"Did you come here to see Coach?" Liam asks innocently.

"Actually, I was hoping to speak to you." I keep eye contact and wonder how nobody else can tell we've had sex. It's so obvious.

"Why?" Pan asks. I force my eyes away from Liam, and Pan narrows his eyes at me.

"I have some plans for a campaign that Liam is part of."

"I could help with that."

When I first met him, Pan seemed shy and reluctant, but as I've gotten to know him, I've learned that he puts hockey first. Always. He's eager to learn about every aspect of hockey, the NHL and creating a serious career for himself. He's a teacher's pet type of guy, and right now, he sees me as the teacher.

"It's ok, I'm sure we'll work together on something else." I try to let him down easy, and he nods and seems to be ok with it.

"Yeah, well, if you need help..."

"Oh, remember the public skate is on Wednesday. It'd be great if you could come."

"I'll be there," Pan says seriously.

"Great."

"Come on," Ethan says. "Liam, we'll see you later?"

"Later," Liam says and hangs back with me as the others leave.

"You have time to go over some stuff?" I ask, glancing at the backs of the hockey players.

121

"Sure."

I look around for a place where we can talk without anyone disturbing us and we move to one of the seating areas near the entrance.

"You look nice," Liam says as we sit down and I instantly don't know what to say. I'm not even wearing anything special. And my hair did not want to cooperate this morning, so it's a bit wilder than intended.

"Thanks," I finally breathe out.

I try to hide my embarrassment by digging through my bag for the papers I printed out for him.

"What's this about?" He leans back in the chair, and I have to clear my throat before I can speak.

"I have some candidates for you." I pull out the pile of profiles and hand it over. "I've gone through some dating sites and looked for women I think we could approach with the idea."

He glares at me as he takes the papers.

"Really? You really want to do this?"

I half shrug and stare at the low table between us. "It's a good idea."

"Unless it all backfires and makes me look even worse."

"It won't." I'm not going to let it.

He sighs and takes a look at the first profile. "I already slept with her." He hands me the paper.

"Oh, and did that not... end well?"

"It ended fine, but I'm not reconnecting with someone just to ask them to pity date me."

The photo on the profile is of a pretty blonde with a killer smile. She's very photogenic. I swallow hard at the thought of her and Liam.

"You're right," I say. "It shouldn't be someone you've been with." She is off the table. I place the paper on the table with her photo facing down.

He takes a look at the next woman and I hold my breath. "I know her. Can't stand her."

He hands me the paper.

"No redheads." I take the next profile and put it in the pile.

"What do you mean, no redheads?"

He shrugs. "They remind me of someone."

I blink a few times and wonder who. Maybe Cora would know? She could find out. Maybe the woman at Rivers? The equestrian? No. I can't keep using Cora to look into his past. That's not acceptable.

"She's way too into reality TV."

"What's wrong with reality TV?"

"She mentions it five times in her profile. That's excessive."

I accept the paper. "Fair enough."

"Walks on the beach are stupid. Especially since there are no beaches anywhere nearby."

"Ok." We have a routine going by now. One by one, he hands me the profiles, and I put them aside.

"Pretty sure this one is fake. I think this photo is a combination of two actresses, and her answers scream bot."

I wrinkle my forehead and study the profile. "Oh, shit. She does look like a combination of a young Angelina Jolie and Jenna Ortega."

"Right?" He only has one paper left now.

I stare at the bot profile, unsure how I missed that.

He hands me the last paper. "She has too many cats and I'm allergic." With that, he leans back again and looks me over.

"Are you serious?" I pick up the pile and flick through the profiles. "Not one of them works?"

He shrugs. "I'm sure you'll find someone."

"You have to work with me here. I'm doing this for you, you know."

"I never asked for this. I'm doing it for the team."

"And none of them is even tolerable?" One by one, I study the faces in the pile. But he's right. None of them works.

"It has to be believable. Nobody would ever think I was in a relationship with any of them."

"Well," I gather the papers and put them away. "At least I learned a lot about what you don't want."

"Glad I could help." His knuckles are white and I wonder if he's mad.

I hesitate. "I should go. I'll see you Wednesday?"

He nods. "See you Wednesday."

I don't want to leave him. For some odd reason, I'd rather keep spending time with him here, even if it's just to discuss other women. But there's no reason for me to stay.

So I get up and leave. I walk away from him and he watches me go. A small part inside me wants him to say something, to stop me, even if it's just for one more minute. A few more seconds. But he doesn't.

Chapter 25 – The public skate

Liam

My heart hits my throat as I watch Faye squeeze her eyes shut and skate right into the boards. I wince internally as she catches herself and uses the boards to turn around and push off.

"You're doing great," I say to the young girl I'm helping. "You almost have it." She's trying to learn how to come to do a double-footed hockey stop without falling. She can't be much older than eight or nine and her mom is anxiously watching over her as she falls over and over. The kid is great, though. Full of determination. And doesn't seem to mind a few bumps and bruises.

"I'll get it." She takes off again, and this time she's almost come to a stop when she loses her balance and topples over.

"Just keep practicing," I say.

She nods and gets up to do it again. I skate over to JD and match his pace.

"Hey," his eyes are scanning the ice. "How's it going?"

"Great, I'm pretty sure she'll be part of the team in ten years' time." I gesture to the girl who's fallen over yet again.

"I guess that's what it's all about."

The ice is almost crowded with so many of the Lions being here. They all seem to be doing a good job.

Faye is filming Pan as he helps a small kid, barely old enough to stand on a pair of skates. The kid is doing better than her. She's trying so hard to stay upright on her skates, but it's wobbly as fuck.

"I hope she's getting some usable footage," JD mutters.

"What do you mean?" I watch her almost lose her balance, waving the camera all over the place. "Oh. Yeah, I see what you mean."

"Should we do something?"

Faye seems to stumble over her feet yet again. And I hold my breath. She doesn't fall.

"I got it," I say and feel thrilled to finally have an excuse to approach her.

"Be nice to her," JD calls after me.

I pull up to her and come to a halt so suddenly she's thrown off balance.

"Oh, shit," she mutters and flails with her arms. I reach out and catch her.

"Getting any good photos?" I ask with a half smile and she glares at me.

"I don't see why I have to wear skates. I'd be much better off in my shoes."

I shake my head. "I've seen you try that. It's not much better."

She looks defeated as she studies the screen on the camera. "This sucks. I've got some good photos, because I don't have to move for those, but I can't get the videos I want."

"What do you need?"

"To know how to skate?"

She's so cute when she's upset. Her cheeks have little red dots and her eyes are laser focused.

"That doesn't seem to be an option right now." I smirk down at her feet.

"Well, then I need someone to film for me." She holds out the camera.

I shake my head. "That's a hard no. I am no good with cameras."

"You film dance videos all the time."

"I know how to set up a camera and stand in front of it. Not skate around and film people."

She sighs. "I'll just hope I get a lot better very quickly then."

"I have an idea. So you need to follow Pan?"

"Yeah, but there's too many people and I keep falling over and I don't know where he's going."

"Relax, Roses. I got you."

I grab her waist.

"What are you doing?"

"Helping you get what you need. Now, do you trust me?"

She nods. "Yes." The word warms my heart, and I have to fight off a smile.

I start moving across the ice and pull her body as close to mine as I can do in a rink filled with people watching. I lift her slightly and she inhales so quietly I almost think I imagined it.

"Liam." Her voice is pleading, but I don't know for what.

"JD is worried you won't get any good footage," I tell her. "So you better start filming."

She holds up the camera and I weave between the people, trying to place her so she can get an unobstructed view of Pan and the kid.

I slowly pass them so she can get their faces in the video. When I'm ahead of them, I stop and put her down temporarily. Instead of holding her waist, I wrap my arm around her so she can film behind us as I try to keep just ahead of them.

"Great," she says when she's done and looks around. "Thank you."

"What else?" I ask.

"Oh. Maybe Enzo and Cole?"

I spot them skating next to a group of preteen boys and head on over. They're just chatting with them, but the boys' faces are lighting up. I move ahead of them and Faye films the interaction. Cole is answering questions without a single hint of a smile on his face, but it doesn't seem to matter. He shows them some exercises and they're listening to him so intently it's almost funny.

Enzo seems slightly more human and even cracks a couple of jokes with them.

I circle around them and make sure Faye gets the footage she needs.

"Ok. Good."

"You got that?" I put her down on the ice and grab her elbow as she almost tumbles over.

"Yeah."

"What else do you want?"

She bites her lip. "I'm sure this is fine. You don't have to carry me around anymore."

"Faye, what do you need?"

Our eyes meet.

"Just some general images of the people skating."

"Ok. We'll make a few laps and you tell me what to do."

She seems to blush at that. "Ok."

I grab her again and just as I set off; I meet Ethan's eyes. His forehead is furrowed, and he looks slightly confused and worried.

Oh, fuck. I almost forgot I told him about Faye. Well, I told him about the first time. As far as he knows, it never happened again.

I look away and focus on my task.

Once the skate comes to an end, Faye seems happy.

"I think I got a lot of stuff I can use." She puts her camera away.

"That's good." I've already let go of her. More than one of the players was eyeing us suspiciously and I don't want to give them any more ammunition than necessary.

"I didn't really get many shots of you, though." She seems so concerned with that. I almost laugh.

"That's ok. There will be other events."

"Yeah, but we're trying to improve your image."

128

"I guess you're going to have to learn how to skate."

Her cheeks redden, and I want to tell her I lied. As long as I'm around, she never has to learn to skate. But I don't.

"I will," she says.

"Do you need help to get to the entrance?" I ask and she judges the distance.

"Umm, yeah."

This time I take her hand and try to ignore the jolt of electricity that shoots up my arm. "Ok, try to skate for me, Roses."

"Why do you call me that?" She takes some careful steps and I make sure to hold her steady.

"Why not?"

"It's an odd nickname."

I pull her along slightly as she works her way to the entrance.

"You don't like it?"

"I didn't say that." We reach the boards, and at the same time, JD comes up to us.

"Did you get anything usable?" he asks Faye.

"Thanks to Liam," she smiles, and my heart wants to explode. It's too much. I can't be this close to her.

"Yeah, that was... unconventional."

I shrug. "It worked. And you told me to help her." I nod at them and leave them to discuss whatever it is they talk about. Mostly, I just have to get away from her before I do something I'll regret. Like kiss her in front of everyone. Or throw her over my shoulder and find a quiet corner.

I need a shower. A cold one.

Chapter 26 – Call it what it is

Faye

I barely make it inside the apartment before I lean back against the door and close my eyes. The way he held me all day long... Fuck, but it did things to me. He lifted me up as if I weighed nothing and made sure I got the perfect footage.

And somehow he did it without making anyone suspicious. Oh, god, I hope nobody got suspicious.

"What's up with you?" Cora asks as she comes out of the kitchen and heads into the living room with a bowl of ice cream.

"He touched me."

"Inappropriately?" She furrows her brow.

"No. Not even a little."

"Ok, sit down and tell me."

I shake off my jacket and step out of my shoes, leaving my bag behind.

"Tonight was the public skate," I say as I curl up on the couch with my back against the armrests. She mirrors my position. We've had many conversations like this.

"Ok."

"And I was supposed to film it." I shift in my seat.

"I'm with you so far."

"But I don't know how to skate."

"Oh, yeah. I forgot about that. You fell once when you were seven and refused to put on skates again."

"Whatever. It's not like you were great at it."

"I'll have you know I'm absolutely decent at skating." She smiles at me and takes a spoonful of ice cream.

"Well, I wasn't getting the footage I needed, because I kept stumbling and falling over."

"Did he come to save you?"

I nod. "He kind of did." I stare at my hands as I remember how strong his were on my waist.

"Tell me."

"He pretty much carried me around."

Her eyebrow shoots up. "Really? Just like that?"

I can't stop smiling. "It was so... strange. But he made sure I got what I needed."

"Hm? Maybe it's time to invite him over again, then?" She wiggles her eyebrow. "Or do the phone thing. Now that I know you do that, I won't barge in again."

My cheeks burn. "We don't do that."

"I beg to differ. I thought you were being attacked in there."

"It happened once."

"And apparently he's pretty good at it." She's teasing me, and it's working.

"That's not... Just stop talking about it, please."

She gives me a small shrug. "So, tell me. What was it like having him cart you around today? And what do you mean there was no inappropriate touching? Shouldn't there have been?"

"Oh, Cora. It was... fucking amazing. I never knew how strong he is. But his hands didn't stray, not even once. Is that bad?"

"I don't know. I mean, you were in public. And he does know about the rules, and how important the job is to you."

"True. But it was so hard not to touch him."

She smiles mischievously. "He set a little fire in your loins, didn't he?"

I clear my throat and avoid looking at her.

"What do I do now?" I ask.

"Now, you call it what it is and go for it."

"What is it?"

"You're clearly friends with benefits."

"Argh." I bury my face in the back of the couch. "We can't be friends with benefits."

"Why not?" Cora eats her ice cream as if this is just another boring conversation.

"It's against the rules."

"So? You've both already broken the rules. Do you really think anyone is going to ask how many times you've slept together if they find out? Are you going to be more fired if the answer is higher?"

"No." I admit sheepishly.

"There you go. Besides, nobody has to find out, and it's only for a few months."

"What?" I look up at the mention of a deadline. Nobody said anything about a deadline to me.

"Yeah, I mean, he's graduating, right? And hockey season is coming to an end."

Right. I guess that is the deadline.

"They have a real shot at the Frozen Four this year. If they win, it'll really put them on the map. That's why it's so important that their reputations are good." I really want my team to do well. They're working so hard to get better and win their games. Each and everyone of them wants this. And I want it for them.

"Focus, Faye. You just turned into a social media manager. That's not what we're doing right now."

"Sorry."

"You should talk to Liam."

"And say what?" My stomach flips at the thought of talking to him again.

"Talk about what you're doing. You need to clear things up."

"I've never done that before." I furrow my brows.

"You've never talked to a guy about sex?"

"Well, no. I mean, not like this. I've never slept with someone I wasn't in a relationship with before."

"Well, you've slept with Liam like three times already, and it sounds like it's going to happen again. So you might as well be honest with him and talk about what you're doing. It's the only way you won't get hurt."

I chew on my bottom lip as I contemplate what she's saying. "You're right. I should talk to him." Shit, that's going to be an awkward conversation. I freeze. "What if he doesn't want to?"

Cora sighs deeply. "He's not allowed to sleep around, and he doesn't want a relationship. You already know he finds you attractive. What's there to object to? Guys love knowing women want to sleep with them. You just need to tell him."

I nod. "Yeah, you're right. I'll tell him. Maybe tomorrow."

"Just be honest about what you want and expect of him."

"Fuck, Cora, how are you so mature about all of this?"

"Experience, my dear cousin." She winks at me and smiles.

"And yet, you're having ice cream for dinner."

"I had a protein bar earlier. It evens out."

Shaking my head, I get up and head to the kitchen to see if I can find something more appropriate than ice cream to have for dinner.

Chapter 27 – The kiss

Faye

I chose to work at the Den the following day. The Lions have practice, so I watch them as I create posts and answer comments. I've actually come to like being here while they practice. There's something about the determination and motivation that hangs in the air.

And of course, there's Liam.

My eyes keep finding him whenever I glance up from my phone and I catch him looking at me a few times as well. I want to talk to him, but there's too many people around. I could text him, but his phone is probably in his bag.

After the guys go to shower and change, I take my time before slowly making my way back there.

I feel a bit silly hanging around pretending to be typing on my phone, but none of the players seem to find it odd as they leave.

When the door opens and Liam comes out with Ethan and JD, my heart sinks.

"You're still here," JD says.

"Just finishing up some things." I try to ignore the fact that I could do my job anywhere and hold up my phone as if to prove a point.

"Do you need a ride?" JD asks, and I shake my head.

"No, I'm good. I'll see you later."

My eyes meet Liam's and I almost miss the suspicious look Ethan is giving us before I hide my blushing cheeks and pretend to be utterly engrossed in my phone.

"See you around," JD says and keeps walking.

"Yeah, see you," Ethan says.

"Uh-uh. See you." I don't look at them.

Liam follows them down the hallway, and my shoulders sink. So much for that plan. I guess I could call him, but what I want to say isn't really something you say over the phone.

A couple of stragglers leave the locker room and I put away my phone and slowly follow them toward the front of the building.

"Yeah, I probably left it somewhere." Liam's voice rings out and I slow my steps. "No, you go ahead. I'll catch up with you later."

My feet stop in place and my heartbeat spikes.

Liam appears around a corner and passes the stragglers. As he walks toward me, he makes a gesture with his head, as if he wants me to go with him.

I make sure nobody is watching before I join him.

We walk to the locker room in silence. Liam opens the door and pokes his head in.

"Nobody's here."

I take a deep breath and follow him inside.

The door barely closes behind me before he's backing me up against the wall. He rests his forearm on the wall near my head and I can barely breathe.

"Hey," he says in a low voice.

"Hi."

"You looked like you were waiting for me."

I swallow and nod. No time like the present. I might as well get this over with.

"I want to do it again."

He blinks. "Are you serious?"

Doubt immediately takes over my brain.

"Unless you don't want to. I mean, we don't have to. I was just thinking."

A slow smile spreads on his lips. "Oh, I'll do it. I'll fuck your brains out if that's what you want."

"And don't worry," I say, and try to ignore how close he is to me. "I'm not suggesting a relationship. All I'm saying is that I'm busy with my studies and job and I don't have time to socialize and find a boyfriend." Oh, shit. I'm babbling again. "And since you don't suck in bed, I was thinking we could have an arrangement."

He places his free hand on my waist and I feel deliciously trapped. "That works for me, since I'm no longer allowed to sleep around."

"Good."

The kiss takes me by surprise. And for a moment, I think he's just as surprised as I am. His lips on mine feel so right. He tastes me tenderly and I open up for him and lose myself in the kiss.

I could kiss him for hours. I place my hands on his waist and he pulls me away from the wall so he can sink his hand into my hair.

"Oh, fuck," he says when he finally pulls away from me.

He rests his forehead against mine and we're both panting. My head is spinning and I'm glad he's still holding on to me because I'm not sure my legs would carry me right now.

"Yeah," I say.

He clears his throat. "I think we can work something out."

"We'd..." I'm trying so hard to focus and get my breathing under control. "We'd be exclusive, right? I mean, you'd let me know before sleeping with someone else."

"Yeah. I don't cheat."

"Well, it wouldn't be cheating. Not really." I have to remind myself that this is not a relationship. He's in no way agreeing to be my boyfriend.

Our eyes lock and I see his determination. "I won't sleep with anyone else while we're doing this."

"Good. Then I want you to get tested."

He seems to take some time to register what I just said. "What?"

"I'll get tested too, of course. And if we're both clean, I'd like to skip the condoms."

His mouth falls open. "You... What?"

"I've never been a fan." I shrug and ignore my burning cheeks. "I just prefer it without."

He's still gaping at me, not saying anything.

"Do you think you could get tested?" I finally ask.

He nods slowly.

"Ok. Good. We can talk more about this later."

As I open the door and walk away, I hope he didn't see how red my face is. I've had conversations before about getting tested and condoms, but it feels so very different knowing he's not my boyfriend. Whatever we do is just for sex. And somehow, it has my pulse racing. I almost wanted to do it right there, in the locker room.

But that would be stupid. Right? We're at the Den. Anyone could walk in on us. I sigh. And if they catch us, I lose my job and I don't even know what happens to Liam. I can't imagine it's good.

We're going to have to be very, very careful.

Chapter 28 – Interviews

Liam

I know it's game day. I'm going through the motions and doing all the things I normally do on game day. So it has to be game day. But I did make one exception.

Earlier today, I made a visit to a clinic.

Fuck me. She asked me to get tested. I don't even want to think of what that means.

I sit in the locker room, geared up and ready to head out on the ice for warm-ups. Coach is talking, but I can't hear a single word.

She wants to skip the condoms.

That's what she said.

For some reason, that has me way too excited. I've always used condoms. Sure, when I've been in relationships, I've suggested a few times we try without. But that's a two person decision. And not one you take easily.

But she wants me to get tested. Because she doesn't like condoms.

My entire body shivers in anticipation, and I shift in my seat to hide it.

"Everyone clear on that?" Coach asks.

The rest of the room nods and several of the players say yes, so I play along. He could have been telling us the plan is to slap the other team with fish, and I'd have no idea.

"Great," Coach says. "We're going to have a good game tonight. Before we go out there, I believe our social media manager had something to say."

My head snaps up and I see the door is open. She must have been waiting right outside, because she comes into the room and smiles at everyone but me.

"Hi guys, I hope you're ready to win tonight."

The room cheers. They all like her. She fits in so well with us.

"Good. I'm glad to hear it. So, what I'm doing tonight is I want to get some short clips of you guys answering questions. I'll film the answers and post them sometime in the next few weeks. If you don't want to answer the question, you don't have to. But I want to do this at several of your games and then, eventually, make a little short thing about your way to the Frozen Four."

She's so good at her job. Everyone is giving her their full attention and what she's saying actually sounds like a really good idea.

"How long should the answers be?" Pan asks.

"Short." She doesn't miss a beat. "A sentence or two is fine. The questions today will be more about your background. Why you play hockey, how you train, what was it like to join the Lions. Stuff like that."

She scans the room. "Any other questions?"

"Why are you doing it today?" Cayden asks. "Wouldn't it be better to do it during practice?"

He almost sounds accusatory, and I narrow my eyes at him, but Faye doesn't blink.

"I'm doing it today because I want the adrenaline. I want the game in the background. I want the crowd and the excitement. Having all of that will make the clips come alive."

Cayden nods and seems satisfied with the answer.

"Faye will be hanging out with us tonight, and please work with her. But your main focus is the game. Don't forget that." Coach eyes us all. "Now let's get out there and win."

Coach leaves. Several of the players instantly follow him. I sit tight as Faye moves into the room and stops in front of Pan.

"Do you want the first question?"

His entire face lights up. I don't know if she's doing it on purpose, but I'm pretty sure she just made his night.

"Of course." He sits up straight and Faye turns on the camera.

"Have you always wanted to be a hockey player?"

Pan's face softens.

"I used to go to games with my grandad when I was a kid. I was at hockey games before I could walk. And as soon as he was able to fit a pair of skates on my feet, he took me out on the ice. He used to be a coach, and I loved hanging out with him. He taught me so much and he made me love hockey."

Faye lowers the camera. "That was perfect. Thank you." She hesitates. "You said loved. Is he....?"

"He died three years ago. But every time I play, it's like he's here with me."

I notice a couple of the other guys are staring at Pan. I never knew. I knew he loved hockey. He's obsessed with hockey. But I don't think he's ever mentioned his grandfather before.

"I'm sorry for your loss," Faye says.

Pan shrugs and gets up. "Thanks. I should warm up."

She nods and steps aside.

I get up to follow the others when Faye turns to me. She raises the camera with a raised eyebrow, and I nod and hold my breath.

"How has it been to be part of the Lions for the last few years?"

"Oh, it's been great." I try not to look at the camera. Or to stare at her. "We've formed close bonds and you really feel like you're part of a team with these guys. We're all working toward the same goal and even if we sometimes have our differences, at the end of the day, we're teammates."

"Thank you." She lowers the camera. We're the only ones left in the locker room. "You should head out there." She's keeping her eyes on the camera in front of her.

"Yeah, I should go." I force my feet to move so I can pass by her. I can't stop. Not here. Not now. She does things to me. Makes me forget what I should be doing. She could ruin my life.

We get to the ice and she films the warm-ups. So what if I make sure to flex a little for her? I'm just doing my best.

After warm-ups, she's talking to more of the guys. I try to not pay attention. It's not like it matters. She's doing her job. I'll probably see the clips at some point.

But I still listen in as she stops our goalie and interviews him.

"Hi, Hudson. Mind answering a question?"

He glances over at Coach, who keeps an eye on him.

"Sure, I guess."

"What does a typical week look like when it comes to getting ready for a game like this one today?"

"We have practice every day. Different types of drills and working on skills and skating. I lift three times a week and try to make sure I get enough sleep."

"Sounds like a rough schedule."

"You have to eat enough to have energy for it all. And make sure you don't skip stretches and cool downs."

Hudson never smiles, but at least he's giving her more than one-word answers.

"Thanks. I appreciate it."

"No problem." With that, he turns and leaves.

Faye spots Walter and raises the camera again.

"Hey, Walter."

"What?" He looks around anxiously.

"Can you tell me what your thoughts are right before a game?"

"To win." He blinks at her.

"Right. But do you do anything to be ready to hit the ice?"

"I mean, I guess I make sure my equipment is all good."

I smile as I sense Faye's frustration.

"Ok. What about the opposing team? Does it matter who you're up against?"

Walter looks at her as if she's stupid.

"Yeah. They all have different strengths and weaknesses. You have to take that into account."

"Ok." Faye chews her bottom lip.

"Was that all?"

"Yes, thank you, Walter."

"Sure."

She at least waits until he can't see to roll her eyes. I guess they can't all give good answers.

Once the game starts, Faye takes her place in the audience and I set my mind to the game.

When we raise our arms in yet another victory, all I want is to find her and celebrate. But Ethan is already suspicious and Coach isn't stupid. So I tell myself that it doesn't matter and try my hardest not to look in her direction.

We leave the ice and she greets us with the camera, asking a few more questions and getting more footage.

By the time I'm showered and changed, she's already gone. For a moment, I think I should text her, or call. But I don't.

Chapter 29 – Test results

Faye

It's Tuesday afternoon and I'm still at the Den after they finish practice. I spent the entire weekend working on a project for one of my classes and wondering if I should call Liam.

I've never had a friend with benefits before, so I have no idea what's expected of me. How often are we supposed to meet up? Just when one of us wants sex? Are we actually friends? I mean, I doubt he'd want to just hang out and watch a movie or something, so maybe it's more about the benefits?

Either way, I got myself tested, like I said I would, and I really hope he did too.

If I'm honest with myself, part of the reason I've been avoiding him is that I'm embarrassed about how forward I was. I probably shouldn't have come straight out and told him what I did. But it's too late to do anything about it now.

And in an effort to be braver, and because Cora is starting to make fun of me, I'm hanging back after practice to see if I can talk to him.

When the players leave, my eyes scan over them anxiously. If he doesn't notice me, I don't know what to do. What if he comes out with a bunch of his friends and doesn't want to talk to me?

Fuck. I should just text him or something.

I wave at Pan and Dustin as they walk by and try to make up my mind if I should pack up my things and pretend I wasn't waiting for him, or just suck it up.

I barely notice him as he comes out into the lobby, sees me, turns around and goes back toward the locker room.

Well, I guess that's some form of answer. I slowly start putting my things away. Maybe today isn't a good day?

No. I put my bag down. Today is the day. I need to talk to him before I chicken out.

Jonathan gives me a little wave as he leaves and I wave back.

Liam knows I'm here, and I'm not going to let him get away. I get up again and grab my bag. Heading toward the back, I'm on a mission. If I've counted correctly, most of the guys should be gone by now.

"Hi, Faye, what's up?" JD glances up from his phone.

"Not much. Has everyone left already?"

"Hm?" He's on the phone again. "Yeah, I think I'm the last one aside from Liam and Ethan."

"Coach left?"

"Yeah, he had a meeting earlier."

"Ok, thanks."

"See you tomorrow."

Hopefully, JD didn't find that suspicious.

Ok. Ethan is still here. How do I get rid of him? Maybe if I wait, he'll leave? I mean, he's not going to stay here all night.

I slow my steps and take a few deep breaths. The locker room door opens and Ethan emerges.

He does a double take when he sees me.

"Faye? What are you doing here?"

"I dropped a mitten. I was looking for it."

"Oh, I didn't see any." He narrows his eyes.

"I'm sure it's here somewhere."

"Yeah. Well, I'll see you later." I don't think he believes me. Does he know?

"Bye." I give him a cheery wave and walk past the locker room door. Keeping up the pretense and pretending to search for the mitten that's in my pocket.

Once Ethan is gone, the door opens again. This time it's Liam. He looks around and startles at the sight of me.

"Hey."

"Hi, I wanted to talk to you."

He nods. Then he holds open the door to the locker room. "In here?"

I hesitate. If I go in there with him, I'm not sure what will happen. I shake my head.

He drops the door and comes up to me.

Oh, fuck. I'm in trouble out here as well.

"I have something to show you," Liam says and takes out his phone. I inhale his scent as I wait for him to find whatever it is. "Here."

He turns the screen to me, and I breathe out a sigh of relief. I have a very similar document on my phone.

"Hold on," I say and bring it up. I hand him my phone as I take his.

I trust him, but I feel like I should make sure his test results are all good before we do this. And I expect him to care enough about his health to do the same with mine.

"Looks good to me," he says and we switch back to our own phones.

I nod. "Yeah."

"So." He clears his throat. "Are you on birth control?"

I nod. "I have an implant."

He takes a deep, shaky breath. "Ok."

"Are you ok?" He seems odd.

Nodding, he puts away his phone and takes a step closer. "Are you seriously going to let me do it without a condom?" His voice is low and excited.

I look him in the eyes and blink. "Yes. Why wouldn't I?"

He shrugs. "I've never done that before."

A smile takes over my face. "You're a raw virgin?"

"Most women insist on condoms, and I've always respected that. Besides, I'm too young to be a dad."

"If you want, you can still use one."

His hands grip my upper arms and he pushes me against the wall. His body presses against mine and I can feel something hard against my stomach.

"Hell, no," he says in a low, menacing voice that gives me shivers. "I'm going to fuck you with nothing in between and fill you up with my cum."

My insides melt. I had no idea dirty talk would turn me on like this.

"What else are you going to do to me?"

He lowers his head, and I part my lips.

"So much. I'm going to make you beg for-"

"Liam!" Ethan's voice rings out.

He jumps away from me, and I close my eyes at the disappointment.

"Coming," Liam yells back.

"Fuck you," I say and try to calm myself down.

Liam smirks. "Sorry, Roses, I have to go. I have a thing with Ethan. And he's going to get suspicious if he has to wait any longer."

I nod. "I'll see you tomorrow for the game."

"Tomorrow."

He's gone and I'm left feeling robbed. But we're doing this. And he wants it just as much as I do. When I finally trust my knees to carry me, I smile as I leave the Den. This is going to be interesting. Very interesting.

Chapter 30 – You still wanna?

Faye

Liam looks uncomfortable. I'm in the locker room right before the game, and he keeps glancing over at me and adjusting his gear.

His words from yesterday ring in my ears, and I keep losing my train of thought.

I'm trying to get a few more interviews done today. And I find myself caught up in the excitement of getting closer to the Frozen Four.

If I understand it correctly, they need to win the game tonight and a couple more games to have a chance at getting to the regional finals. And everyone is on edge.

The Lions are good, and they should be able to win, but for a few of them, this is the first time they're experiencing this kind of pressure.

I focus on my interview with Cole and do my best to make him look human. Then again, he's one of the scarier players and I think part of the reason he's such a good forward is because everyone is intimidated by him.

"Thank you so much," I say when he's finished. I turn off the camera and look around. I have more questions I could ask, but they're all distracted by the upcoming game. So instead I walk over to Pan. His post garnered a lot of attention.

"Oh, Pan. I don't know if you read any of the comments under the post I made, but if you didn't, I wanted to let you know that a lot of people offered their condolences about your grandfather and there were also a few comments about how cute you are."

Pan's embarrasses easily so I don't go into details.

"I haven't looked," he says, but I'm not sure I believe him.

"Maybe you should. People seem to like you."

Pan needs to gain some more confidence. He's starting to bulk out and mature, but he's still nervous around women.

When it's time for the boys to head to the ice, I move to the side so I won't be in their way. I film them as they pass me by and cheer them on.

Liam comes right up to me and I make sure nobody's within earshot before I put the camera away.

"Any feedback on my video?" he asks as the last of the guys walk by. He lowers his voice and his eyes turn dark. "When can I fuck you?"

Oh, god. Why does he do this to me? How can I be expected to think when he says five words and has me wet?

But, fuck, it's empowering that he wants me.

I smile and raise an eyebrow in an attempt to be flirty. "Eager much?"

"Like you aren't?" He's got me there. I had a hard time sleeping last night thinking of what we've started.

"How about...?" I mask my insecurities by putting a finger to my lip and pretending to think. "How about if you win the game tonight, you can come over to my place?"

I lower my hand and have to physically stop myself from placing it on his chest.

"Is that what it takes? A win?" Why does he make it sound like a threat?

I shake my head. "Just get out there and win."

The little smirk he gives me before he hurries after his teammates is devilish. And somehow, I know they're going to win tonight. If they don't, it won't be because of Liam.

I find Morgan in the audience and join her to watch the game. We're still not very close, but I do like hanging out with her.

The Lions win.

I don't think anyone's surprised when Cole scores the winning goal and does his celebration looking as if smiling is beneath him.

The enthusiasm of the crowd is infectious and by the time I remember I'm supposed to do more interviews, the teams have already left the ice.

"Ah, shit," I say when I realize I fucked up.

"What's wrong?" Morgan asks. We're waiting to get out of our row.

"It doesn't matter. I just forgot something I was supposed to do. But it's fine. No big deal."

"Do you need a ride home? Me and JD can take you."

"Yeah, sure." What I really want is to wait for Liam and have him fuck me right here and now, but this might be less suspicious.

I hang out with Morgan as we wait for the team to appear. We discuss her mom's exhibit, and it's cute how Morgan wants to learn more about photography for JD.

JD is among the first of the players to show up. He greets those waiting for him, and I take out the camera as Morgan gives him a hug.

"So, Captain, how does it feel to have another win on the road to the Frozen Four?"

He gives me a little eye roll and keeps his arm around Morgan's shoulders, but humors me. "Feels good. The team is strong this year and I'm confident we'll have one of our best years ever. Everybody has been working hard, and it's really a team effort."

"What's your biggest challenge now?"

"Oh," he looks off in the distance for a while. "Injuries are always a risk, but other than that, I don't think anything can stop us from doing our best."

"Thanks."

"You don't mind taking Faye home, right?" Morgan asks, still holding on to JD.

I busy myself with putting away the camera and avoid looking at them. It must be nice to be so open with a relationship. To be able to show affection in public.

I shake my head. It's not that I want a relationship with Liam. That's just sex, and I know that. But it's been a while since I had a boyfriend, and I kind of miss it.

"I don't mind," JD says.

"Great." I smile as we head to his car.

The whole way to my place, I listen to Morgan and JD joke and tease each other, and it makes me feel sad and lonely.

As soon as I enter the apartment, my phone rings.

"Hey," Cora says. She's sitting on the couch putting on her boots.

"Hi." I grab my phone. It's Liam. "Hey." I really hope I don't sound as breathless as I think.

"Hey, you left."

"Oh, yeah. JD and Morgan gave me a ride home." I fiddle with my sleeve.

"Oh."

"I'm at my apartment now." Do I sound weird? I feel weird.

"You still want to fuck?"

"Yes." Oh, god do I want to.

"Ok, I'll be right over."

"See you soon."

I hang up and exhale.

Cora laughs. "What the hell was that?"

"Liam is coming over."

"Good for you." She gets up and grabs her jacket. "So it's friends with benefits?"

"Yes. Fuck, this is a bad idea. We're so going to get caught."

"You worry too much. I'm sure you'll be fine. And I'll help cover if you need it. I will swear up and down I was here all night, and all you did was discuss social media strategies. And have pizza. Pepperoni and chicken. Because details are important." She winks at me.

"You don't mind that he's coming over, do you?"

"Nope, I'm headed out. Feel free to be as loud as you want."

"Where are you going?" I take in her outfit. She's wearing leather pants and knee-high boots. Her jacket is black and padded and she's holding a pair of gloves.

"I just found out about these race meets. I'm not really sure what to expect, but I figured I'd take Carlos and go check it out."

"Carlos is going to a race?"

Carlos is Cora's childhood friend. He's the sweetest guy imaginable, but Cora's complete opposite. Where Cora is wild and reckless, he's in bed with a cup of tea. Chamomile, because any amount of caffeine after six pm is bad.

"Well, I said I'd go alone if he didn't come with me."

"You use him."

"What's the point of having a six foot five, bodybuilder friend if I can't make him be my bodyguard once in a while?"

I shake my head. "Take it easy on him, ok?"

"I always do."

She gives me a little wave, grabs her helmet and leaves.

I take a deep breath and view the apartment. Liam is going to be here in a few minutes. I should probably get ready.

Chapter 31 – Nothing between us

Faye

I'm not ready when the doorbell rings. And I'm so eager I could explode.

I'm almost shaking as I go to open the door. But I can't tell if it's from nerves or from excitement. All I know is that I need to see him.

"Hey." He leans against the doorframe and looks at me with darkened eyes. If it wasn't for his chest moving more rapidly than usual, I'd think he was completely unaffected.

"Hey." I can't blame him, though. It's hard to breathe normally around him. Especially when he's looking at me like he wants to do very wicked things to me.

"Can I come in?"

I nod and step aside. This shouldn't be weird. He's been here before, and we've done this. More than once.

He takes off his jacket and shoes and looks around.

Why does it feel like a first time? Why am I so nervous?

"Is your roommate here?"

"No. She's out." It hits me at that moment that we're all alone. Just him and me. "If anyone asks, she was here the entire time, and we had pizza. Pepperoni and chicken."

"Ok." He wrinkles his forehead. "Is the alibi for us or her?"

"Us. I think. I hope. It might be a bit for her, too. I don't always ask what she gets up to."

"We have the apartment to ourselves?"

I clear my throat. "Yes."

All it takes is one look between us and we're drawn together like magnets. His hands are on me and I hold on to his shirt. He grabs a fistful of my hair and tilts my head back as he lowers his lips to mine.

I'm drowning.

I know I should fight this, but I can't for the life of me figure out why. As I fall deeper and deeper into the kiss, there's a small voice warning me of something. But it's so hard to care when he makes me feel so good.

The warning fades away, and everything is right. His lips belong on mine, and I need to be close to him.

I rub myself against him and shiver when he moans. That sound sends waves of desire through me and I start tugging at his shirt.

As I struggle to pull it over his head, he runs his tongue over my lower lip.

"Liam," I gasp and he pulls back just long enough to get his shirt off.

I spread my palms on his chest, feeling his heartbeat under my fingers.

His hands are under my shirt, trailing up my back. I move in closer to him and feel my bra come undone.

"Take it all off," he says without removing his lips from mine.

Together we get the top and bra off and Liam shifts his attention from my lips to my breasts. His mouth covers one nipple. I arch my back and close my eyes.

His tongue flicks over the hard nipple, and I grab his head.

"You can still change your mind." His hands are hesitating at the button on my pants.

"I want you."

His mouth clamps down on my nipple, and he sucks hard. I lose my breath for a moment.

"I want you to put that cock inside me. I want to feel you, with nothing between us."

He growls and hot air rushes over the nipple, drying the saliva he's left there. "You're going to fucking feel it. I'm going to bury myself so deep inside you I'll be all that you can feel."

He's somehow managed to undo my pants and pulls them down. I'm already wet for him as he sinks down to his knees.

Stepping out of the pants, I reach back. We're still in the small hallway. Behind me is a narrow side table. I stumble against it and knock down a scented candle and a bowl of ornamental pinecones my mom insisted we needed.

I grab the edge of the table. Liam smiles up at me and pushes me back so I'm almost sitting on it. Then he grabs my knees and slowly opens them.

Looking down at his blond head has me gasping in anticipation. I grip the table as if my life depends on it. He kisses my inner thigh, and I spread wider for him.

Slow kisses move closer and closer and by the time he reaches my core, I'm breathing heavily.

He rubs a finger up and down between my lips.

"This is going to be mine," he says, almost to himself. He leans in and kisses me. As he does, he places his finger at my opening. Moving the tip in a small circle, he's driving me mad with lust. "You're so wet for me. I don't think I'm the only one eager for this."

"Liam," is all I can say.

His tongue darts out and tastes me. I lift a leg and place my foot on his shoulder.

"Liam." I'm vaguely aware that we should move to the bedroom, but as his finger dives deeper and his tongue finds my clit, I don't have the ability to say anything. Much less protest.

Heat and tension build inside me and I moan.

"Fucking hell," Liam says and stands up. I whine in disappointment as he undoes his pants. "I need you now."

The pants hit the floor and his throbbing cock stands straight out. I don't get long to admire it. Liam immediately steps between my legs. He's trembling as he stops just out of reach.

"Are you sure?"

I meet his eyes. "Fuck me."

He takes the final step forward, and his cock is touching me. I gasp, still looking into his eyes. He takes a few seconds to cover the tip in my wetness, then he slowly starts pushing inside me.

"Oh, fuck." His mouth covers mine, and I move my hands to his shoulders as he buries himself in me. The kiss is passionate and eager, and I tremble from an overload of emotions. He nips at my lower lip before resting his forehead against mine.

"Fuck, that feels good." He starts moving. Pulling out in one long, smooth motion. Then he fills me up again.

He grabs my legs and moves faster. I hold on to the table as he picks up speed. A book falls to the floor, but I couldn't care less. Closing my eyes, all I can focus on is how he feels as he thrusts into me. The pace is almost furious now. He's making small noises that tingle along my spine.

When I open my eyes, he does too. It's as if he can sense me looking. His forehead is covered in a thin layer of sweat.

I don't expect it, maybe it's the angle or pace, but all of a sudden I feel the buildup. I've never come from just penetration before, so it takes me by surprise. My mouth falls open and my breathing is hard.

"Fuck, Faye. This feels too good," he says.

"Don't stop." I'm panting. "Please. Don't stop."

He doesn't. His face sets in determination, and I can tell he's struggling to hold back. But he keeps going. My orgasm builds and builds until it finally ruptures. I throw my head back as my muscles start to spasm and pleasure crashes over me.

"Fuck." I don't know which of us is screaming. And then I feel him come inside me.

He slams into me as if he never wants to be apart from me. His body convulses as he finishes, and I pull his face to mine so I can kiss him. His arms wrap around me and he lifts me up. My legs cling to his waist. I love feeling him joined with me.

Chapter 32 – Three times

Faye

"I'm really sorry," I say on the phone to Cora as I approach the Den. "I promise I'll clean it up later. I woke up late and had to hurry to make it to class."

"That's not why I'm calling," Cora says. "I need details, Faye. This wasn't an innocent booty call. You practically destroyed the hallway. And do I have to sanitize the couch before I sit on it?"

"What? No. Of course not. I'm sorry about the hallway, but we moved to my bedroom after that."

"Really?" Cora sounds too pleased with the answer. "So you did it more than once?"

I slow my steps and make sure no one is nearby. Damn Cora and her nosiness. I can't stop the smile as I think of last night. "Yes. Three times."

"How was it?"

"Cora, I'm not telling you."

"Oh, come on. I struck out last night. I need to live vicariously through you. Just tell me the highlights."

I sigh. "The first time was insane. It was like we couldn't keep our hands off each other."

"And the second time?"

"Was slow and sensual." I sigh at the memory of him kissing me all over and keeping eye contact while fucking me. "And that was in my bed, so no need to freak out about the couch."

"And the third time?"

After he took me in the hallway, he carried me to the bedroom while he was still inside me. He put me down carefully on the bed and asked me if I was ok. All I could do was nod.

When he lay beside me, it was natural. As if he belonged in my bed. He apologized for it being over so soon. I assured him I had no regrets. Then he slid his hand between my legs, rested his head on his arm as he laid next to me, and started touching me.

For the next few minutes, I just lied there while he got me and himself all worked up again. We took our time, exploring every inch of each other and finding out what turns us on.

When he slid into me again, I was finally capable of fully embracing the experience of having no barrier between us. We moved as if it was always meant to be us and when we came, stars exploded.

After the second time, we both fell asleep. I woke up an hour later, in his arms. When I moved, he held onto me. And got hard again. So I kissed him and asked if I could ride him. He laughed, told me the answer was always going to be yes.

I climbed on top of him and took my pleasure. And he gave me his.

How do I explain that to Cora? What happened last night was so much more than sex. It was intimacy. But it wasn't supposed to be.

"The third time was... It was all good, Cora."

She sighs. "I'm jealous. It's been way too long since I had someone I wanted to do it with three times in one night."

I don't tell her that I would have been willing to do it plenty more times, but Liam grabbed his things and left and now I don't know how to act around him.

"I have to go, Cora. I'm at the Den."

"Ok. Well, I appreciate you not having sex on the couch."

"Bye." I shake my head and hang up as I go inside.

It's strange how familiar I've become with this place. I nod at the security guard as he walks by and find myself in the hallway where Coach's office is.

"Faye," his voice calls out as I pass by. His door is open and I stop.

"Hey, Coach. How's it going?"

"Good. Could you come in and close the door? It'll be quick."

"Sure." I move into his office and sit down opposite him. "What's up?"

"I was just wondering how things are going with Liam. I've seen a few posts about him, but shouldn't there be more?"

"Right. Well, I was hoping to work it in without making it seem like we're trying to reform him. I know he has a lot of eyes on him right now, but if we go all out, it's going to look like we're trying too hard. I want it to feel more organic."

"You think people would think it's all fake?"

"Yes. It has to come naturally."

"And what about this plan to find him a fake girlfriend? Is that still happening?"

I squirm in my seat. "I've been looking at candidates." I had hoped it would all blow over and everyone would forget it. Maybe think of it as a silly idea that they couldn't believe they ever thought was good.

Coach nods. "It might be good to get something out there soon. After this weekend, of course. I just heard from a couple of the alumni. One of them has a daughter here at UNI and was not happy with the Lions getting a reputation as fuckboys."

I swallow. "I'm sure people will forget all about that soon."

Coach takes a deep breath and leans back. "Well, so far you've been doing a great job, so I trust you'll handle this as well. I think you should maybe focus a bit more on Liam's reputation, but I acknowledge that you've done a lot for the team as a whole."

"Thank you," I say and stand.

"And I must say I'm impressed with the way you've turned Liam's behavior around."

I furrow my brow and adjust my bag. "I haven't really done much."

"I wouldn't be so sure about that. He's listening now. And he doesn't show up to practice trying to hide a hangover. Whatever you're doing, keep up the good work."

Nodding, I try not to let my imagination run wild. "Will do."

I quickly leave his office before all the things I've been doing to Liam floods my brain.

Chapter 33 – Insights

Liam

"Wait, she's coming with us?" Pan says as I enter the locker room.

I'm a minute late, but it looks like is Coach already talking to the team. I sneak past him to get to my spot, but stumble when I see Faye standing next to him.

"Nice of you to join us, Liam," Coach says.

"Sorry, class ran over." I ignore Faye and sit down. "What'd I miss?"

"Faye's coming with us tomorrow," Pan says excitedly.

My stomach lurches and I meet her eyes. She's smiling like the professional goddess she is, but I can tell there's a hint of uncertainty there.

"To the game?" I ask and blink.

"No, to the Bahamas," Cole says sarcastically. "Yes, of course, to the game."

Glaring at Cole, I remind myself that Coach is in the room. And Faye.

"Yes," Coach says. "Faye will be coming on the bus with us. She will be staying at the same hotel as us, and she will be at the game. It's important that you remember she's there to work. Please make her job easier if you can."

I glance up at Faye. Her eyes are on me. Will she have her own room? She has to, right? As far as I know, she's the only woman coming with us. It's not like they're going to let her share with one of the guys.

"Tomorrow's game is important." Coach goes on. "If we win, we move on to the regional semifinals. Our goal this year is the Frozen

161

Four. I expect you all to do your best and come to the game rested and ready to fight for that. Do you understand?"

We answer him, and Faye takes some photos as he continues his pep talk.

"Ok, get changed," Coach finally says. "I'll see you on the ice in five."

He leaves the room and Faye follows. I instantly miss her.

"I'm not sure I like this," Hudson says.

"Don't like what?" I ask.

"Her coming along. Is she really going to be on the bus with us?"

Anger grows, but I do my best to keep it down. "Yeah. So?"

"So, she's changing the routine."

"What routine? You can still fall asleep to your stupid podcast." I start putting my gear on while not looking at him.

"Yeah, but it's going to be different with a woman on the bus."

I shake my head. "She's one extra person. Suck it up. Don't be an asshole about it."

He narrows his eyes at me. "You're one to talk."

"What's that supposed to mean?"

"If anyone's been acting like an asshole lately, it's you. You've been acting as if the whole world revolves around you."

"Fuck you. No, I haven't."

"I've seen you hungover several times, or tired because you were hooking up with some puck bunny. Get it together, man. You're supposed to be part of a team." He gets up and leaves the room. I stare after him for a bit before I continue getting ready.

Have I really been that bad? I admit, I've been a bit distant. And maybe I was drinking too much. And not showing up in the best of shape always. But it's not like it was bad.

I want to tell myself that nobody noticed when I spiraled out of control.

I blink at the room. Maybe I was feeling a bit of self pity. But it's not like I let it take over. I was just going through something.

"Hey," I nod at Ethan, and he comes closer.

"What's up?"

How do I even ask this? He's my best friend and part of me wants to think he would have told me if I was acting like a douche. A vague memory of him bringing it up comes to mind.

"Have I been different lately?"

"The fuck is this coming from?"

I shrug.

Ethan inhales. "I mean, you took the whole Kaitlynn thing pretty hard. But you've been better lately. I guess your new guardian has seen to that."

"Guardian?" I squint at him. "What the fuck are you talking about?"

"Faye. Everyone knows she's been whipping you into shape."

I stare at him with my mouth open.

"What?" He acts all innocent. "It's pretty obvious that she's been talking to you and making you change your behavior. We all assumed that's part of the reason she was hired."

"She's not my guardian."

He shrugs. "Whatever. She's made you less of an asshole."

Fuck, I have been an asshole. Ethan heads to the ice, leaving me with my thoughts. I've been an asshole, sleeping around and drinking too much. Fuck.

And then there's her. She's polite and professional. Except when I have her naked and she's wild and eager for my cock. I can make her lose control and moan loud enough for the neighbors to hear.

Here at the Den, she's the epitome of a good girl, and I'm not even worthy of breathing the same air as her. And it's not like she's just here for me. She's here for all of us, the whole team.

In her apartment, it's just her and me. Fuck, I miss that apartment. More accurately, I miss the things we did in that apartment.

As I take the ice, she's talking to Coach off to one side. She's coming with us tomorrow. I push back the smile that's taken over my chest. I really shouldn't care that she's coming with us.

I start warming up as she finishes her conversation and walks away. She'll be on the bus with us. At the same hotel. Fuck, that shouldn't make me happy. But it does. Even if we don't get a chance to hook up.

Chapter 34 – Busride

Faye

I arrive at the Den early on Friday morning with my bag and camera. The guys are already there, and I can't help but look for Liam.

He's talking to Ethan, but glances in my direction.

"All ready to spend a day with these idiots?" Coach asks with a smile.

"I'm all set."

"Great. Let me know if you need anything."

"Thanks." I get a few photos and some footage of the bus being loaded with more gear than I would have ever thought necessary.

At least the camera makes me feel less awkward. I also use my phone to film a short snippet. I could probably make a short video on travelling to an away game and what it's like.

"Hey, Faye." Pan comes up to me and I'm glad to have someone to talk to.

"Hi, are you excited about the game?"

"Sure. I like away games."

"Oh? How so?"

"We get to see other arenas, and it's fun riding the bus with everyone."

"Like a bonding experience?"

"Yeah."

"So, do you have assigned seats, or...?" All night I was trying to think of scenarios where I could end up sitting next to Liam. None of them seems feasible.

"Not really, but people kind of stick to the same seats."

Coach walks up to the front of the bus and looks around at the players.

"Listen up," he yells and everyone quiets down. "The bus trip will take about six hours. We'll stop for a bathroom break about half-way. Let's try to behave today, ok?"

He gestures for us to start boarding, and I hurry to position myself so I can film the guys getting on the bus.

As Liam walks by me, he avoids looking at the camera. It seems we have some unspoken agreement to ignore each other, and I understand it, but I'm not sure I like it.

Liam is standing in the aisle as I find a seat closer to the front of the bus.

"You need help with that?" Liam asks, pointing to my bag.

Was he waiting for me so he could help?

"Thanks." I let him put my bag in the overhead compartment. Someone bumps into him, and I instinctively raise a hand as he stumbles toward me. His muscles are hard under the hoodie and he smells enticing.

"Sorry," he says and closes the compartment.

I remove my hand. "So, do you usually sit alone?"

I notice most of the guys are paired up, but a few of them have a seat to themselves.

He points to my seat. "Yeah, but I don't mind sitting with Ethan."

I blink at him. "I took your seat?" I glance back at it, but there's no sign anyone is sitting there.

"We figured you might want your own."

I meet his eyes. "I appreciate that," I say quietly, not sure I mean it.

He nods and walks back to where Ethan is sitting. I take my seat and wait for us to get moving.

For some reason, I thought I might be able to get some more sleep on the bus. Looking around, I do see some of the guys sleeping in awkward positions here and there, but most of them have no thoughts on sleep.

Within half an hour, some of them are deep into a card game, a couple are occupied by a video game, and all around me I hear talking and laughing. I make sure to document it all.

When I sit down and look out the window, my phone buzzes.

It's a text from Liam.

Do you have a room for yourself at the hotel?

Yes. Why?

I turn around and locate him. Ethan has fallen asleep next to him.

I thought of some things I want to do with you. And since I'm sharing a room with Ethan...

You want to hook up at the hotel? The hotel everyone is staying at?

I bite my lip and can't hide the smile. It would be a lie to say that it never crossed my mind. But wouldn't it be too risky? What if we get caught?

I can't stop thinking of the way your entire body shudders when you come.

Oh, fuck. I glance back at him, and he smirks and raises an eyebrow. Does he really want to play this game here?

I do have fond memories of your tongue exploring certain parts of me.

He coughs, and I almost burst out laughing.

"I hope they're not too loud for you." I almost jump out of my seat when Coach speaks. Instinctively, I hide my phone screen.

"Not at all. I have to admit, it's slightly more chaotic than I imagined." I smile just as some commotion breaks out. I strain my neck and look back. And freeze.

Silas and Ash are trying to take Liam's phone from him. My heart stops as they get hold of it. Silas screams in laughter.

"What's this? Liam's got something happening here."

"I need my earplugs," Coach says with a shake of his head as he retreats back to his seat.

My panicked eyes meet Liam's for a brief second.

"Give that back, asshole," he says and lunges for the phone.

Silas backs away. "This guy is sexting someone."

I can't take it. My stomach is roiling as I sit back down. What the hell do I do now? Fuck, this is bad.

There's a chorus of voices teasing Liam, and I can't breathe. I do my best to hide from all of them. This is the worst possible time for this to happen. I'm stuck on this trip with them. If I get fired now, it's going to be so bad.

It takes me a while to realize nobody has mentioned my name.

"Who is she?" Ash asks. "And why the fuck is she saved as Iceberg? Is she frigid or something?"

My panic turns to confusion. He doesn't have me saved under my name?

"How the fuck do you save someone as Iceberg when they're writing stuff like that?" Silas says and laughs.

"Call her," Cole says with a grin.

I scramble to grab my phone and make sure it's on silent. Not trusting it, I turn it off while there's even more commotion.

"You're all fucking assholes." Liam sounds angry. I peek between the seats and he's got his phone back. He pushes Ash aside.

"Hey, watch it," Silas says as he catches Ash.

"Fuck off, all of you." Liam moves away from them and comes up to the seat opposite and one back from mine. He sits down next to Hudson, who seems to be able to sleep through anything.

I turn my phone back on. My heart is still beating a mile a minute and my fingers are shaking as I type.

168

You have me saved as Iceberg?

He squirms.

Yeah.

I stare at him. He stares back. He has another nickname for me? He didn't even explain what Roses was about. And now he has me saved as Iceberg? What the hell is that?

It's a good thing you didn't have me as my name. It's unusual enough they might have figured it out.

Our eyes meet again, and I don't know what to think. Hudson shifts in the seat next to him and wakes up. I pick up a book I brought and start reading.

Chapter 35 – A wall of hockey players

Faye

I get a lot of good footage of the guys preparing for the game and warming up. They goof off and tease each other. Until they get serious. Well, maybe a bit after too.

Being on the road trip with them is enlightening. I see more clearly how they interact and who tends to group up. I'm not surprised that Ethan and Liam stick together.

I am, however, a bit surprised to see Pan and Cayden hanging out. In my mind, Pan is a rule-following younger brother type. He's eager to please and a bit insecure.

Cayden is the complete opposite. There are very few rules he hasn't broken. Sometimes, it seems his entire life's goal is to break as many rules as possible.

Pan wants to be liked and respected. Cayden isn't afraid of stepping on toes to get what he wants.

They shouldn't work together, but somehow they seem to enjoy each other's company. Maybe it's the way they both take hockey so seriously? I don't understand it.

Before I know, it's time for them to hit the ice. They take it with force and the other team, Grainer, doesn't stand a chance.

Despite Cayden spending quite a bit of time in the penalty box and Enzo getting a bloody nose when he defends a bit too hard, it's an easy win. Hudson is excellent in the goal, and all I have to do is look over at Pan to see the mixed emotions. He wants to be out there, but he's also proud of Hudson. When it's clear the Lions are going to win, he gets his chance. Coach pulls out Hudson and gives Pan some ice time.

As the guys get changed, I make my way to the bus that'll take us back to the hotel. It's dark outside, and the air is cold. The bus is parked at the side of the arena.

The visitors' parking is to the back and the other side and I can see and hear excited fans as they leave. Most of them are disappointed, but here and there I see a car filled with the Lions black and yellow. It seems many of them have made a road trip out of it.

I hurry up to one of the cars and ask if I can take some photos. They are more than happy to oblige and pose for me. As I walk back to the bus, I'm already thinking of what I could do surrounding the fans. Maybe I should highlight them more, interview some of them?

The guys still aren't at the bus, so I head in the opposite direction toward the front of the arena, thinking I can take some photos of it to use.

There's very few people in the front. Part of the players' parking lot is hidden from the road by a stone wall. I take some photos from the front, but the road is too close, so I move to the stone wall to check out the angle.

I get my photos and check them on the camera. Satisfied, I look up and realize I'm pretty far from the bus, and I've ended up in a dark part of the parking lot. There are some cars here, most of them probably belong to the players or the staff.

I start walking back when I spot someone heading to one of the cars. Figuring it's one of the Grainer players, I grab my phone but don't feel too worried.

"Hey," he leaves the car and comes toward me. "I saw you with the Lions, right?"

My heart is beating fast, and I glance at my phone as I unlock it.

"Yeah, I'm their social media manager."

"Really?" He smiles and stops in front of me, blocking my path.

"Did you play tonight?" I try to remember if I saw him, but honestly, with the helmets and my obsession with Liam, I have no idea who played on the other team.

"Nah, not tonight. I had a small injury. So you hang out with the Lions a lot then?"

I don't like his smile.

"Some. They're good guys." I try to glance at my phone without him noticing.

"You know, if you want to hang out with me and my boys, we could arrange that."

"Thanks, but I'm not interested. I should get back to the bus."

The laugh is scary. Not because it's evil, but because it's so condescending. Almost as if the laugh is calling me a liar.

"What's your name, sweetie?"

"Oh. Uh. Faye." My eyes flicker across the parking lot, but there's nobody close by.

"It's very nice to meet you, Faye. But we can both be real here. I'm sure you would rather go have some dinner with me than sit on a sweaty bus."

I try to step to one side so I can get past him, but he blocks my path and comes closer. "I appreciate the offer, but I really have to get on that bus. It's my job."

I glance at my phone again. I've managed to find Liam's number.

"Come on. No need to be shy. You deserve to be with winners, sweetie."

I dial and pray he answers as I hide the phone behind my back.

"Don't call me sweetie. And didn't you just lose to the Lions?"

"Yeah, but that's because I wasn't on the ice. Trust me, if I had been playing, we would have won and you could have celebrated with a real winner."

"I'm sure. But I really should head back to the bus now."

"We have time. If you don't want to go anywhere, we can get to know each other here."

"I don't think so."

"What do you mean, sweetie?" He steps even closer and reaches out to stroke my cheek. I shy back and turn my head away.

"I mean, I'd rather just leave, if you don't mind."

He laughs. "But sweetie, I know you don't mean that."

"I do. I really want to go."

I step to the side, but he's quick to follow.

"I think we got off on the wrong foot," he says. "Let's try this again."

I swallow.

"You're very beautiful."

"Thank you." My voice is little more than a whisper.

"One of the prettiest girls I've ever seen."

"I... I should go." Again, I try to sidestep him. And again, he blocks me.

"Now, now, is that any way to show gratitude?"

"Gratitude?" I furrow my brow. "For what?"

"Did I not just compliment you?"

"Yes. But I didn't ask for it."

He shakes his head. "You really need to learn to appreciate when a man pays attention to you."

"I have to go." I try to pass him by, but he grabs my wrist. Panic bubbles up inside me. "Let go of me."

"Why? We're having such a pleasant conversation."

"Listen, I'm not interested. Can't you just let me go?"

"At least give me your number. I think I've earned that much."

My mind is baffled. How exactly does he think he's earned that? Does he think I owe him something because he gave me a compliment?

I shake my head. He yanks at my wrist, and I yelp as I feel the shock throughout my body. It's violent enough that my phone goes flying.

"Oh, you like that?" He pulls me closer.

"What? No. Stop it."

"Come on, sweetie, don't be like that. We could have a really good time." He puts his hand on my waist and I try to push him away.

"Asshole," Liam's voice calls out. "She told you to stop it."

I peer behind the guy and see not only Liam, but half the hockey team, with more of them appearing to the sides. Some of them are in only t-shirts.

"Relax," the guy says. "We're just having some fun." He starts to turn and sees Hudson and Cayden. Then he keeps turning and his face pales as he sees how many of them are out there.

"Let her go, dirtbag," Dustin says.

"You want us to kick your ass off the ice as well?" Ethan says.

Liam's knuckles are white as he clenches his fists by his side. His face is tight and his entire body is on edge. I can tell he's holding back.

"Chill, guys. It's just another slut, no need to get worked up."

Pan approaches with his fist clenched, but before he can do anything, Liam's fist has connected with the guy's jaw.

He lets go of me and someone else grabs my arm. I get pulled out of the way and end up behind Cayden and Hudson. More of the guys surround me as others raise their voices and start berating the guy.

Surrounded by a wall of hockey players, I have never felt safer. Even if I hear more of the Grainer players approaching, I am able to breathe again.

"You ok?" Walter asks and looks me over.

I nod. "Yeah, more scared than anything." I rub my wrist where he grabbed me. I don't like that he had his fingers on me. Even through the thick jacket.

"You're ok," Cole says. "We won't let him hurt you."

"Thanks." I sigh in relief.

"Is this yours?" Dustin asks and hands me a phone.

I take it with shaky fingers. The screen is cracked, but right now, I don't care.

Liam pushes past the others and grabs my elbows. With worried eyes, he bends down and studies my face. "Did he hurt you? Because if he did, I will fuck him up."

I shake my head. "No. Thanks for coming."

His hands twitch, and I instinctively know he wants to hug me.

"Yeah, sure, anytime." He lets go of me and steps back. Then he runs a hand through his hair. "What were you thinking, Faye? Going out alone. It's not safe." He's working himself up into a frenzy and raises his voice. "What would you have done if I didn't answer? You can't just walk around alone in the dark."

"I wanted some photos," I say weakly. The adrenaline is leaving me and him shouting at me is enough to bring me to tears. I fight them as best I can.

"I don't give a fuck if you want photos. You can't just wander around alone. Anything could have happened to you. Don't you understand how stupid that is?"

His rant goes on even though someone puts a hand on his shoulder and tries to stop him. I can't tell who, because to my horror, the tears are now flooding my eyes. I try to inhale, but it turns to a sob.

Liam instantly stops ranting and looks at me. He looks pale. I sob again and tears stream down my cheeks.

"Oh, fuck, you did it now," Hudson says.

"Shit. I'm sorry." Liam steps in and embraces me. "I'm sorry for yelling."

I bury my face in his t-shirt and let the sobs out. He holds me tight in front of everyone as I try to regain some form of composure.

All I want is to stay in Liam's arms and breathe in his scent. That woodsy vanilla is like home to me now. It's the perfect scent to calm me down.

But his friends surround us and any one of them could get me fired if they found out what was really going on. So I place my hands against his chest and push him away.

It takes him a heartbeat to understand what I'm doing. Then he releases me.

Ethan pats me on the back. "Let's get you to the bus."

I nod and they surround me as we walk.

"Do you want to report this to anyone?" Pan asks.

Part of me wants the guy to get what he deserves, but he didn't actually do anything to me. Liam hit him.

I shake my head. "No. He didn't hurt me and you guys could get in trouble." I glance up at Liam, who's shaking his hand. "And Liam can't handle any more bad press right now. Can we just forget it ever happened?"

The guys seem to understand where I'm coming from. They grumble a bit, then they get their things and we slowly take our seats.

Coach seems to be a bit confused why they all stormed out all of a sudden, but they play it down and we have a quiet drive back to the hotel.

Chapter 36 – Roses

Liam

My heart is racing. Ethan is talking to me, but I can barely hear him over the pounding in my ears. The bus ride to the hotel takes an eternity, and I can't even sit next to her.

Her hands are shaking, and I almost want to kiss Pan when he goes to sit by her. I strain to hear what they're saying, but there's too much noise around me. All I catch is Pan asking her if she's ok.

At least she's not alone.

The bus stops in the hotel parking lot, and we file out. I make sure to walk close to Faye. I can't just leave her, not now.

"Hey, are you coming with to the dinner?" Ethan asks.

That's right, we're supposed to have a team dinner tonight. And Faye is supposed to be there.

"Hold on."

I jog up to Faye. "Do you still want to come to dinner with us?"

She shakes her head. "No, I think I just want to go to my room."

"That's understandable," Ethan says, and I notice he joined us.

"I'll walk you there." I hold my breath, waiting for either of them to say something.

Faye just nods.

"I'm sure you could get some room service," Ethan says. "Or we can bring you something."

"I'm fine. I had a hot dog earlier."

We enter the hotel, and some of the guys break off to discuss the upcoming dinner. It's at a restaurant not too far from the hotel.

"I'll make sure she's ok," I tell Ethan. "And I'll probably skip the dinner."

His eyes narrow, and for a panicked second, I think he's about to smile. "Sounds good." He turns and walks away.

"You don't have to see me up," Faye says as I follow her into the elevator.

She pushes the button for her floor. The doors close and we're alone.

"I'm sorry I yelled at you." I run a hand through my hair. "I shouldn't have done that. None of what happened was your fault. I was just so fucking scared."

She takes a shaky breath. "Ok."

Her eyes are focused on the display over the door. I stand next to her, wondering if I fucked up badly.

The doors open before I can gather my thoughts and we get out together. She stops at her door and puts the card in the reader.

"Thanks for walking me."

I clear my throat. "Listen... I was... Can I come in for a bit?"

She nods and pushes the door open. Her room is pretty much a copy of the room I share with Ethan. Except, only one of the beds is occupied. When she closes the door after us, it's like we're all alone in the world. She takes off her jacket and throws it on the unused bed. I unzip mine, but leave it on.

"When you called me and I realized what was going on, I freaked out. I almost threw up. I didn't know what to do. So I put it on speaker. JD was the one who got us moving. I've never been that scared in my life."

"But you found me." She sounds so fragile.

"When you screamed..."

I want to see her eyes. I want to make sure she's still here with me. But she's looking away.

"I just wanted to take some photos of the arena. I thought they might come in handy." She bites her lower lip. "I wasn't thinking. I shouldn't have been alone."

"You don't have to do those things alone. Just tell someone. We'll come with you."

She inhales, and it ends in a small sob.

"Roses." I wrap my arms around her and hold her. She sinks into me and in the middle of everything horrible happening, I can't help but enjoy that feeling.

After a while, her body stops shaking.

"Do you want me to go?"

"No," she says into my chest. So I stroke her hair and keep holding her.

"Are you ok? If you want, I'll go find that guy and fuck him up."

"I'm ok." She snuggles closer and presses her body against mine.

My body instantly reacts. I try to shift away from her, but she won't let me.

Her arms sneak under my jacket and I feel my hard cock press against her stomach.

"Sorry about that. Just ignore it." She must think I'm a heartless asshole for getting hard after what she just went through.

"Ok." She wiggles against me and I bite back a groan.

"Roses? What are you doing?"

"Nothing." She holds me tighter and keeps moving. I almost laugh out loud. She's teasing me.

"You're evil."

"I like you."

I look down at her, and she leans her head back so our eyes meet. Her cheeks turn bright red.

"I mean... Not like... I just..."

"You want to fuck me?" I ask and push aside the disappointment.

She nods.

I stroke her hair. "Are you sure?"

"Only if you want to."

I take my jacket off as fast as humanly possible. Without thinking, I let the shirt follow.

"I'll take that as a yes." She places her hands on my chest and electricity courses through me.

"Take off your clothes for me," I say, and pull down my pants.

I sit down on her bed and watch as she starts to strip. She takes her time, slowly removing each piece of clothing. I watch her face carefully, wanting to make sure she's into this.

I want her to know she's in full control and can stop at any time. She doesn't.

When she finally pulls down her panties, my cock is almost painfully hard. She walks up to me where I'm sitting and puts a knee on the bed next to me. With one hand, she pushes at my chest until I lie down. I grab her waist.

"Tell me what you want, Roses."

She lowers her lips to mine and I'm almost scared to demand anything from her. But she kisses me, slowly and sensually, in a way that makes me feel it all the way to my toes.

"I want you," she says.

"You have me."

Her naked body presses against mine and I can't resist pinching her nipple. I grab her boob and enjoy the feeling of it in my hand. Her hand disappears between us and I almost swear when I feel her fingers around my cock.

"Let me get you ready," I mumble and prepare to eat her out.

But she shakes her head and sits up. "You already did." She shifts so she can place the tip between her lips. She's so wet. "You came for me." She drags it up and down. "You held me." She places it at her opening. "You stroked my hair." She lowers herself slightly and gasps as the tip enters her. "You made sure I was ok." Her eyes are closed, and she's slowly taking my cock. "You care about me."

I don't even know what to say to that, because at the same time she drops down completely and I'm fully inside her.

"Oh, fuck."

She starts moving and I'm lost. She's part of me and I'm part of her. Her head is thrown back, and she's clearly enjoying herself. I watch her bounce up and down on my cock and reach up to grab her tits. She's perfect.

So fucking perfect.

Once she slows down a bit, I sit up and hold her waist. She groans as the angle shifts and starts moving in more of a circular motion.

"Fuck me," she says and pushes down to get me as deep inside her as possible. She stops moving and opens her eyes. "I'm so close," she whispers. She reaches down between us and, still holding eye contact, starts stimulating her clit.

My breath catches and all I can do is sit still and hold her as she pushes herself over the edge.

"Oh, fuck. Liam." When her eyes close, her pussy spasms around my cock and my mouth falls open as I do my best not to come. She comes with me inside her and my fingers clench her hips, holding her still so I can enjoy every bit of it.

When she finally relaxes and shivers a bit, I hug her and spin us around so she's under me.

"That was fucking amazing," I say and move my hips.

She moans.

"But now, it's my turn."

I pull out and thrust into her. Again and again as she gasps for air.

"Liam."

"Yes, Roses?"

"Liam."

I place my thumb on her still sensitive clit, and she startles. I rub her gently a few times before grabbing her legs and bracing myself so I can fuck her properly.

"You want my cock, Roses?"

"Yes."

I pound into her, already too close to coming.

"Where do you want my cum, Roses?" I groan as she takes her time answering.

"On my stomach," she finally says and I pull out of her. I grab the tip of my cock and stroke it furiously as the climax builds. When I start coming, I don't know how to stop. The release is powerful, and I cover her stomach with it.

As soon as I can see again, I shimmy back and lower my head between her legs. I'll be damned if I'm not responsible for at least one of her orgasms tonight.

I find her clit with my tongue and start working it. It doesn't take long before she's fisting my hair and begging me for something.

I'm learning to read her body like an open book and when she's about to come for me, I push two fingers inside her so I can stroke that spot inside her that I hope will make her see stars.

Her entire body bucks and thrashes as she comes for me.

I ease up and let her relax as I give her a final lick and move next to her.

"Shit," she says in a drawn out, sleepy voice.

"Good?" I ask and kiss her lips.

"Yeah. I'd say." She puts an arm over her eyes and I feel an odd sense of pride.

As she recovers, I reach for the tissues on the nightstand and start wiping her stomach.

"I made a mess." I don't think I hide the triumph in my voice.

She laughs. "Why did you have me saved as Iceberg? That feels a bit cruel."

I throw away the tissues and lie closer to her so I can spoon her and hold her in my arms.

"My grandma has a garden. When I was a kid, I used to love playing there. My favorite spot was between these rose bushes. My grandma was very proud of them, but she would always let me pick a rose if I wanted one. Sometimes, I'd take my toys there and play for hours. Or I'd lie on a blanket and read." I push aside the thought that I used to feel almost as content then, as I do now with her in my arms.

"That doesn't answer my question."

"You smell like the roses," I lean in and take a deep whiff of her neck. "You remind me of that garden."

"Is that why you call me Roses?"

I nod against her neck. "They were Iceberg roses. I didn't think I could name you Roses in my phone, because in my mind, everyone knows what you smell like. It's so obvious."

She shifts slightly backwards into my arms. "So you went with Iceberg."

"It wasn't meant to be cruel."

"It's not."

Chapter 37 – Morgan's angry

Faye

I was safe. All night after the incident, I felt safe. Liam stayed with me. He held me, and when I woke up from a nightmare, he was there.

He whispered comforting words to me and stroked my hair. And I curled up closer to him and fell asleep.

He was gone in the morning. Probably to lessen any suspicions about us spending the night together. I'm not sure if it actually worked. He was sharing a room with Ethan. Surely Ethan must have figured it out? But maybe Liam lied and said he hooked up with a puck bunny or something?

Walking down to breakfast was awkward, but other than a few stray looks, nobody acted any differently, and I don't think Coach had any idea about the incident.

So I pretended nothing happened. I took photos of the guys on the bus, interviewed them about winning the game, and that was that.

We arrived back at UNI, and I immediately drowned myself in work. Aside from my schoolwork, I had footage and photos to edit and posts to make.

It's not until Monday after class that I have time to reflect on what happened. I know I'm very lucky to have gotten away. And maybe nothing would have happened if the guys hadn't showed up. Maybe I overreacted and everything would have been fine?

I enter the Den, ready to ask a few more questions and do some of my work while I watch them practice. It's become almost a routine that I work here. I like the atmosphere.

JD is standing with Morgan, and I wave at him. He says something and Morgan whips her head around so her green hair goes flying, then she grabs JD's hand and pulls him over to me.

"Hey," I say when they get closer.

"Are you ok?" Morgan asks.

I look over at JD and he blushes a bit. It's clear he's told her what happened.

"I'm fine. What's up?"

Morgan studies me as if she thinks I'm lying. JD clears his throat.

"I've talked with the guys. We won't bring this up to Coach if you don't want to, but we agreed that when you come to the away games, one of us should always be with you."

"What?" I stare at him.

"We all heard you on the phone. I don't think any of us can forget how scared you sounded. Hell, I still want to punch that guy."

"He can't get away with something like this." Morgan is angry.

"I appreciate it, but it wasn't that big of a deal."

"Don't do that." Morgan raises a finger in my face. "Don't make excuses."

I swallow. Ever since it happened, I've been telling myself that it was just in my head. That he probably didn't mean any harm.

"I'm fine," I say to her as much as to myself.

"Of course you are." She embraces me in a bear hug. "No man can break you. Everything will be fine." She holds me at arm's length and my eyes tear up. "If you ever want to talk about it, you call me, ok? I know we don't really know each other like that, but I'll listen. And if you want to beat his ass, I can teach you how."

"I appreciate it, but he didn't hurt me."

"He grabbed your wrist. JD told me he was holding on to it when they showed up."

I nod and something inside me snaps. "It was scary." I sob.

"I know." She hugs me again. "I don't talk about it much, but something similar happened to me. This guy I kind of knew thought he could... Well, it doesn't matter right now. Just know that if you want to talk, I'm here. Hell, if you want to drink or punch something, I'm also with you."

"Thanks." I blink away the tears. Having someone take it so seriously feels like a relief, like a confirmation that I'm not going crazy. What the guys did was great, but somehow, I needed to hear this from Morgan.

"Meanwhile, if you ever don't feel safe, you call me, or JD, or any of the Lions. If they don't show up for you, I will break their nose. You can ask JD how serious I am about that."

I look over at him, and he smiles and grimaces.

Morgan takes something out of her pocket. "Here, I got you some info about people you can talk to if you need it."

I grab the pile of pamphlets. "You didn't have to do that." At a quick glance, I see information about some therapists, and psychologists and a private detective. I'm not entirely sure what I'd do with that, but I take it anyway.

"Just in case. And you have my number. I have to go now. I have class. But I wanted to make sure you knew I'm here if you need me."

"I really appreciate that, Morgan. Thank you."

"Anytime. See you around." She turns and gives JD a kiss. "Bye, babe."

"Bye." He watches her leave.

"She's... something," I say.

"Yeah." He clears his throat. "I know I probably shouldn't have told her, but I don't keep secrets from her, and I figured since you know each other..."

"It's fine. I like Morgan. She's probably really good to have around in a crisis."

"She is. And she wasn't kidding about breaking their noses. She broke mine once. Before we started dating."

"Did you have it coming?"

"Well... Yeah. Kind of."

I nod to myself. "I figured."

"I'll see you on the ice."

He turns toward the locker room, and I make my way to the ice. Coach is placing some small cones at regular intervals when he spots me. He skates up to me.

"Faye. I was meaning to ask, now that the trip is over, do you have any progress when it comes to Liam?"

"Oh, right. Yes. I have a candidate that I think might work. I know he has the food drive this afternoon, so she's going to meet us there just so I can see if they're believable at all. If they hit it off, we can use photos of the both of them. If not, she's just there helping out like any other volunteer."

"That sounds like a plan. Does Liam know?"

"Not yet. I talked to her last night. I figured I'd not give him a chance to come up with any excuse."

Or myself. Because if I start to think about what I'm doing, I'm going to scream. I'm setting him up with someone else. Someone who isn't me.

And I hate it.

Chapter 38 – Food drive

Liam

I rub my hands together to keep warm as I wait for the next donation. The food drive is well underway and my job is to greet people and carry their donations inside, where they can be sorted and repackaged.

I'm not surprised when Faye shows up with her camera. I figured she'd take some photos. But she's not alone.

I smile at the man handing over a bag with canned goods and thank him on behalf of the Lions as I keep an eye on Faye and the woman she came with. Their body language tells me they don't want anyone to overhear them. The woman looks a bit upset, then she rolls her eyes and sighs.

Faye says a few more words to her before they both head over.

I quickly look away and check the cans in the bag I was just handed. It's all ready to eat pasta. I bring it to the right pile and stack the cans before I go back to the donation table.

"Liam, hey." Faye looks suspiciously innocent. "Have you met Ava?"

Her voice quivers slightly as she steps aside to reveal Ava.

"It's so nice to meet you," Ava says with a smile. There's something about this that I don't like.

"You too," I say and shake her hand. She's not a bad-looking woman, she's a bit taller than Faye and has blonde curls that frame her heart-shaped face.

I raise an eyebrow at Faye.

"I'll let you two get to know each other," Faye says. "Liam, will you show Ava what to do?"

"Sure." I narrow my eyes at her as she backs away. Not wanting to be rude, I turn to Ava. "So, are you here to volunteer?"

"Something like that." She sighs as she looks around.

"And how do you know Faye?"

"I don't. Not really. We just met."

"Ok." A woman in her thirties comes up with a box, and I hurry to help her.

"So, what we do," I say after thanking the woman, "is basically we accept the donations and then we sort them over here." I take the box inside and gesture to the area with my elbow.

"There's not a lot of heavy lifting, is there? I don't like lifting things."

"Uh, well, some. I guess. But it's for a good cause."

Ava looks me up and down. "You look really strong."

"Thanks. So if any cans are dented or bloated, we put them over here. Other than that, we have categories for what we get."

"Yeah, I can read the signs. But I'm bored now. Tell me about yourself."

"Me?" I look around the area to see if I can spot Faye. I'm not sure what's going on here, but I'm pretty sure I don't like it. "What do you want to know about me?"

"Anything. Faye said you're a good guy."

"I hope so. Well, I play hockey for the UNI Lions. And I study chemistry."

"Really? That's so interesting."

I glance over at Faye. She's taking pictures of us from afar.

"Excuse me for a moment."

I leave Ava to deal with the donations and go up to Faye.

"Can I speak to you?" I give her a glare and walk past her and into an empty hallway.

"What's up?" Faye asks and avoids looking at me.

"What's going on here?" I study her as she squirms.

189

"What do you mean?"

"I mean, who is Ava?"

Faye clears her throat. "She's a volunteer. Just like you?"

"Like hell she is." I cross my arms.

Faye sighs. "Fine, I brought her here to see if you would hit it off. She's a candidate for being your fake relationship."

My eyes go wide. "Are you serious?"

"Well, I have to do something. Coach was asking. "

"So you chose her?" I nod in Ava's direction.

"There's nothing wrong with her. She's pretty and smart. She doesn't really care about hockey, but that shouldn't be a deal breaker."

"I'm not interested in her." I speak through clenched teeth.

"Why not?"

"Why not? Why would I be?"

"It's not like you have to like her, or anything. It's all fake."

I rub my temples. "This is madness. You can't just spring someone on me like that."

"Well, what's wrong with her?"

"She's not..." I stop myself before I say something I'd regret. The word that almost escapes has taken me by surprise and I end up just staring at her. You. She's not you. "She's not right. It wouldn't work."

Faye sighs. "You need to help me out. How am I supposed to find someone for you when you're being so stubborn?"

I shake my head. "I don't want you to find anyone for me."

"Well, I do." She takes a stance with her hands on her hips. "Because it's my job, and I need to do a good job here. This may all be a joke to you, but it's my career."

I take a step closer. I hate that she's mad. "Don't you think I know that? What do you think is keeping me from kissing you right now?" I raise an eyebrow.

She blinks and looks surprised. "What?"

"If I wasn't thinking about your job, I'd drag you into a corner and do things to you that would make you scream out my name. Did you know that?"

She swallows and shakes her head.

I take a deep breath. "Ava won't work. I can already tell I won't be able to stand her."

"I'll... I'll find someone else."

She's really insistent about this. I don't understand why. There haven't been any bad rumors about me for a while now.

"Fine." Does she not care? I can't believe she's willing to stand by as I pretend to be dating someone else. But if that's what she wants, then I guess that's what will happen. "I need to get back to work."

I resist the urge to kiss her head as I walk past her. Fuck, this is confusing. How the fuck am I supposed to feel about all of this?

Chapter 39 – Another setup?

Liam

I still can't believe she tried to set me up yesterday. Maybe she's just doing her job, but I really thought... I don't know what I thought.

I keep glancing over at her during practice. She's absorbed by her work and barely looks back. But fuck, when she does... I feel that down to my toes.

I shake it off and focus on the practice. We're ending with a quick-fire drill where the last person to score a goal has to do twenty push-ups and fifty crunches. Pan is in the goal and his objective is to get through as many rounds as possible. He's getting a lot better and I can tell he's taking this seriously and working to improve himself.

I score my goal on the second try, and head to the side to cheer Pan on. He does his best but one after another; the players score on him until there is only one remaining.

We make fun of Enzo as he malds and quickly leaves the ice. Since we're not monsters, he gets to remove his gear before he completes his punishment.

As I turn to the exit, I notice we have more onlookers. It's a group of figure skaters waiting to use the ice. Several of them are frowning at the ice as if they think we've deliberately tried to cut it up for them.

"Hey, you're Liam, right?" a woman in tight pants and an oversized crop top asks me.

"Uh, yeah." I stop and step to the side so the rest of the guys can pass by.

"Hi, I'm Helena." She tilts her head and blinks rapidly a few times.

"I'm sorry, do I know you?" Her blonde hair is up in a ponytail and I'm trying to remember if I've met her before.

"I've seen you around. You're very good at hockey."

"Oh, thanks."

"I wonder what else you're good at." She looks me up and down so slowly it makes me uncomfortable."

"Well, I'm decent at Halo." I shift on my skates, wondering how to get away. Is this another set up by Faye? Is she going to get mad at me if I brush this woman off? Why can't she just talk to me about these things instead of springing random women on me?

"You like computer games?" She is definitely trying something here.

"Sure. Do you?" How the fuck do I know if Faye sent her? Would she send a figure skater? Or would that be too close to the hockey team since we share the ice?

"I play Stardew Valley."

"Nice." Where is Faye? She should really be here for this.

"We could play something together sometime." She twirls her ponytail and takes a small step closer.

"I don't know about that. Most of my time goes to hockey."

"Maybe you could squeeze me in? I think we would play very nicely together." She steps even closer and tilts her head back to look up at me.

I swallow. Then my entire body tingles and I look up in time to see Faye's face fall. She's staring at us.

Clearing my throat, I return my attention to the woman in front of me. "Listen, I'm sure you're very nice and all, but I'm not looking for anything like that."

"Why not?" She's pouting now and stepping even closer.

"I just..." Fuck. I glance over at Faye, but her expression is composed and I have no idea what she wants me to do here. "Listen, I'm not... I mean..."

SOFIA M KAY

"I'm sure I could think of several games you'd find interesting."

Shaking my head, I step back. The only games I want to play are with Faye. "No thanks. It's not going to happen."

I look up, but Faye's gone. Shit.

"Let me at least give you my number so you can call me if you change your mind."

"Uh." I can't see where she went. "Maybe another time."

I leave the woman there and start walking in the direction Faye left. Fuck the skates. If I wasn't wearing them, I'd run. Luckily, I find her not too far from the ice. She's stopped just around the corner and out of view from everyone else.

"Faye."

"Oh, hi. How was practice?" She's not looking at me.

"Fine. Did... Was that another of your setups?" I gesture back to the figure skater.

"What? No. No, you're free to see her on your own time."

I desperately try to catch her eyes. "She just came up to me and started talking."

"That's ok. It's not like you're bound to me or anything." She clears her throat and crosses her arms in front of her.

"You're upset." I stand right in front of her.

"No." She shakes her head. "Of course not. It's just... If you're going to see someone else, it would mess up the plans I have."

I straighten. "Right. That's the only reason."

"What other reason could there be?"

She finally looks at me, and I drown in her eyes. But there's a hardness there. A shield that I don't like.

"She came up to me. I wasn't going to say yes to anything."

She gives me the smallest of nods. "Ok. I mean, you can, if you want. Just let me know if you want to break our agreement."

"I don't. I like our agreement." The faintest hint of a small smile ghosts over her lips and I lean a gloved hand on the wall behind her.

194

"Speaking of our agreement." I lower my voice. "How about we meet up tonight? I could stop by the apartment?"

Her body instinctively moves closer to mine, and I'm not even sure she's aware of doing it. I love it, the way she's so comfortable around me.

"I can't," she says. "I have to go to a party?"

"A party?"

She nods. "It's a birthday party for a friend. I'm going with Cora."

Fuck, that makes my chest hurt. Maybe I overdid it on the ice.

"Oh." I stand back up and try not to let my disappointment show. "I should go get changed. I guess I'll see you later."

"I'll be around for a while. I have a meeting with Coach and some other people in a bit over an hour."

An idea takes form in my mind. "So, you're saying you'll be here when I'm done showering?"

She nods. "Probably. Why?"

I smirk. "I'll see you in a bit." Then I walk off before I lose every ounce of control that is keeping me from pouncing her right here and now.

Chapter 40 – So close

Faye

Liam walks off toward the locker room to shower and I find a small sitting area near Coach's office. I sometimes sit out front because I like the huge open space and the big walls of windows, but today I'm in more of a backroom mood.

My plan yesterday to find Liam a fake date failed miserably. And to top it off, I had to deal with a rejected Ava afterwards. She did not get over it until I offered to invite her to another team event so she could meet some of the other players.

And then I find Liam flirting with a cute figure skater. Not that I care. I don't. It's none of my business who he flirts with. He can marry her for all I care.

I sit down and grab a notebook where I keep ideas for posts. I have just over an hour to kill, so I might as well get some work done.

It's not that I was jealous. That would be silly. I have nothing to be jealous about. He was talking to someone else. He's allowed to do that. And I don't care. At all.

I do my best to keep my brain from thinking too closely about what I felt when I saw that woman flirting with him. I probably shouldn't examine my feelings too closely.

Liam must have showered in record time. My heart skips a beat when he comes toward me with a small smile and darkness in his eyes.

"Come on." He makes a gesture with his head as he quietly urges me to follow.

"Why?" I ask, but I'm already grabbing my things.

"I want to show you something."

His head swivels from side to side as we pass an intersecting corridor. It's a maze down here and even though I'm getting familiar with it, I'm not sure where he's taking me.

We cross an open area with rows of pillars and head down another corridor.

"Where are we going?" I keep my voice down, because whatever we're doing, I don't think we should be announcing it to the world.

"Here."

He stops at a door and opens it. It's a small lounge with a couple of couches and a mini fridge.

"What is this?" I ask as he closes the door after us.

"It's for visiting teams."

"Oh." I drop my bag and jacket on one of the couches. "And what are we doing here?"

"Whatever you want." He comes closer and I inhale in anticipation. "You have an hour to kill, right? Well, I'd be willing to help you do that."

His hands land on my hips, and I melt like ice in a hot drink.

"Really?" My voice is husky. "This was your plan? To get me alone in a room with a couch?"

"A couch, a desk, a wall... I can make anything work."

I want to tease him, but there's not a doubt in my mind that he's telling the truth.

He pulls me closer, and I inhale him. The hint of vanilla has become an aphrodisiac and my stomach tightens.

"So, you want to have sex?" I ask.

"Don't you?" He lowers his mouth and kisses my jaw. I curse my body as it comes to life under his touch.

"Yes," I whine. His mouth moves along my jawline all the way to my ear. He grabs my earlobe between his teeth and pulls gently.

His lips cover the sensitive part just below my ear, and I tilt my head to give him better access. My hands sneak around him.

"You smell so good." He presses his nose to my neck and takes a deep inhale.

"What if someone comes in here?"

"They won't. The room isn't in use."

"Are you sure?"

He nods and nips at my neck with his lips. "I'm sure."

"Ok." I take his face in my hands and press my lips against his.

It's explosive. My body needs his kiss. I close my eyes. The crazy thing is that I trust him. He could have brought me out on the ice and told me no one would see us and I would believe him.

His hands are pulling at my clothes, and suddenly my urges are desperate. I let go of his face and start doing the same. I pull at his shirt, but I don't want to stop kissing him, so I move to the pants and try to pull them down. He's wearing sweats, so I have more luck than he does. He curses as he tugs at my pants.

I laugh against his mouth. He bites my lower lip playfully. Then he breaks the kiss and leans back so he can get a look at my pants. I watch him as he manages to get the zipper open and pull them down. As I step out of the pants, he's pulling my sweater over my head.

"Fuck, yes," he says when he sees my bra. "Your tits are perfect."

Instead of waiting for an answer, he reaches back and unhooks my bra. I shiver as I stand naked in front of him.

In two seconds, he's removed his own clothes, and it's just him and me, naked. He steps up to me and lets one hand slide down my back until he's groping my ass. Then he squeezes it and pulls me closer. I gasp as his hard cock presses into my stomach.

"I'm going to need you to be quiet today," he says and gives me a quick kiss.

"I can be quiet. Can you?"

He raises an eyebrow. "Is that a challenge?"

I slip a hand between us and slowly wrap it around his cock. "Maybe." With a smile on my lips, I sink onto my knees. Liam gasps and looks down at me.

Taking his cock in my mouth, I feel extra dirty. I'm naked in a room at the Den, doing something I'm not supposed to. But there's a thrill to it that I find exciting.

"Oh, fuck," Liam says and buries his face in his hands as I take him deeper. I love how hard he gets for me. There's no question in my mind whether he enjoys what I'm doing. I can tell with every pulsating throb of his rock hard cock.

I want to take my time and work him into a frenzy, but his hands cover my temples and pushes gently. I release him from my mouth and meet his eyes.

"You're going to make me come down your throat."

I smile. He's panting and almost shaking.

"I don't mind." I turn back to the shaft in front of me, but he grabs my upper arms and pulls me up.

"I do," he says and pushes me backward.

My back hits the wall, and he places one hand between my legs. I inhale and shudder against him.

"You're so wet for me." Our eyes are locked as he explores me and covers his fingers with my wetness. I lean back against the wall and he places one hand by my head. The other is still between my legs.

One finger pushes into my opening, and I gasp. Except for his hand, he's not touching me. I see the lust in his eyes as he pushes a second finger inside. His thumb finds my clit and I'm about to combust.

"Liam."

"Shh. Quiet, remember?" He's teasing me and I wish I could reply with something snappy, but he has a knack for finding just the right rhythm. My knees go weak, and I grab his arms and lean against him. He continues to rub my clit and move his fingers.

"Liam." I bury my face against his shoulder and try to stifle my moan.

"That's it. Come for me, Roses."

I whimper and let go of any hesitation. His free arm wraps around my waist, holding me up as I come.

I keep my lips pressed against his skin and resist the urge to cry out his name.

"Fuck, yes," he says when I finally come to my senses. "You're amazing."

"Liam," I feel weak, but still need more.

"Yes?"

I twist my way out of his arms and walk up to the back of the couch. Feeling brave, I look back over my shoulder as I lean forward and place my elbows on the backrest.

"Fuck me."

The dark lust that comes over him is almost scary. Not only does his face change, but as he moves toward me, his movements remind me of a tiger hunting its prey.

He says nothing as he stops behind me and grabs my hips. I spread my legs a little and wait. His hand caresses my ass, and I'm almost nervous in anticipation.

Then I feel him lining up. I expect him to take it slow, but he's barely there before he thrusts into me.

"Oh, fuck," I cry out in pleasure.

His fingers dig into my hips as he tries to get deeper. I hold on to the couch and he pulls out and slams into me again.

"Quiet, Roses," he says and repeats the motion.

"Umm." I don't dare open my mouth for fear I might scream out his name. This is a new position for us, and I love it. I love his fingers gripping me as if he needs me. I love how exposed I feel and yet in control. And I especially love how his cock hits just right.

His pace turns frantic and all I can do is take it and hold on to the couch. Each stroke is painting a picture of my pleasure and I lose track of time and place.

"Fuck, Faye." His groan is so intense I feel it to my spine. It's what pushes me over the edge.

"Liam." I barely have enough awareness to keep my voice down as wave after wave of pleasure crashes into me.

Liam grabs my waist and pulls me up against his chest. I turn my head and his lips find mine. He shudders against me as he comes inside me while kissing me.

"Fuck," he finally says and rests his forehead against mine.

"Yeah." I'm still out of breath.

He hugs me tighter and I give myself a moment to enjoy the sensation of him so close to me.

I'm brought back to reality when he clears his throat.

"We should get dressed."

"Right." I take a step away from him and start looking for my underwear, still feeling wobbly.

"I think there's a bathroom there?" He points to a door in the corner.

I pull on my panties and nod. I quickly get dressed and flee into the small room.

After cleaning up as best I can, I make sure my hair isn't too wild, but there's not much I can do about the rosy tint to my cheeks. Hopefully, they'll return to normal before my meeting.

When I look presentable, I leave the bathroom. Liam is waiting for me, all dressed and looking almost as if nothing happened.

"Ready?" he asks and I nod. He opens the door and together we step out of the room.

"Liam," a deep voice says. I freeze. It's Mickey Gordon, the equipment manager.

"Hey, what's up?"

I don't know how Liam can sound so casual. I try to hide behind him as I, once more, make sure my clothes aren't inside out.

"Not much, just checking some stuff. What are you guys doing?" His eyes narrow as he looks from Liam to me.

"We were going over some of Faye's PR plans for me." Liam rolls his eyes. "I still think you're exaggerating, but she takes her job seriously." He shrugs as if it's all on me and he's just trying to comply.

"It's not just my job," I say, trying to not be suspicious. "What you do affects the entire team."

"You were meeting here?" Gordon says and looks past us to the now empty room.

Liam shrugs. "I don't want everyone to know my private business."

"Fair enough. Well, I won't keep you."

He hurries off. I almost want to throw up as I follow Liam in the opposite direction.

"That was too close." My hands are shaking.

"I don't think he suspects anything."

I hate that Liam is so calm.

"He almost caught us," I whisper shout.

"But he didn't."

"What we did was stupid."

"What we did was awesome," he says and smiles as if our careers didn't almost just end.

"Liam, I'm serious."

"So am I, and I know you liked it. You came so hard on my-"

"Liam!" I look around to make sure no one is within hearing distance.

"Listen, Roses. We had a close call, and yeah, in the future we should probably be more careful. But we didn't get caught."

I nod, but my insides are a twisted ball of anxiety and I'm no longer sure this relationship was a good idea.

Chapter 41 – Calling mom

Liam

I know almost getting caught affected her more than she wanted to let on. The fear was so clearly written in her face I wanted to hold her and tell her everything will be fine. But at that moment, we reached the busier parts of the Den and there were people around us.

She broke off and went back to waiting for her meeting with Coach. And I had no choice but to walk away.

Part of me feels bad for not caring as much as she does. I'd never do anything to put her career in jeopardy. Well, except for what we are already doing. But another part is envious that she knows what she's passionate about and wants to do with her life.

For many years, I assumed hockey would be my life. I thought it would be something I would always want to do. That certainty has faded. For many reasons.

I'm not as good at it as I assumed when I was younger. I dreamt of going to a major NHL team and being the star of the show. Coming to UNI forced me to face reality. I'm good, but not that good.

I've seen my teammates excel on the ice and get contacted by the teams I dreamed of.

Whenever they get good news, it pushes me further away from the future I thought I would have.

I still love hockey, and I will always want to play. But I'm more and more leaning towards playing for fun in some amateur league.

I lock myself in my room and do something I haven't done in a while. Something I should have done. I call my mom.

"Hi, sweetie. Is everything ok?"

"Hi, mom. Yeah, everything is fine. How's work?"

"Work is good. I finally got the new marketing manager to realize I'm his boss. Only took him six months and a formal write-up." She says it with a smile. Mom has always taken challenges in stride. She's fought for everything she's accomplished and she's accomplished a lot.

"How did you know what you wanted to do? Did you always want to work in a big company?"

She laughs. "What's this about? No. When I was younger, I wanted to be a ballerina. You know this. I was good. I've shown you the videos. Until I messed up my knee, I thought I could make a career out of it. Maybe I would have."

"Do you regret not doing that?"

"Yes, and no. If I had, you wouldn't be here. I was obsessed with dancing. If I would have thought I had any chance at making it, I wouldn't have kept you. Blowing out my knee was the best thing that happened to me."

"But you just started a new job. How did you know where to go from there?"

"Honey, I created this career for you. When I first saw you, I was determined to give you whatever you want in this world. Why are you asking?"

"I appreciate that, mom. But I don't know what I want."

"It's not hockey?" There's no judgment in her voice. There never has been. She's been my number one supporter since I can remember. But she does not give a fuck what I do. She'll just be there for me.

"I don't think it is. But I don't know how to figure it out."

"Is it chemistry?"

"Maybe. I think I could be happy doing that."

"Do this for me, honey. Close your eyes."

"Ok." I sit on my bed and close my eyes.

"Now imagine your life in five years. A quick glance at your day. How you feel, what you're excited about. Now, do the same, but it's your sixtieth birthday. What do you want in your life when you turn sixty? Is there one constant? Something that popped up in both scenarios?"

"Faye."

Her name escapes me before I can stop it.

"Really?" Mom teases. "And who is Faye?"

I clear my throat. "She's nobody. Just this woman I've been... seeing."

"Tell me all about her."

I can easily imagine mom settling into her comfy armchair and preparing to drag every detail out of me.

"It's not like that. We're not dating or anything. We can't. She's the new social media manager, and she'd lose her job."

"But she's the one you thought of?"

"It's probably because I saw her earlier and... I don't want to be alone."

"Do you like her?"

My heart hammers in my chest so hard I think I'm about to pass out.

"She's ok, I guess. Pretty. Smells nice."

"Does she like you?"

"I don't know. But it doesn't matter. We've decided it's just... sex."

"Sex that's against the rules?"

"Yeah."

She takes a deep breath and I can feel the disappointment over the phone. "Liam. Are you putting her job at risk?"

I feel like an ass. "We're careful."

"Liam. That's not fair to her."

"She's an adult. She knows what she's doing. She could call it off at any time."

"You need to take responsibility for your actions. I did not raise you to put people's futures so blatantly at risk. Still, I'm very glad you're not acting like a fuckboy anymore."

"What? Mom! I have not been acting like a fuckboy."

"I'm not stupid, Liam. I follow you on social media and I've seen the pictures."

My cheeks burn. "So, you knew about that?"

"Yes, I'm always going to keep tabs on you. You're my only child. You're the most important person in my life. But I figured you needed to go through a wild phase. Lord knows, I did. It's all part of finding yourself, which is what college is for."

"I don't want to know about your wild phase," I grumble.

"If you care about this woman, you need to take her needs and wants into consideration. You can't risk her career for your own selfish needs. Not if you care about her."

I fall back onto the bed and stare at the ceiling. "I don't know what to do."

"Be careful. Think things through."

"I will. I'll figure it out."

"I have to go now. I have to get ready for a date. Give my best to Ethan."

"Will do. Have fun."

"Oh, I intend to."

Shaking my head, I hang up on her and keep staring at the ceiling.

Should I end things with Faye? It would be the right thing to do. I hate how scared she looked earlier, how terrified the thought of getting caught made her.

I go back and forth for a long time until my thoughts are interrupted by a knock at the door.

"Yeah?" I shout without getting up.

"Hey, man, you want to join us for dinner?" Ethan pops in his head.

"Who's us?"

"Me and Lily, JD and Morgan, and Jonathan and his new girl."

I grimace at the lineup of couples.

"Nah, I'm good. I don't feel like being a seventh wheel."

"Come on. You hardly ever come out with us anymore. Are you not seeing anyone?"

The air gets tense, as if there's a crackle of energy waiting to erupt.

"Nope." I say and feel bad for lying. But am I? We're not seeing each other. We have an arrangement.

"So you'd be ok if I set you up with someone?"

I shrug. "I'm in no mood to meet anyone tonight."

"Huh."

I can't look at him. I'm lying to my best friend and I hate it. Maybe mom is right and I need to stop all of this. Things are starting to get way too complicated.

"Ok, well, let me know if you change your mind," Ethan says and closes the door.

I take a deep breath. What the fuck has my life become?

Chapter 42 – Well… Fuck…

Faye

If I didn't know better, I'd think Liam was avoiding me.

It's been almost a week since our encounter at the Den and he's barely looked at me since. Whenever I've reached out, he's claimed to be busy.

But he can't stay away from me forever.

After we almost got caught, I admit I freaked out a bit. It took Cora a while to talk me down, but she did. I think it helps that she takes risks all the time and to her, it's no big deal. She's convinced that I'll find a new job easily, even if the worst happens. Which she says won't.

And it's not like it's out of the ordinary for me and Liam to hang out, so barring someone walking in on us in the middle of having sex, we can probably talk our way out of it.

All we have to do is not have sex at the Den again. Or anywhere else in public.

I bite my lip. Not that I regret it. There was something so hot about sneaking off to do it and nobody else knowing.

Liam might be regretting it, though. Or I suppose he could be over me. It was never supposed to be a relationship, so I don't know why that thought hurts. His actions lately have thrown me for a loop. I'm not sure what to think about the lack of communication.

I take a deep breath as I approach the chemistry building. I don't know if there will be other people here. If there are, we won't be able to talk. But if there aren't, then maybe I'll get some answers to questions I'm not sure I even want to ask.

"Hey." Liam stands outside the door, waiting for me.

"Hi."

He looks cold. His hands are tucked deep into his pockets and he's pulled the scarf up to his hat.

"Let's get inside." He flashes a key fob and opens the door. "There shouldn't be too many people here at this hour. Hopefully, we can set everything up and get it done pretty quickly."

"Ok." I adjust the camera bag as I follow him across the open space toward an elevator. A group of two women and a man in white lab coats cross the floor. The man is using a blue, disposable glove to hold a package as they take the stairs to the next floor.

Liam clears his throat. "I got your messages."

I nod. "I figured."

"I was going to answer, but I've been really busy."

"That's fine. You don't owe me anything."

He takes a short breath as if he's preparing to say something, but changes his mind.

The elevator door opens and we walk down a corridor past several closed doors.

"I was thinking this lab would work," Liam says and opens a door. He turns on the lights and reveals several rows of white counters with giant metal contraptions at the end of each row.

"It looks so... professional," I say. There are more of the contraptions against the wall. The front looks like a glass window you can move up and down. The one closest to me has a complicated-looking setup with vials and chemistry things.

"Oh, I remember this," I say and point. "It's a bunsen burner, right?"

"Yeah."

I nod. "This will work. Just give me a minute to set up."

"Good. I'll get changed."

I remove my jacket and take out the camera. Liam leaves the room so I take a couple of slow laps, trying out angles and checking the lighting. I try turning some of the lights off, but it seems whoever planned this room was not thinking about flattering lighting and good photo opportunities.

"Where do you want me?"

I swivel, and my jaw drops when I see Liam in his lab coat. He puts on a pair of safety glasses and I swallow.

"Um. Can you do something chemically over here?" I point to one of the spots I want to try.

"Sure." He grabs a few items and fills a beaker with water. Then he starts pipetting the water into tiny vials.

I step back and take his photo. Fuck, he looks hot.

"You actually look like you know what you're doing."

He glares at me. "That's because I do."

"Right." I keep forgetting that he's more than just a hockey player. "Could you hold up that thing a little?"

He does and I take more photos. While I tell him where to look and what to do, my heart is beating so incredibly fast I'm certain I'm about to have a heart attack.

It should be illegal for someone to be this sexy. But when he smiles at me, I'm ready to drop my panties for him in public again.

"You want me to wear gloves?" he asks. I shake my head. I don't like the gloves, I like imagining his hands on me. His fingers trailing places.

"This is going to be great," I say to distract myself.

"I hope so." He smiles and our eyes meet.

My stomach gets warm. I can't for the life of me remember what I'm supposed to be doing. The warmth spreads to my chest. That smile is dangerous. No, it's worse. It's seductive.

Fuck. My brain catches up with my body.

"Oh, fuck." I whisper to myself.

"What was that?" He picks up a flask and puts some water into it.

His movements are calm and collected. Unlike my brain. My thoughts are racing. But the loudest one is crystal clear. And it's not what I want to hear.

Blinking, I try to get rid of it. It's wrong. It has to be.

I'm in love with him.

Nope, I won't allow it. Something's misfired in my brain and as soon as I figure out what, I can laugh at the most ridiculous idea I've gotten in a long time.

I force myself to snap more photos so he won't get suspicious.

I've been wrong before.

But not about this.

It could be a mistake.

Is it?

It's as if my brain takes a pause to think it over.

Well, fuck.

What do I do now?

Do I tell him?

"I never thought I would be able to keep up with both hockey and chemistry," Liam says.

"Oh? Why not?"

"They're both time consuming. And very different."

"But you have."

His satisfied smirk is making me want to tear off his clothes. "Yeah. It hasn't been easy. The people here don't really get why I've focused so much of my time on hockey. And sometimes, on road trips, I've barely been aware of where we are because I've been so focused on chemistry homework."

"Could you... could you lean back against the counter and cross your arms?"

"Like this?" He takes the pose and I bite my lip.

"Uh-uh. Just like that."

Fuck, this image might just go into my personal collection.

"I really was going to call you."

He must be taking my silence for something it's not.

"Yeah?"

"Yeah. I'm sorry about last time. It was a stupid idea."

I shrug. "We probably shouldn't do that again." But fuck do I want to.

"Right." He looks away. "Are we done here?"

"I have what I need." I start packing up the camera.

"Great."

I take a deep breath as he's about to leave the room. "Want to come to my place?"

It's just sex. Purely physical. That's all my body wants. And I'm going to prove it to myself.

"Yeah."

He nods at me before he goes to change.

Chapter 43 – Slow

Faye

It's the first time I'm in his car. I tell myself that if anyone sees us, we can say he was driving me home. That's the polite thing to do and something any of the players probably would have offered.

I hold the camera bag in my lap as if it's a shield that will protect me. And I don't even know what I need protecting from.

"So, you think those photos will work?" Liam sounds strange. As if there's tension between us.

"Oh, yeah. I think they'll be great for your reputation." I can't look at him. My stupid brain is insane for thinking I have feelings for him. I don't.

It's awkward as he parks the car near my building.

"Will your roommate be home?" He shuts off the engine and I take a breath.

"No. She's out." Fuck, I didn't even think about that. Good thing Cora has plans with Carlos tonight.

"Ok."

I get out of the car and adjust my bags. It's just sex. No big deal.

We walk together into the building.

"Are you ok?" He looks at me with concern as he pushes the button for the elevator.

"Yeah, I'm fine."

"You know we don't have to do this, right?"

"I want to." If only I could stop being so fucking nervous. What's that even about? I force myself to look at him and smile.

The elevator doors open and we get in.

He hits the button for my floor and I inhale. The scent of vanilla and wood fill my nostrils and some of the nerves fall away.

We stand in silence as the elevator reaches my floor.

I brush past him, intentionally touching him as I walk up to the door. His presence soothes me. And puts me on edge.

I enter the apartment and put down my bags as Liam closes the door behind us and we're all alone.

"Hey." Liam's voice is soft and I turn to face him.

"Yeah?"

He carefully puts his hands on my waist, and my entire body flutters.

His face lowers, and gentle lips find mine. There's nothing strange or wrong about the kiss. I put my arms around his neck and answer it.

It feels right.

I don't know how else to put it. Kissing Liam is what I was always meant to do.

Before the kiss gets too deep, he pulls away.

"That's better," he says and rubs a thumb along my bottom lip.

"Better?" My head is spinning from being so close to him.

"You're starting to relax."

"Oh."

"I bet I can make you forget about whatever it is that's on your mind." He leans in and kisses my cheek. His mouth trails down to my ear and the sensitive skin below.

"I'm sure you can," I say and decide to just give in. I could fight this, but why? He can bring me so much pleasure, it would be stupid not to let him. Besides, it's just sex.

He opens my jacket and slowly takes it off. Our lips meet again and it's nothing like the last time we stood in this hallway.

This time, our hands explore cautiously. We slowly remove each item of clothing as we make our way toward my bedroom.

He steps out of his pants, and finally there is nothing between us. I press my body against his and feel him respond to my touch.

"You're so beautiful." His mouth barely leaves mine to whisper the words.

His hands caress my sides and I shiver in anticipation.

"Liam."

He teases his tongue into my mouth and I squeeze my eyes shut. I want so much from him. All of him.

I entangle my hands into his hair and hold him close. My skin burns where his hands trail down my sides and back up. Our tongues play and I could melt into him.

I gasp as his palms cover my breasts. My nipples are instantly hard and straining.

"I need you, Faye."

"Take me."

Our eyes meet, and he backs me up. The bed hits my knees and I sit down. Still maintaining eye contact, I move further up the bed. Then I open my legs to invite him in.

He takes a quick breath and holds it for a second. As he releases, he joins me on the bed. He sits between my legs, and my breathing turns shallow.

The atmosphere is heavy with electricity, and my core is pulsating with need. He grabs my ankles and lifts them up. I grab hold under my knees and swallow, feeling exposed. He gives me a small smile, as if to tell me I'm doing good.

He raises an eyebrow as he grabs his hardness, and I nod. I'm ready. I want him. No, I need him.

We've done this before. I've felt him inside me many times. But it's never been this slow. This sensual.

He takes his time until I want to scream. Slowly filling me up.

Once he's buried inside me, he holds still. I breathe into all the emotions coursing through me. He leans forward and kisses me. His lips are hot and tender on mine.

The movements are leisurely. He pulls out as if he has all the time in the world.

"Liam," I gasp against his lips. I've never experienced anything like this before. Gone is the frantic need for immediate release. Somehow we've converged on this path to slow satisfaction.

Each thrust is meticulous. His lips cover mine as I pant, and explore my jaw and neck when it becomes too much.

When he presses his cheek to mine and increases the pace, I hold on to him and wrap my legs around his waist.

A single tear escapes because I realize it's not just sex.

I keep my face hidden from his and take what he gives me.

I lose track of time and place. His hands hold on to me and he moves us around. He ends up sitting with his back against the headboard and I'm in his lap.

All of a sudden, I'm in control. Grabbing the headboard, I continue the pace he set. His hands are now free to explore my breasts, my back, my ass. Everywhere he touches, he leaves a trail of heat and need.

With one hand buried in my hair and the other pinching my nipple, he increases the pace. I move up and down, faster and faster until my orgasm starts building.

His mouth covers my nipple and his fingers are homing in on my clit. I throw my head back as the pressure builds, desperate for the release.

It still takes me by surprise. The force of it almost knocks me over, but Liam's hands hold me securely. He lowers me onto my back and pounds into me. I'm surrounded by pleasure as he takes what he needs and finishes inside me.

His body is heavy on top of me, and I am completely relaxed.

"Wow," Liam says in a voice so soft I can barely hear him.

I want to hug him, keep him close, but he pulls out of me and lies next to me on his back.

"Yeah," I say and squeeze my eyes shut to keep the tears from starting.

"This is so crazy." I can feel the bed move as she shakes his head.

"What do you mean?" I can barely speak as my sated body tries to become one with the bed.

"I could be having sex with anyone."

My eyes shoot open. I stare at the ceiling.

"Yeah?"

"And I ended up with you."

He's still shaking his head. I try not to let the panic inside me show. No, not panic. What is that feeling? Why is it so chilling?

He lets out a small laugh. "Nobody would ever believe this. You and me." He laughs. "Or maybe everyone would."

My heart is racing. My mouth is dry. "Please don't tell anyone." I'm dizzy. I can't do this. I don't know what the fuck is going on, but I can't lose my job. I love this job.

"I won't."

He sounds so nonchalant about all of this. And to my horror, I realize it's because this isn't a big deal to him.

And why does my heart hurt?

"I don't know if I can do this anymore." The words reach out of me and I think I'm as surprised as he is.

He gets up on an elbow and looks at me. "What do you mean?"

"It's... it's too big of a risk. We might get caught. I can't do it."

"No. Faye. Roses. Don't say that. We'll be more careful. Is this because we had sex at the Den? We'll never do that again."

Fuck, this is hard. He reminds me of a little boy, desperate to hold on to me.

"I don't know." Why am I faltering? I need to be strong.

"Listen, Faye. We have a good thing going. And we just have to be more careful. How about this: outside of this apartment, we're nothing but player and social media manager? Ok? We won't let anything on. Nobody will ever be able to figure it out."

I hate myself for giving in. My heart is about to be shattered. But as his hand rests on my stomach, how can I say no?

So I nod. "Ok."

The smile lights up his face. "You won't regret it. I promise." He leans in and kisses me. As he slowly starts a trail of kisses down my body, all I can think about is that I already do.

But it's just sex. Purely physical.

That's it.

Chapter 44 – Just a crush?

Faye

"I don't know what changed."

I'm sitting on the couch with Cora warming my hands on a mug of tea.

Through the open door, I can see my bed. It's made and there's no sign of what happened last night. When I woke up, the bed smelled like him. But I've been in classes all day, and now, I'm scared to check if it still does. Scared, because I don't know what I want the answer to be.

After he went down on me and made me come yet again, we had another session. It was still more sensual than frantic, and when I came, I was overwhelmed by emotions.

Luckily, Liam rolled over on his back and rested with an arm over his eyes. It took everything in me to collect myself.

"What do you mean?" Cora says and sips her tea. "Did he change?"

I tilt my head and stare at the bed. "No. Well... No. Yes. I don't know. I mean, the sex was different last night. Slower."

"Better?"

"Yes? Maybe. It was different."

The sex had been awesome, but as soon as it was over, Liam left like he always does. It was as if he barely gave himself time to catch his breath before he jumped out of the bed and told me he'd see me around.

"But something changed?" Cora is furrowing her brow.

I shake my head. "Nevermind. It doesn't matter."

"Faye. Come on. Just tell me."

With a sigh, I close my eyes. "I think I like him."

"You are sleeping with the guy."

"Yeah, but it was only supposed to be sex."

She sits up. "Wait. You mean you like him like him?"

I nod.

"Holy shit. Well, does he like you back?"

I shake my head. "It's just an arrangement to him. Sex."

Cora leans back with a thoughtful look on her face. "Right."

"Gah! It's so stupid. I was taking photos of him yesterday and he was in a lab coat. It was the first time I've seen him look so... sciency."

"I didn't know you had a thing for nerds."

"I don't. Not usually."

"What do you want to do now?"

I shrug and stare at the tea. "What we agreed to, I guess. It's not like I can do anything else. We talked about it a little yesterday. We'll only have sex here, and when we're not here, we're professional." I glance up at her. "What? Why are you looking at me like that?"

"Are you going to get hurt?"

"No. Of course not." I stare back down at the dark liquid in my mug. "I can keep things separate. I'm a professional."

God, I hope I can manage my emotions. I have to.

"So, you're still going to find him someone to date?" she raises her eyebrow at me, as if it's a challenge.

"Yes. Of course I will."

"Have you been looking?"

"I..." I close my mouth. I have. But not seriously. Every time I start, I get this funny feeling and an urge to... not. "I'm working on it."

"Because if you think you can do this, that shouldn't be an issue, right?"

"Right." I take a breath. She's right. It stings. But I should find someone for him. That way, whatever feelings I think I might have will disappear. And I'll see he's not for me.

Cora narrows her eyes. "Seriously?"

"Yeah. I'm going to find him someone. It's no big deal."

She makes a weird strangled noise and throws her hand up, almost spilling her tea. "What the fuck, Faye?"

"What?"

"What do you mean, you'll find someone for him? What the hell is that about?"

"You asked about the fake dating. It's my job."

"Fuck that. If you like him, what you should be looking for is a way to be with him."

"Cora."

"You should not be setting him up with other women."

"I have to. It's my job. And we agreed to keep things professional."

"Faye, you like this guy. You don't have to torture yourself like this."

I put the cold tea down and rub my temples. "It's my job, Cora. My career. I can't get fired this early on. Do you have any idea what that would do to my reputation?"

She shakes her head. "Then you better work on your poker face."

"What do you mean?"

"Your face does weird things when you talk about him. Even mentioning him dating someone else makes you look like you want to commit murder."

"It does not."

"I'm just saying." She puts her mug next to mine and takes my hands. "I will always be here for you. I'd love to see this work out like you want. But I don't think it will."

"I'll be fine."

"No, you won't. But when everything blows up, I'll be here with a shoulder to cry on and a bottle of tequila."

I smile. "Things will not blow up, because it's just sex and I can control my feelings. It's probably just a little crush that will be over in no time. There will be no need to get drunk or spend an evening crying on your shoulder." I get up and grab the mugs.

"I hope you're right. But just in case, I'm getting more ice cream."

"You just want to get more ice cream so you can have it for dinner." Shaking my head, I take the mugs to the kitchen.

"It's made from milk. Basically, it's protein. And sometimes it has berries. Which are super healthy."

I smile at her logic as I bring the mugs to the sink.

She's being overprotective. Nothing bad is going to happen. Even if I maybe, possibly, have a small crush on Liam, it doesn't matter. Crushes are temporary and it won't keep me from doing my job or anything.

In fact, I'm going to find him someone great to date.

I will.

Chapter 45 – Introducing Shana

Faye

My hands are shaking.

I smile reassuringly at the woman standing next to me.

"Thank you so much for doing this."

"Of course," Shana says. "I should be thanking you."

"I'm sorry you have to do this. I mean, in general. It shouldn't be that way."

She shrugs. "They have a lot of flaws, but I still love my grandparents. Do I wish they accepted me for who I am? Of course, but it is what it is."

"You never thought about telling them?"

We're a bit early, waiting outside the restaurant. It's a surprisingly warm day, and the sun is shining.

"I did. Several times, but something always stopped me. Grandma doesn't have much time left and we've decided to just leave it and focus on making her last months as pleasant as possible."

I keep an eye on the road, looking for Liam's car. I honestly can't say what I would do in Shana's position. Having to hide who you are must suck. But I also kind of understand her wanting to shield her grandma. With a deep breath, all I can feel is gratitude that I'm not the one making the decision.

"And there's the money," Shana adds casually. "If she finds out, she'll remove me from the will. This way, I can take some of that money and help others in my position or worse. There's this one charity that focuses on helping teens that have been kicked out of their homes after coming out to their parents. I'm going to donate a good chunk to that."

I smile. "I see." Suddenly, her choice makes a lot more sense.

My stomach flutters as a car pulls in. "That's him." I nod at Liam getting out of the car.

"He's not bad looking." Shana tilts her head. "Just the kind of man my grandma would want to see me with." Her voice sounds dead.

"Come on, let me introduce you."

I walk on ahead, my stomach in knots. Maybe I should have warned him?

"Liam?"

"Hey, Roses." He smiles at me and almost breaks my heart. "I didn't think you'd want to meet in public. But I guess this is far enough away that we can avoid prying eyes."

He takes a step toward me and I quickly step back and to the side.

"This is Shana," I say and can't tear my eyes away from his.

His face drops, and I can almost imagine a look of hurt betrayal. Then he looks over at her and smiles politely.

"Shana?" He holds out a hand.

"Shana, this is Liam." Every word scrapes my chest raw as I speak. "I met Shana a while back when I took some photos for her."

"It's a pleasure," Shana says and looks him up and down. She winks at me. "I can work with this."

"Hi, can you give us a moment?" Liam holds up a finger at Shana, who just nods. When he grabs my arm, electricity shoots through me. I follow him off to the side.

"What the hell, Faye? I thought we were... What is she doing here?"

"Shana? She's your date. I figured you two could have lunch here and get to know each other. I'll take some photos of you guys and if things work out, which I think they will, because she's great, then we'll leak the photos in time for the game on Friday."

He looks at me as if he hasn't heard a word I just said.

"What are you doing, Faye?"

"My job."

"Your job?"

"Yes, remember?"

"So you want me to go on a date with this woman?"

I nod. Worried I might choke on the word.

"How can you set me up with someone just like that?"

"You knew we were going to do this. We talked about it. And Shana is perfect. Don't you think she's pretty?"

"Yeah, but I don't want to date her."

"I tried getting you out of this, but everyone is dead set on the idea." I spoke to Coach again this morning, desperate for a way out. "There was nothing I could do."

"Nothing but pimp me out?"

Fuck, that hurts. The way he looks at me hurts. The disappointment in his words hurt.

"Liam. You know it's not like that."

"I never agreed to this." His narrowed eyes are dark and intense.

"You can walk away," I whisper. God, I want him to walk away. Even knowing that it's fake, I want him to walk away.

"Not with your job on the line," he mutters so quietly I'm not sure I hear him right.

Shana takes a step closer. "Are we doing this?" She tilts her head and smiles.

I close my eyes and turn my head away. Liam's eyes practically burn my skin before he faces her.

"Yeah, it's so nice to meet you. Are you hungry?"

"Starving." Her smile is genuine and radiating, and my chest contracts as they walk into the restaurant together.

I take a few moments to myself before I follow them. I sit at a table where I have an unobstructed view of them. With my phone, I snap a few photos of them before I order some soup.

They talk and laugh and I hate how natural Shana makes it look. I have to remind myself that I gave her instructions, and that she has no interest in Liam whatsoever.

The soup is almost inedible because of the tightening feeling in my stomach. I get a few really good photos and try to convince myself I don't care that she's touching his arm.

They take their time with the lunch and when my soup is gone, I can't take it anymore. I send a quick text to Liam that I got what I needed and have to head out. He looks over at me as I'm paying the bill. It's the first time he's paid me any attention since we sat down, and I don't know how to feel about that.

He soon texts me back, letting me know that he's driving Shana back to her place. I get up and give him a quick nod before I almost sprint out of the restaurant.

I chose a place where I was fairly certain we wouldn't run into anyone we know, and I'm grateful for that as I hurry away. Because if Cora is right and I don't have a poker face, then I certainly don't want to run into anyone with any sort of questions right now.

Not when I have no answers.

Chapter 46 – A new friend

Liam

Shana is great. She's easy to talk to, funny, and seems like a really good person. I thought hanging out with her would be strange, like it was with the last woman Faye tried to set me up with. It's not. We found things to talk about and she even made me laugh.

But the entire time, all I could think of was Faye at the other table, not giving a fuck that I was on a date with another woman.

I don't get how it's so easy for her to set me up with someone else. I was starting to think that we have something. Something more than just sex. But I guess I was wrong.

It's good that she's not jealous, I guess. Makes all of this fake dating a lot easier.

"Thanks for driving me," Shana says as we get in the car. "Faye chose a place a bit out of my usual way."

"Yeah, I guess she didn't want to run into anyone we know." My knuckles whiten on the steering wheel. When she asked me to meet her here, I thought... Fuck, it doesn't matter. I was wrong.

"I had a good time." Shana takes out her phone.

"Me too." Not as good as it would have been with Faye. But I guess that's not an option.

Shana shifts in her seat, and the scent of her perfume hits me. It's not roses.

"Listen," I keep my eyes on the road.

"Yes?"

"I don't know what Faye told you, but I'm not interested in a relationship with you. I'm sorry."

Her laughter fills the car. "Don't worry. She told me what's going on. Besides, my girlfriend probably wouldn't like that."

"Oh, you're gay?" Relief floods over me and I feel less guilty for driving her home.

"Didn't Faye tell you?" She sounds amused.

I shake my head. "No, she didn't really tell me anything about you." That's why she wasn't jealous. My chest stops constricting and I want to smile.

"Well, I am. So you don't need to worry about that."

Nodding, I turn down her street. "So, why are you doing this?"

"It's complicated. But basically, my grandmother is... old fashioned. She's not doing well, and she's starting to ask a lot of questions about my dating life. When Faye brought this up, I figured it would put her mind at ease and keep her off my back."

"Why don't you just tell her the truth?"

She sighs. "I know I should. And believe me, I've been contemplating doing that many, many times. We were close when I grew up and I do love her and part of me doesn't want to let her down. She usually keeps her opinions to herself, but she has made it clear it's something she doesn't accept. I got really close to telling her a few years back, but then her friend's grandson came out, and her reaction was... vile."

"Man, that sucks." I want to focus on the things Shana is telling me. I want to feel bad for her, but all I can think of is Faye and what she's doing now. Should I call her?

"Yeah. It sucks. I'd like for her to meet my girlfriend, but I know that's not possible."

"What about your parents?" I pull up to the house marked on the gps.

"They're supportive. I mean, they weren't happy when I came out, but they've come around. But when it comes to grandma, they say to just let it be and don't upset her. She doesn't have that much time left. And her mind isn't all there anymore."

"Oh. Sorry about that."

"It is what it is. I can still see a lot of good in her, and I know she loves me. I'm just not sure she loves me enough to accept who I am. Not when it goes against everything she was raised to believe in."

"Yeah, that sucks."

She undoes her seatbelt. "Yeah. It does. Anyway, you don't have to worry about me. It was very clear from the start that you and Faye have something going on." She puts her hand on the handle and my brain does a double take, trying to figure out what she just said.

"What? No, we don't."

"Oh, please. You like her."

"It's not like that."

She settles in the seat again. "Then what's it like? Because from where I was sitting, you like her."

"Nah. We.... I mean, yeah, she's ok. But... Ok, so we are kind of having sex. But that's it. She's too busy to have a boyfriend, and I'm doing this," I motion between her and me, "to improve my reputation."

"Ha! I knew it. I'm never wrong about these things."

"I'm not... in love... with her or anything." My chest constricts again. "And you can't tell anyone."

She raises an eyebrow. "I can't tell anyone that you're not in love with her?"

"No, I mean about the sex. I probably shouldn't have said anything." I take a deep breath. "It's against the rules. If anyone finds out, she could get fired, and I'd get kicked off the team."

"What? Why?"

"Apparently there was a big scandal a few years back, before my time, and the social media manager dated one of the players. They broke up, and she went scorched earth and published a whole bunch of stuff she shouldn't have."

"Oh."

"So they made it a rule not to allow relationships."

"And the first thing the two of you did was start sleeping together?"

I don't like the grin on her face.

"We didn't just... We had a one-night stand. Before we knew who the other one was. Ok? It's not like we planned it."

Her grin turns wider. "So you had a one-night stand, found out you weren't allowed to see each other, and immediately thought you need to have sex on a regular basis?"

"It's not like that. We're good in bed. That's it."

"Uh-uh. I'm sure that's all it is."

"Don't make this weird. She doesn't even like me."

"Do you like her?"

Without waiting for an answer, she gets out of the car.

It's not like that. I want to scream after her, let her know she has it all wrong. That whatever romantic ideas she has are wrong. But she just gives me a wave and hurries into the building.

Fuck. Now she's going to think there's something going on.

There's not.

I don't do relationships anymore. At all.

And Faye... Well, she can't, can she? She has her job, and she's already freaking out about losing it. She may say she's not, but I could see the panic on her face when we almost got caught. She cares about this job, and if I was a decent person, I would break it off and let her have it. Risk free.

If I was a decent person, I would let her go. Not text her asking if I can come over tonight.

Chapter 47 – Leaks

Liam

It's time for another away game and we're gathered at the Den, getting ready to board the bus. This time, Faye won't be coming with us, and I kind of hate that. But she has some big photography project due that apparently is going to take all weekend.

I spent yesterday evening with her, and she mentioned it. I know all she wants from me is sex, but those moments when we're catching our breaths and just lie next to each other have become some of my favorites.

"Hey, I didn't know you were seeing someone?"

My heart jumps to my throat and I stare at Ethan as he comes up to me with his phone.

"What?" Did they find out about Faye? How the fuck did that happen? She's going to kill me for this. Did someone see me leaving her place? Fuck, what do I do now?

Ethan shows me his screen. It's a picture of me and Shana.

"Oh." Fuck, that was terrifying. "Yeah. I guess."

Ethan shakes his head. "You know, I actually thought... Never mind. It's kind of stupid now."

"You thought what?"

"It doesn't matter. Congratulations, man. Who is she?"

I blink. He knows who Faye is. Then it hits me. I shake my head. "Oh, her. Yeah, her name is Shana. I met her a couple of weeks ago and we really hit it off."

We discussed a story to tell people, but it all seems so contrived and ridiculous now.

"Well, I knew something was going on," Ethan says. "You've been so weird lately."

"I haven't been weird."

My spine tingles and I spin around. Faye is here. She's taking pictures of us from a distance.

I swallow. She must have done this, so she already knows. She's the one who set everything up. Why the fuck do I feel like I want to keep this from her? Like I want to shield her from this?

"Liam, why the secrecy?" Hudson asks as he comes up to us. "Are you ashamed of us?"

Faye is walking in our direction as more of the guys crowd around.

"Fuck off. It's none of your business."

JD is giving me a look, and I know what's going on in his head. He's wondering if this is real or fake. He knows about the plan, but I don't think he's in the loop with all the details.

"Are you in love?" Dustin asks, just as Faye reaches us. She almost drops her camera and freezes.

"What kind of question is that?" I ask.

Dustin's cheeks go red and he shrugs.

"Well?" Cole asks with a raised eyebrow. "Are you?" He's mocking Dustin as much as he's mocking me.

"Fuck off. It's new."

I keep glancing at Faye. I don't like the expression on her face. It's too hidden. To anyone else, she probably looks uninterested, but I know her. I can see the hurt in her eyes.

"How about we get moving," JD says. "Faye, did you need something before we leave?"

She startles as he mentions her name.

"Oh, I'd like a photo, if you wouldn't mind lining up in front of the bus."

Everyone moves for her. I love how they respect her already. It doesn't take long before we're posing by the bus and she's clicking away on her camera.

"Hey, you must be glad now," Pan says when the photo session is over.

"How so?" Faye asks.

"Now that Liam is someone else's problem. We've all seen you try yo wrangle him."

She forces a smile on her face and I wonder if anyone believes it's real.

"It's one less thing for me to worry about."

"Liam, when do we get to meet this woman?" Ethan comes up and puts an arm around my neck.

"With the way you behave? Probably never." I shrug out of his grip and move to get on the bus.

"Are you saying we don't know how to behave?" He follows me as I find my seat.

"It's new," is all I say.

I try to ignore the comments. Faye is laughing with Pan outside my window. She looks so pretty when she's happy.

Pan finally leaves her alone and gets on the bus. Faye takes a couple of photos of the bus and waves us off as we start moving.

I check my phone and find a bunch of comments and messages about the photo with Shana. I ignore them all.

We win the regional semifinals. When I skate around the ice, celebrating, my eyes stray over the audience, but I'm only looking for one face. It could be drowning in the sea of onlookers, but I know she's not there. I can feel her absence.

She will be watching, though. There are cameras here filming and she'll be posting about the victory.

If I could go to her, I would. There would be no better way to celebrate. But since I can't, I go with the guys to dinner and then back to my room.

Is it too late to call? I haven't spoken to her since last night. I hesitate for a while, then I can't resist and tap the icon.

"Hi." Her voice is soft and calm.

"Hi. We won."

"I know. I was watching."

I kick off my shoes and sit on the bed.

"I figured you were."

"It's kind of my job."

"So, you posted the photo."

"That was ok, right? You said you approve of Shana. I spoke to her as well, and she's happy with the arrangement."

I arrange the pillows behind me so I can lean back.

"Yeah, that's fine. It's what the plan was all along."

"So, you're at the hotel tonight?"

"Yeah, I'm sharing a room with Ethan, but he's not here right now."

"Oh."

"Are you out celebrating?" I close my eyes. There's no sound in the background. I know she's not out.

"No, I'm at home."

"Good."

"Good?"

"Well, I just mean, I'm glad I didn't interrupt anything." I cringe at myself. "Unless you were sleeping?"

"No, I was watching a movie."

"What kind of movie?"

"Umm... It doesn't matter." I can almost hear the blush in her voice.

My ears instantly perk, and she has my full attention. "What's that supposed to mean?"

"Nothing."

"What movie was it, Roses?"

"Why do you care?"

"Was it porn?"

"No! Of course not."

I smile to myself. "Unless you tell me, I'm just going to assume it was porn."

She sighs. "It was Legally Blonde, ok? It's one of my favorites."

"Ok. That's about the lawyer, right?"

"She's a law student, but yeah."

"Ok, well, I'll let you get back to it. Maybe I'll watch something as well."

I try to remember if I've seen Legally Blonde. I know the gist of the movie, but it might just be through trailers and what people have told me. Maybe I need to watch it to see what the fuss is about?

"Porn?"

I laugh. "With Ethan in the room?"

"You said he's not there."

"But he will be."

"Hm, would that really stop you?"

"Good night, Roses."

"Good night."

I shake my head as I hang up the phone. I like that she teases me.

As I'm trying to find Legally Blonde, I get a message from Faye. My brows furrow when I notice it's a short video. The message accompanying it just says: hope Ethan catches you.

I click the video and almost choke on air.

It's Faye. I know it is. Even with no face visible, I'd know her body anywhere. And her bed. Because, fuck me, that's her bed.

The video starts with her hand sliding over her chest. She's wearing a black, lacy top. Her hand moves between her breasts and down to the visible skin on her stomach. I hold my breath as it moves even further and the tips of her fingers glide into her panties. Her entire body arches and I ache for her.

The video cuts off there and I have never felt that amount of frustration in my life.

I watch it over and over and imagine the scent of her on my skin.

She gets her wish. I'm too distracted by the video that I only notice Ethan when he opens the door. I quickly sit up and face away from him. Praying that he didn't notice the effect she has on me.

Chapter 48 – Official

Faye

The crowd goes wild. The Lions win the regional semifinals and the entire Den is celebrating.

I smile and take photos of them on the ice.

Last night, Liam came over. We barely spoke ten words to each other. His hands, and his tongue, did all the talking.

It's desperate now. I don't think he can feel it. But every time we have sex, it's like I'm struggling to keep hold of him. Like I never want to let him go.

It's pointless. I know it can't stay like this. But for one more night, I let myself believe that maybe it can. I do that every time, because one day will actually be the last time.

"I don't know why I'm nervous," Shana says next to me.

"Come on. Let's wait outside." I walk down the hallway toward the players' parking lot. "All you have to do is give him a hug." I can't look at her. We met up before the game and talked about what we want from this interaction. I already spoke with Liam and he's onboard with the whole thing.

She looks very cute with his jersey over a sweater. The front is tucked into the jeans, making her look stylish and effortless.

It's his name on her back.

Because, officially, she's his girl.

Fuck, that hurts.

"I know. It's silly. I guess it's just the first time we'll be together in public. You know, with people who know him."

"I know." We leave the Den and wait with the people already there. "But you've talked about this. If anyone asks you questions, just tell them what we've practiced. Some of the guys might tease you, or act like the twelve-year-olds they really are, but you can ignore that."

"Thank you for waiting with me. I know you need the photos, but I appreciate it."

"No worries."

I keep an eye on the door as I post another photo of the team. They're closer to the Frozen Four than ever, and we're starting to get some attention. I take my time making sure the posts are good, and even answer some comments.

Next to me, Shana shifts on her feet.

"They should be coming out soon," I smile at her. I can't even hate her. She's nice. She's considerate and friendly and I actually like her. Which, somehow, makes it all worse.

As I look back, the door opens. I put my phone away and grab the camera. This is it. A moment I've been dreading.

"I'll see you later," Shana says as Liam emerges. "Thanks again."

I nod at her. "See you later."

My job is simple. I point the camera at the happy couple and document this win. Their celebration.

So why does it feel like it's tearing out my heart?

Liam sees me. His eyes soften for a split second. Then they shift to Shana, who's approaching him.

He smiles. I raise the camera and start taking photos. They find each other. Both of them smile. There's a moment's hesitation, then they embrace.

My chest tightens as I preserve this moment forever. Or until the digital evidence is gone. I make sure I have plenty of photos to choose from.

I move back as Pan and Cole come up to them. Shana smiles and looks blushingly happy. I know she wants to be an actress, but she almost seems too good at this. She's talking to the guys as more of the team gathers around, and I can hear them laughing. I move further away.

All eyes are on Liam and Shana and from where I'm standing, they look like the perfect couple. Morgan is there with JD. Ethan has his girlfriend Lily with him and I see a few more of the guys join them with or without dates.

I know they're all planning to go to Lucky's to celebrate, so I withdraw even further and make my escape before they see me and ask me to join them.

I tell myself I have work to do. That I need to edit the pictures I took and create some more posts to upload in the next few days.

The apartment is empty when I get there. Cora must be out again. Which is probably for the best. She said I'd get hurt doing this, and I'm starting to think she was right.

Unable to sleep, I get to work on the photos instead. I scrutinize the pictures of Liam and Shana and try to read more into them than there is. I know there's nothing going on between them. There's not even a chance of anything happening. But seeing them, surrounded by his teammates, standing so close to each other, it does something to me.

I don't even know how long I've been staring at the photos when my phone buzzes. I take a breath and check it. It's from Liam. He's asking if I'm asleep.

I stare at the notification as it stays on the screen for a while.

Closing my eyes, I shake my head. I'm not the other woman.

Shana isn't his girlfriend. But now, everyone thinks she is.

I grab my phone, but instead of replying to him, I check Instagram. And get nauseous. There are several images of him and Shana there. They're eating and drinking and laughing. They look like they're having fun together.

It's great. From a PR standpoint, this is exactly what we wanted. And it's showing up from other people. Not from the Lions' account.

This is good, I tell myself as I fight back the tears.
Liam and Shana are now an official couple.

Chapter 49 – Bad feelings

Liam

I waited for a reply from Faye last night until I fell asleep. It's embarrassing how eager I was to rush out and meet her. But I guess she had already gone to bed when I texted. I can't blame her. It was late.

This morning, I texted her again, just telling her good morning. And yeah, part of me really wanted to see her again. Sometimes it feels like torture only seeing her at the Den.

I know she saw my text, but she didn't answer.

Disappointed, I get on with my day. It's not like it matters. I don't care if she replies. Why would I?

After my classes, I head to the Den. It's Friday today and for once, we don't have a game. The regional finals are tomorrow, so we're taking it easy today.

I don't give a fuck.

As I enter the arena, I don't care about hockey. Sure, it's in the back of my mind, but for once, something else feels more important.

I stop dead in my tracks when my thoughts catch up to me. Hockey has been part of my life for so long. For years, it was the most important thing in my life. I would have given up everything for a chance to hit the ice.

So what changed?

I slowly stroll toward the locker room. Maybe it's time? For a couple of years now, I've known that I'll never have a career in the NHL like I wanted. I've seen the other players surpass me and put in more effort, be more disciplined, and want it more than me.

Maybe a small part of me still thought I'd get discovered. That somehow I'd still end up in the NHL. I must have been holding on to a fool's hope. Because now, that's gone as well.

Hockey has moved from a priority to something I do, a hobby.

I enter the locker room and stand by the door for a while. The others are getting ready for practice and I feel out of place.

I'm proud of what we've done so far and I still want to win the Frozen Four, but the passion isn't there anymore.

I grab my phone and find Iceberg. The guys all assume Iceberg is Shana. I scoff to myself, as if any other woman could measure up to Roses.

Still standing by the door, I try to figure out what to write so she'll text me back. Not that I care. She's not my girlfriend or anything. We're not in a relationship. I just miss the sex.

I guess I could say that? Ask if she wants to meet up tonight?

I delete and retype the message a few times before actually hitting send. Then I just stand there, staring at the phone.

Sorry. Busy.

I keep staring. Something must have happened. Is she avoiding me? Did I do something? I wrack my brain, trying to come up with something I could have done wrong.

The door opens behind me. Ethan, JD, and a few of the other guys come in, followed by Coach and Faye.

I'm frozen to my spot as I put the phone away.

"Gather around," Coach says. "Tomorrow is a big day, and Faye will be with us as we get ready. She wants to document everything and I think it's a good idea to put out some good publicity. I've spoken to several alumni, and things are looking up. There's been talk about some donations to get a cold water pool put in and possibly a hot tub. So when you're on the ice tomorrow, remember that."

Faye has stopped next to me. She's so close I could reach out and touch her. But she's not looking at me.

Coach talks about tomorrow, and what the day will look like. I couldn't care less. All of my attention is on the woman next to me.

Everyone is focused on Coach, so I shift myself closer to her. Her body stiffens as I casually stand so close to her I inhale her scent.

I don't look at her. But I turn my body so nobody can see when I reach out a pinky to touch hers. She holds her breath. I want to take her hand in mine, but before I can do more than graze against her, she moves away and takes out her phone.

I wait. Is she texting me? Is she upset? I probably shouldn't have done that. But nobody knows. There's no way anyone could have seen us.

After a while, I check my phone.

Nothing.

Shit. Is she texting someone else?

I glance over at her just as Coach says something and turns to her.

"Thank you," she says and steps forward. "I'll make sure to do that. And if any of you are worried about the interviews, I'd be happy to go over some questions with you. I have a list of do's and don'ts, but it's mostly pretty self explanatory stuff. Be polite, don't trash talk the other team too harshly, be approachable and candid, but don't be long winded and too detail-oriented." She smiles and lights up the room. "I'm sure you'll all do great."

"Thank you Faye," Coach says.

I study her face as she steps back and lets him take over again.

I can't take this anymore. I text her.

Can we talk?

She closes her eyes before she picks up her phone.

Stop staring at me. And I can't talk today. I'm busy.

Did I do something?

"Ok," Coach says. "Get changed and I'll see you on the ice."

He turns to Faye and they leave together.

Everything is fine. I'm just busy.

Bullshit. I know it is, but I can't very well tell her that. I have no idea what's going on. It's as if she wants to end things between us.

My insides twist and burn. That can't be it.

There is no way she wants to end this. I mean, it's only sex. But it's good sex and I know she likes it. I grab my phone.

"Liam," JD raises his voice, and I look up. "Get changed. You can text Shana later."

I blink at him and almost correct him. Then I clear my throat. Everyone else is almost ready to head out, and I haven't even started putting on my gear.

"Sure," I say and put away the phone. I'm going to have to find a way to talk to her. Maybe not here at the Den, but I have to do something.

Chapter 50 – Maybe?

Liam

The moment the puck hits the net and there's less than a minute left on the clock, there's a noticeable shift all around me. It's two to one and if we can hold out for fifty-three seconds, we win. Fifty-three seconds to the Frozen Four. Fifty-three seconds to the best year in a long time for the UNI Lions.

In fifty-three seconds, all eyes will be on us.

UNI alumni will be cheering for us in bars, telling their co-workers that they used to go here. Proud parents will brag about how their kids know someone on the team.

Our parents will receive congratulation messages and phone calls. They'll beam with pride and wear the UNI Lions jerseys.

Talent scouts will take an extra look at the game footage. Maybe they'll spot a player with potential.

Fifty-three seconds can change lives. If we keep the lead, we win. If we fumble and Grainer evens the score, it could go either way.

I get back on the ice with one goal in mind. To run out the clock.

The seconds tick down, and we keep control of the puck. Of the game. Of our futures.

The tension on Coach's face intensifies. Pride is mixing in there. Everyone looks proud.

I get the puck and break away. It doesn't matter if I score. I take my time, line up the shot. Another goal would clench it. It would add insult to injury for Granier.

The puck flies straight. The goalie is panicking. I can tell by his movements, he knows how important this game is. He lunges for it. And misses.

The buzzer sounds and I raise my arms. There's seven seconds left. I just assured our win. The crowd is loud. Adrenaline is pumping through me and I know this is one of the best moments of my entire hockey career.

I'm going to miss this. This very moment, when something big is decided by my action. I'm going to miss it. But I don't belong here.

My eyes scan the crowd. I already know where she's sitting. The girl that smells like roses. She's right next to the woman everyone thinks I'm dating. They're both cheering.

The last seconds fly by and we've won.

What happens next is a flurry. Time runs out and everyone rushes onto the ice. I'm in the midst of my teammates, shouting and cheering as we hug and celebrate. It hits me that we did it. We made it to the Frozen Four.

Around us, the fans are cheering us on. We shake hands with Granier, people congratulate us, others want interviews.

I take a moment to study my teammates. This is a moment we'll all remember for the rest of our lives.

"Looks like you're getting that pool," Coach says when he sees me. "And good on you for going along with the PR campaign."

"Yeah," I glance over at the two women. "I guess it's all working out."

Coach pats my back as he moves on.

Everything is perfect for me. Coach is happy. The team is happy. We've made it to the Frozen Four. The sponsors are happy. And yet...

As soon as I can get off the ice, I do. I take my time showering and calming down from the adrenaline rush. It doesn't take long before hunger takes over. It always does after a game.

But food isn't what I want. I know I have to go out there and hug Shana and let people get more pictures of us. But that's not what I want.

Faye started a group chat with me, Shana, and JD. In all honesty, I'm not sure JD cares all that much, but he's in on the idea and, I don't know, maybe it makes Faye feel better to have him there. Or I guess it might be for Shana's benefit.

Either way, he's the one that suggested we kiss if the Lions won tonight. Me and Shana. He wants us to kiss. I told him he's pushing it, but he insisted it has to look real for the cameras. Since I have a reputation of not being shy when it comes to public displays of affection, he says it'll be weird if we don't.

Faye didn't say anything.

Shana, to my surprise, agreed to do it.

I'm still not going to. They're just going to have to make do with a hug. If that's not enough for them, they can fuck right off.

I leave the locker room and head outside. Everyone is there. Shana immediately comes up to me and I hug her.

"Congratulations, babe." She looks happy. I know it's fake, but she's really good at this.

"Thanks."

Faye is talking to Coach. I move closer. She's supposed to be taking pictures.

"...just want you to know that," Coach says. "You've done really well, and no matter what happens now, we're very happy to have you on the team."

"Thank you," Faye says and glances over at me. "I appreciate that. But I should get some photos right now."

"Of course. I'll leave you to it." Coach spots someone else to talk to and walks off.

Faye closes her eyes for a moment before raising the camera at me and Shana.

"Pretend I'm not here," she says with a fake smile.

Shana hugs me again. "You did so well tonight. I can't believe you scored a goal."

"Thanks," I say and force myself to focus on her. "It was really a team effort, though."

"You all did great."

I turn to the guys. "I think we're all heading to Lucky's. Want to come?"

Shana grimaces. "I'm sorry, I have a really early morning tomorrow."

"Ok. No problem. Faye? Are you coming?" I deliberately ask her loudly enough that Pan overhears.

"You're coming, right?" he instantly asks. "You're part of the team now."

Faye looks uncomfortable, then she smiles. "I'd love to."

"I should go," Shana says and I remember the woman next to me.

"You have your car?"

"Yeah, it's right over there." She points towards the parking lot.

"I'll walk you."

"This is tough on you, isn't it?" Shana asks when we're out of earshot of the others.

"What is?"

"Being with the wrong woman."

I clear my throat. "I have no idea what you mean."

"Right. Well, I'm sorry you can't be with her."

"It's not like that."

"So you keep saying. But the world has to be blind not to notice the way you two look at each other."

"It doesn't matter anymore. I think she's over me."

"What do you mean?"

I shrug. "She's not answering texts. She's too busy to hang out." This really shouldn't bother me.

"I'm sorry."

"It's good though. She has her job to think about. Everyone says she's been doing such a good job. I don't blame her for wanting to keep that safe."

"And what about your feelings? Are you over her?"

I can't help it. I look over to where she's standing. "I never..." I never had feelings for her, is what I want to say. But the words get stuck in my throat. I've gotten into trouble like this before. With Eve and Kaitlynn. I let feelings come before common sense.

No. That was never like this. Neither Eve nor Kaitlynn ever did this to me.

"Do you want a relationship with her?"

We're at her car now. I stop and wait as she unlocks it and gets in. What's the answer to that question? Do I?

"I don't think it matters. We said it was only sex. And I assumed it wouldn't last long. I just thought it would last... longer."

"Maybe it's not over?"

I give her a weak smile. "Maybe. Good night."

I make sure she gets in the car and watch as she drives off.

Maybe it's not over? I wish I knew what to do, though. All I know is that I'm not ready for this to be the end.

Chapter 51 – Goodbye

Faye

The smile hurts when he walks away with her. But I keep it on my face. This is my big break as much as it's theirs. I'm seeing loads of interaction with the posts I've made and several people have told me I'm doing a good job. Including Coach.

It was a dirty trick Liam pulled when he made Pan insist on me joining them. Then again, maybe a night out is just what I need.

They're talking, looking like a real couple, as he walks her to the car. It's not supposed to be this way. He's supposed to be with me.

I blink. That's not what I was thinking. That's not what I was supposed to think.

"You need a ride?" Pan asks, and I snap out of it.

"Yeah, if you don't mind."

"Not at all. JD is driving."

I follow Pan to the car and get into the backseat with Pan and Dustin. Morgan is up front and I do my best to not give away my tumultuous feelings.

"I can't believe you won," Morgan says.

"I can," Pan says. "And I bet you we'll win the Frozen Four as well."

JD shakes his head. "I don't know about that. We're up against some great teams."

"How about we celebrate tonight and worry about that tomorrow?" Dustin smiles at me. He's a good guy, maybe a bit too... nice? I keep getting virgin vibes from him. Not that there's anything wrong with that.

"You getting drunk tonight, Faye?" Morgan asks. "Because I'm in the mood to go a bit crazy."

She smiles at me, and I nod. "You know what? I think I will." If I'm drunk, I won't be obsessing over Liam and what he's doing with Shana.

Fuck.

I know nothing is happening. I even met Shana's girlfriend the other day. But it still hurts when he touches her in public and pretends I don't exist.

"Let's go," Morgan says. "JD, you're on guard duty. It's your job to make sure we get home safely."

JD sighs. "You know I will."

He seems exasperated by it, but there's also a seriousness in his voice that's deadly. As if this is now his life's mission and he will let nothing stand in his way.

"Can I leave this in the car?" I ask and hold up the camera.

"Give it here." Morgan takes it and removes a scarf and some random stuff from the glove box. She manages to barely fit the camera and leaves all the other stuff on the floor. As long as the car doesn't get broken into, I think the camera will be safer there than with me if I'm drinking. I can still take photos with my phone.

We pull up at the bar and there's a crowd of people in Lions' jerseys outside. We get out of the car and they immediately start taking photos and ask for selfies. Morgan rolls her eyes, but smiles proudly.

"Come on, let's leave them to it." She takes my hand and almost drags me inside. There are more jersey's in here. This is the unofficial bar for the Lions after all. But there's a strict rule against bothering the players too much.

"What are you drinking? Beer?"

I nod, and she points to a table against the wall. As she heads over to the bar, I have no choice but to join the players at the table.

Liam and Ethan. I don't even know how they got here before us. Maybe JD is a cautious driver. Or it's because Ethan has this ridiculous sports car that someone once said cost over three million dollars.

"Hi," I say and hesitate. I stand by the table, wondering which of them I should sit next to.

"You made it," Ethan says. "Lily will be joining us soon. She's just finishing up her shift." He nods to the bar where his girlfriend is talking to another server.

I nod. The hint is pretty clear. So I move over and sit next to Liam.

"Congratulations," I say to both of them.

"Can you believe we're going out with a bang?" Ethan says. "We're in the Frozen Four."

"You deserve it." I smile at him, and I mean it. I've seen how hard they've worked toward this goal the last few weeks and I'm so happy for them.

"Do you..." Liam clears his throat. "Do you need a drink?"

"Morgan is getting us some," I say and point in her direction, as if to prove I'm not lying.

He nods. "Yeah. Good."

Someone at the next table gets Ethan's attention, and it's just me and Liam. My heart races and I feel lightheaded. The silence is awkward, so I bring out my phone. I make sure all the posts are up and doing well, and scroll a bit.

The photo of Liam and Shana is beautiful. It's dark around them, but they're smiling at each other and sharing a moment. Someone must have taken it when he walked her to her car.

"Can I come over tonight?"

His voice sounds eager, almost desperate. The man in the photo is in a happy relationship with someone who isn't me.

Fuck. Why does it feel like cheating? I know it isn't. Shana isn't his girlfriend.

"I'm spending tonight with Morgan, drinking," I say.

"Oh." He shifts in his seat and his leg presses against mine. "What about tomorrow?"

I'm too busy trying to control my breathing to answer. The photo is still in front of me, so I show him.

"You make a cute couple."

His hand slides onto my leg. "Because you asked me to."

I want him to touch me. I do. But what's the point? We're not together. He doesn't want a girlfriend. At least not one that's real. And even if he did, we can't.

"This isn't working out." At first, I'm not sure he's able to hear me over the noise in the bar.

"What?"

"We should stop." I stare at the photo to give me strength. "You're in a good place with the sponsors, Coach even said so. And he's very happy with the work I've been doing. Everything is working out for the best."

"Faye, what are you talking about?" He pulls away his hand and I miss the warmth.

"If what we're doing comes out, it would ruin everything. Your reputation would be tanked. Especially now that you're officially dating Shana. And I'd lose a job I love."

"Faye. Don't." The hurt in his voice tears my heart apart.

"We always knew this wasn't real."

"Faye. Stop." He sounds angry.

"You told me you don't want a relationship."

"Not here. Not now. We're in a bar full of people."

I know. I want to tell him that's the only thing giving me strength to do this. Reminding me that there is so much at stake.

"I'm sorry."

"No. We'll talk about this later."

I shake my head and blink back the tears. "Good bye, Liam."

He inhales sharply, but before he can say anything, Morgan appears with two beers.

"Oh, my god the bar was crowded." She sits down and slides one of the mugs at me. "Sorry, it took a while."

"That's ok. Thanks." I immediately take a long drink.

"Cheers," Morgan says and joins me.

Next to me, I can feel Liam breathing heavily. I'm not sure what he's thinking right now, and I'm not brave enough to look at him. He's probably relieved that he has an easy out. Maybe he'll miss the sex and regrets not sleeping with me one more time. But whatever he's feeling, he'll be over it soon. He'll realize it never could have worked, and this is for the best.

I'm sure of it.

Chapter 52 – Drunk

Faye

He's torturing me. I know he is.

I laugh at Morgan's joke and finish the drink in front of me. I guess at some point we switched from beer to tequila. I don't even know how that happened.

I ignore Liam next to me as a familiar song some on.

"Oh, let's dance," I say and reach out a hand for Morgan.

"Yes, let's go."

I get up and the world spins. I giggle as I catch my balance and hold on to Morgan.

"You're so drunk," she laughs. Then she stumbles and I break into a fit of laughter.

"So are you."

We make it to the small area where a couple of other people are dancing. I let the music take over and sing along to the lyrics. I don't quite know the words, but it doesn't matter.

I purposely ignore Liam staring at me. He shouldn't be doing that.

My eyes are getting heavy and I stumble again. Morgan laughs.

"Ok," JD says as someone holds me up. "I think that's enough. It's time to go home."

"No," I whine as someone leads me through the room.

I don't want to go home. My room is there. The bed where I've been with Liam. It'll remind me of him. I giggle at myself. Liam is here. That should also remind me of him.

Someone forces a jacket on me and I take a deep breath. Morgan is leaning against a wall.

"This was fun," I tell her.

"I love getting sloppy drunk." She sighs and homes in on JD. Grabbing his shirt, she pulls him close. "I'll show you just how sloppy I am later." She lunges for him and kisses him.

"Ok," I interrupt them. "I don't need to see that."

"Let's get you to the car," JD says and puts his arm around Morgan.

"Yup." I find the door and do my best to walk straight for it.

"Do you need a hand?" I stop leaning against the doorframe as Liam's words warm me up. His whole body used to do that.

"Nah, I got it." JD sounds like a dad. Or an older brother. I've never had an older brother.

"Are you sure? I don't mind."

I turn to Liam. Fuck, I forgot how pretty he is.

Placing a hand on his chest, I try to push him away. "You're with Shana."

He lowers his voice. "You know I'm not."

"But you are. Everyone thinks you are. That's the same."

"It's not the same, Roses."

He's too powerful. He could make me forget everything right here and now.

"I have to go." I find the door again and step outside. The night air is cold and I breathe deep. The drunken fog in my brain clears just a little and I wait for JD and Morgan.

"This way," JD says and I follow him to the car. "IF either of you is going to throw up, please do so now, or let me know so I can stop the car. You do not throw up in the car."

"You're so bossy," Morgan says and snuggles closer to him.

"And you're so drunk," he says with a smile.

"You can take advantage of that later." She raises an eyebrow and now I'm sad. I want what they have. I want to tease someone and flirt like that. Instead, I get secret meetings and codenames on the phone.

I get fake official relationships and feeling like an outsider with the man I'm having sex with.

I get into the backseat and close my eyes. I deserve more than that.

"Come on," JD says and tugs at my arm.

I open my eyes. We're outside my apartment building.

"Did I fall asleep?" I ask and get out of the car.

"You did. Morgan, don't move, I'll be right back."

"I'll pretend you tied me up," Morgan says.

JD shakes his head and leads me inside.

"It's never going to work is it?" I say as we wait for the elevator.

"What is?"

"Liam." I sigh.

"What? The fake dating? It is working. Shana was a good choice. She's really making it seem like he's settled down. I think everyone is happy with that."

The doors open and he nudges me inside. "No, not that."

"Fifth floor?"

I nod and he pushes the button.

"Then what?"

"We're not allowed to do anything," I whisper at him, part of me is yelling to shut up.

"Who isn't?" He frowns at me.

"Me and Liam."

He blinks at me. "Did I miss something?"

I shake my head. "I can't say."

"Faye, did Liam try something?"

I press my lips together.

"Faye?"

The doors open and I stumble out of the elevator.

"He doesn't do relationships." The door is right there. I stare at it for a while, then I remember keys. I look through my pockets.

"You know there's a rule, right? You're not allowed to date any of the hockey players."

"I know." I struggle to fit the key in the lock. "Believe me, I know."

"So, I'm just going to assume that nothing happened between you and Liam, ok?"

"We had sex," I whisper. "And it was great."

"I did not hear that."

I open the door. "I said-"

"Nope. No you didn't. You're just rambling incoherently because you're drunk. But you're home now. Go to bed. Drink some water. Good night." He pushes me inside and closes the door quickly.

I giggle at his rant. He really didn't want to know about me and Liam.

The giggle turns to tears and I sob. There is no me and Liam. Not anymore.

"Faye?" Cora shows up in her pajamas.

"It's over." I sob and she blinks at me.

"What's over?"

"Me and Liam. I told him goodbye."

"Oh."

I close my eyes and feel the tears run down my cheeks.

"Why?" Cora asks.

"Because it hurts. I can't do it anymore. Every time he walks past me and ignores me, it hurts. Seeing whim with Shana hurts."

"You're the one that set that up."

"I know. I'm a fucking idiot. I never should have done that."

Cora's arms wrap around me.

"Damn, Faye, you smell like tequila and regrets."

"I had a good time. Me and Morgan were drinking."

"Let's get you some water. You're going to be hungover tomorrow."

"I'm going to have to see him again. I don't know if I can do that."

Cora leads me to the kitchen where I sit down at the tiny table.

"You can do it. Because you're strong." She opens a bottle of water and puts it in front of me.

"I ended it, Cora. I told him it was all over."

"Well, if that's what you want..."

"I don't. But it's for the best. It's not like we were ever together or anything. I'm just an idiot for getting my heart broken by a guy that just saw me as someone to have sex with."

Cora strokes my hair. "It's going to be ok. You'll get over him."

Tears roll down my cheeks as Cora holds me and comforts me.

"Do you think he ever liked me?"

"I'm sure he did. And you're not an idiot. You just forgot not to fall in love with him."

I nod. "I should have remembered."

Chapter 53 – Getting ready

Faye

I stare at the phone for a while before I dismiss Liam's call.

"Was that him again?" Cora asks.

"It doesn't matter." I grab the comb and smooth back my hair before putting it in a high ponytail.

I'm getting ready for the big game in our hotel room. Cora is dressed in a Lions jersey and ready to cheer UNI on. We arrived here early this morning, and this is the first time all day I've had a moment to myself.

I'm not sure if JD or the guys had anything to do with it, but they told me I could bring a friend. Maybe it's just a perk because it's such an important game, but I kind of think they remember what happened last time and don't want me to be alone.

Cora hesitates next to me.

"Listen, I love that you're protecting your heart. I think you should. I don't want to see you get any more hurt."

"But?"

"But are you sure he has no feelings for you? He's been calling you like fifty times a day. Not to mention the texts and messages. He kept staring at you on the bus. I was sure someone else was going to notice. Fuck, he even sent me a text."

I spin around so fast I almost stab her in the throat with the comb. "He texted you? When? Why? What did he say?"

"The same thing he's been saying since you broke up with him. That he wants to talk."

"What did you say?"

"Nothing. I wasn't sure what you wanted."

I take a deep breath. My chest feels tight. "Ok. Yeah. That's good. Yeah."

"Faye. The boy cares about you. You need to talk to him."

"Do I?"

"Yes?"

I sit down on the bed. "Maybe I do. But I don't want to mess anything up before the game, you know. Maybe I shouldn't have said anything when I did?"

"You can't live a lie, Faye. But right now, I'm not sure what the lie is. I'm sure it's there, but you need to figure it all out."

I stare at the ugly carpet. "I fell in love with him, Cora." My voice is almost a whisper. "I didn't mean to, but I did. I think I fell in love with him a long time ago. If he knew that, he'd probably run for the hills."

"Maybe you should tell him." Cora sits next to me.

Shaking my head, I take a breath. "I've been in contact with Grainer."

"What? Why?"

"They need a new social media manager, and I think it would be a really good position."

"You have a really great position here."

"I know. I'm just seeing if there are options for me."

"Faye, you go to UNI. You can't do that if you work for Grainer."

"They said a transfer might be possible."

Cora closes her eyes.

"You haven't decided anything yet, have you?"

"No. Not yet."

"Good. Because you know Liam's hockey career is almost over. This could very well be the last game of the season."

I breathe and nod. "I forgot about that."

"I know you did. Because you're panicking. You have a great job here. Don't fuck that up. Nobody wants that."

"You're right. I'll just have to tough it out for a while longer." Shaking my head, I try to find some form of clarity in the mess. I grab my phone. "Let's head to the arena. I need to see what's going on."

"Backstage with the hockey team." Cora looks way too smug. "I am all in for that. Any chance we might walk in on them naked?"

"Cora!" She just raises an eyebrow, so I sigh. "Probably not. Come on."

We get a cab to the arena, and I use the time to keep up to date with the social media buzz around the game. I almost choke when I see another picture of Liam and Shana. It's like I can't escape them. Apparently Shana is here as well, and they met up earlier.

Even knowing it's fake, I can't get over how comfortable they look with each other.

"Stop looking at it," Cora says. "You know it's not real."

"I know." I put my phone away as we arrive at the arena.

"So, these badges, will they get us in anywhere?" Cora flashes her badge and a smile at the security guard.

"Don't even think about accidentally stumbling into a room filled with naked hockey players. It's not going to happen."

"You never know. It might."

"No, Cora. Don't even think about it. I work with these people."

"Not with the opposing team." She winks at me, and I can't help but smile.

"Faye."

My smile fades and my stomach clenches as I slowly turn toward the man who said my name.

"Liam."

"I've been trying to call you."

Cora holds up her badge. "I'm going to go try this out." She hurries off before I can stop her.

"What's up?" I don't know what to say.

"Why don't you explain what you meant?"

I can't look at him. My eyes stay locked on the floor.

"You said this isn't real, but not once did you ask me about it."

"Because you already said how you feel. You were very clear that you don't want a relationship. And I can't do the casual sex anymore."

He inhales. "Faye."

"It's fine. We'll just leave it here. We had fun while it lasted. Now it's over."

"Faye, what do you mean?"

His voice is pleading. I force my eyes to meet his. The smile is fake, but maybe he won't notice.

"It was never going to be anything more than what it was. The sex was great. But I can't do it anymore. I'm really busy with the job, and I have to focus on school. You understand how it is."

It kills me to act as if I don't care. But the last thing he needs right before an important game is to worry about me stalking him or whatever.

"Are you sure?"

I nod, still smiling. "I'm sure. Let's just pretend it never happened. You're just another hockey player, and I'm the social media manager." I give a little shrug.

"Is that what you want?"

"It is. Now, shouldn't you be getting ready?"

He nods and walks away. I hold it together until Cora comes back. Then a tear rolls down my cheek.

Chapter 54 – Is it over?

Liam

The adrenaline is unreal as the crowd cheers us on. UNI black and yellow shares the stands with Hallworth blue and navy. The lights above are bright and the cheers have become a familiar background noise that spurs me on.

Everything else leaves my mind as my skates hit the ice. My world is the rink. It's my teammates and the puck. Nothing else matters.

Nothing else should matter.

But as soon as I'm on the bench, thoughts of her flood every cell and I struggle to keep up with what's happening.

Something's very wrong. Maybe with me, but most definitely with her. With her and me.

We were having fun. Sure, it wasn't ideal with the sneaking around and whatnot. But she understood. And maybe I got cold feet for a few moments, but I wasn't going to let that affect us.

She's the one who brought Shana into the mix, but now it's as if she's punishing me for going along with her idea.

I fucking hate it.

I didn't ask to be set up with Shana. She practically begged me to do it. So I did. And then everything changed.

I don't understand. But something has to change.

"Liam!" I look up and realize I'm supposed to be out there. I put everything else out of my mind and focus on hockey.

The game is tied in the third period, and there's ten minutes left. I get on the ice and do my best.

I watch out of the corner of my eye as Enzo crashes into someone in blue and pins them against the board. Cole gets the puck and I get into position. This is it, everything we've worked for.

Cole shoots and I'm ready to go for it.

But the puck never makes it to me. Instead, I watch as Hallworth blue sails past Enzo and Walter. Panic grips me as I rush after them. Hudson has his eyes on the puck, but it's as if I can feel it coming.

They shoot and the puck glides towards Hudson. It bounces off his leg pad and, just as I get there, a stick intercepts it and it bounces. I try in vain to stop what feels inevitable. Hudson throws himself in its path, but it's too late. The puck is over the line and the goal horn sounds.

I close my eyes to avoid seeing the joy on Hallworth's faces. We can still beat this. There's enough time left to turn it around.

But it's as if the possibility of a loss has hit the team hard.

We fight. We would never do anything else. But Hallworth is better. We see that now. All game, we've been struggling to keep up, and it's as if that goal was enough to take away all hope. Maybe we were delusional, thinking we could make it in the Frozen Four?

When they score a third goal to our one, even Coach seems to resign.

It's a hard pill to swallow that we came this far only to lose. But the final buzzer sounds and it's a done deal.

Hallworth beat us and we're out.

Pan's face is harder than I've ever seen it before. He was convinced we'd win the Frozen Four. He's been talking about it for weeks. I imagine it's even harder for him, since he didn't even get any playtime.

Walter sits with his legs outstretched and his back against the boards, breathing heavily. He fought to the last second.

JUST ONE PUCKING NIGHT

Hudson looks like he's ready to beat someone up, and I know he blames himself. He's going to tell us that he's the one who let in the goals and it's all his fault.

I sigh. Everyone is going to be in a crappy mood after this. But JD is already looking as if he's thinking of ways to cheer us up.

The thing is, unless you're the very best, you're going to lose at some point. Would it have been fun to end my college hockey career on top? Sure. Fuck, yeah, it would have. But we made it this far, and I'm not going to bitch about that. It's further than we've made it in years. And I have a feeling the Lions will make it even further next year.

We're a somber group as we wait to shake hands with Hallworth. It's especially hard watching them celebrate. But my mind is already on what I have to do next.

I go through the motions, agree with Ethan that Hallworth is one of the top teams and we were probably never going to beat them. I shake hands and congratulate them, and as we're walking off the ice, a plan is forming in my head.

Coach holds a brief speech before we get changed. It's the usual. He's proud of us and we made it further than anyone thought we would.

I tune out until it's time to shower. Then, I hurry. I still have things to do today.

I walk out into the parking lot to a whole bunch of people waiting for us.

Faye is there.

She's the first one I see. My eyes are instantly drawn to her and I know she notices me, too. But she blinks and turns her head away, talking to Cora. I narrow my eyes and clench my jaw.

Fuck, I hope I'm not wrong. But it doesn't matter. I have to do this.

"Hey, you did so good," Shana says as she comes up to me.

267

"Hey, thanks for coming."

"Yeah, of course. We have to make it look real." She smiles and winks.

"About that...." I say and give her a half smile. "I have to talk to you about something."

"Sure. What is it?"

I gesture with my head. "Follow me." We have time before the bus takes us back to the hotel. Shana walks next to me off to the side. A tingling sensation makes me look over my shoulder. Faye is watching us and I could swear that's sadness in her eyes.

"I have a plan," I say and finally feel a ray of peace inside my chest.

Chapter 55 – Coming clean...

Faye

It's almost a somber bus trip back to UNI the following day. The loss lays like a heavy blanket over everyone. Some of it is probably hangovers though, because I know some of the guys went out drinking last night.

I sit with Cora, who is sleeping. She left the hotel room after I assured her I was ok, and didn't return until early morning. I'm pretty sure she hung out with the Hallworth guys as they celebrated. She has a knack for always finding the most interesting party. Or perhaps the parties are interesting because she's there?

Liam is on his phone a few rows back. Not that I'm keeping track. I wouldn't do that. He can do whatever he wants. And right now, he seems very focused on his phone.

I feel stupid as I check my phone just in case he's sent me a message. He hasn't.

Some of the guys are playing cards and others watching some videos on someone's phone. Cora makes a sound next to me, and Cole turns in his seat to squint at her. I sigh and keep my eyes on the dull landscape outside the window.

I just have to endure a couple more hours on the bus and then I can get away from Liam.

"Is she really sleeping?" Cole asks.

I lean forward and study Cora. She's breathing heavily and seems completely out of it.

"Yeah," I say. "She was out all night."

His eyes narrow further and he shakes his head before facing forward again.

I pick up my phone. Not to check if Liam texted. I wouldn't do that. I have to use it for work.

I check on the social media posts and there's some mean spirited comments about Hallworth being so much better and UNI never should have made it as far as they did, but mostly its supportive messages and well wishes for making it so far.

I make a post about it being a great season and how we're looking forward to next year, trying to make it as positive as possible.

I don't know if I want to scroll and risk seeing more pictures of Shana and Liam. When I finally gather enough courage, I end up seeing photos of Morgan and JD, Ethan and Lily, some of the guys after the game and a short interview with Coach. But nothing with Shana.

I'm not sure what they did last night. I thought they went out together after we returned to the hotel, but maybe I was wrong.

I close my phone and go back to staring out the window. We're almost at UNI. Soon I can leave this bus and his presence.

***

Cora wakes up as we pull into the parking lot at the Den.

"Oh, my god. I needed that," she says and stretches. Cole is frowning at her again, but I ignore him. He's so guarded he probably thinks she's insane for sleeping with other people around.

I gather up my things and get ready to escape the bus as soon as it stops.

"Are we in a hurry?" Cora asks in a dramatic whisper.

"Yes," I whisper back. "I have to get away from him."

"Say less." She stands up and gets her things even before we've come to a full stop. Once she has everything, she grabs my hand. "Excuse us," she says loudly and pushes past Cole and a few other players. "Coming through. Ladies first."

I simply hang on to her hand and smile apologetically as she rudely gets us off the bus. The storage compartments are already open and Cora leaves me towards the front of the bus as she hurries over to grab her duffle bag.

"Here we go," she says and opens the bag. I grab one of the helmets and she takes the other one. She puts on the jacket and zips it up before rolling up the duffle bag. "Let's get you out of here, then."

We head to her bike, and she stows her bag. I make sure my backpack is securely fastened. I had to get one with extra straps for when I ride with her.

I know all eyes are on us when we get on and drive off. I've seen people react to Cora riding her bike. For some reason, men, and women, often stare.

It's why I insisted we arrive early yesterday. I don't need the entire hockey team gawking at me.

Cora drives fast. She takes risks, and it's a wonder she still has her license, or her limbs. But she's good. She grew up riding dirt bikes with her brothers, and I trust her skills completely.

She gets us back to the apartment in one piece. And I want nothing more than to crawl into bed and feel sad for myself for a day or two.

I toss my bag aside and take a quick detour via the kitchen to look for ice cream. I find a carton of vanilla with strawberry chunks. Must be Cora's attempt at convincing herself ice cream can be healthy.

"Oh, my god," Cora says behind me. She's dumped her stuff next to mine and has her phone out.

"What?" I ask and grab a spoon.

"You should probably see this," she says. "But sit down first." She waves a hand toward the living room and I roll my eyes as I walk over and take a seat on the couch. I put the ice cream on the coffee table to thaw and hold out a hand for her phone.

She hands it over and leans on the back of the couch so she can watch with me.

I tense as I see a smiling Shana. She's walking somewhere, outside.

"What is it?" I ask, wanting to stall in case it's bad.

"Just watch it." Cora leans in and hugs me from behind.

"Ok."

I hit play.

"There's been a lot of speculation recently," Shana says in an open and friendly tone. "And it's time to set some things straight."

She's effortless in front of the camera, comfortable.

"Lately, I've been featured in a lot of photos with Liam Greenfield. It's true that I know him and we've been hanging out. What's not true is that we're a couple."

My stomach drops and I pause the video. "What? What is she doing?" I look up at Cora. "This isn't good."

"Just keep watching," Cora says and nods at the phone. "Let's find out what it's all about first."

I take a deep breath before resuming the video.

"I see Liam as a very good friend. We only recently got to know each other, but I can already tell he's a good guy and I'm very glad we met." Her smile widens. "Yes, I have to admit," she rolls her eyes. "At first, I thought maybe something could happen between us. But we were never meant to be. I'm lucky to have him as a friend, but here's the real scoop." She leans in closer and lowers her voice. "He's in love with someone else. All those pictures of us talking were taken while I was helping him figure out a way to win her over." She raises her eyebrows in a mischievous way. "And I hope he does."

The video ends on that.

"What?" I stare at it as it starts over.

"Well, that's a plot twist," Cora says and grabs the phone.

"I don't..." There is so much to digest. My brain stops at the first point. "We worked so hard to set him up. And now this? All the work I did is gone."

"Faye. Honey. You're missing the point."

I blink. "I guess it's not that bad. She did say he's a good friend, and I think that will keep his reputation clear. Besides, the season is pretty much over for us."

"Faye!"

I turn my attention to Cora. "What?"

"The rest of the video. Did you watch it or did your brain shut off?"

I run back through her words. But it's like they're slipping away.

"He's in love with you." Cora looks at me as if I'm supposed to know what that means.

I shake my head. "No."

"Faye, Shana said so. She said he's in love with you."

"No, she didn't. She didn't mention any names."

"Well, of course she's not going to say names. Your job is still on the line."

"He's never shown any interest in me."

"What are you talking about? He always came running as soon as you let him. Did he ever not show up when you asked him to?"

I wrack my brain. "No, he always came. But that was for sex. What if he's in love with someone else?"

"I swear to god, Faye. You need to call him straight away, or I'll tie you up and deliver you to him myself."

"It doesn't matter, Cora. We're still not allowed to date. It's against my contract. She must have been talking about someone else."

Cora shakes her head.

Chapter 56 – White roses

Faye

"Cora, I don't know what to do." I'm pacing the length of the small living room, desperately trying to figure out what all of this means.

"Seems pretty obvious to me," Cora says dryly from the couch. She's much too relaxed for my liking, eating the last of the now melted ice cream.

"I'm serious."

"So am I." She waves the spoon around. "You've been freaking out about this for over an hour now. What you need to do is talk to Liam. Call him."

"But I can't..." I stop and stare at her, trying to force back the tears welling up. "What if it's someone else?"

"Who?" Cora stares at me. "Who would he be in love with if it's not you? Have you seen him show any interest in anyone?"

I slowly shake my head. "But that doesn't mean there isn't someone."

Cora sighs. "I will fucking stab you. I love you, but you're being very annoying right now."

I give her a fake smile. "You keep saying that."

"It's really not that deep. You talk to him, ask him if it's you or someone else, and then you'll know. Either I go out and get more ice cream or you end up having loud phone sex again."

My cheeks burn at the memory and I look for the words to explain to her that it's not that simple.

Before I can come up with a good response, my phone buzzes. Our eyes meet. Panic takes over as I, with trembling fingers, reach for it.

Bile rises in my throat when I see who it is.

"Is it him?" Cora asks.

I shake my head, wondering if it's all over now. "It's Coach."

"Oh. You should answer that."

I nod and take a deep breath. Maybe he doesn't know anything? This could be completely unrelated. Maybe I forgot something on the bus?

"Hi, Coach. What's up?"

Fuck, I probably sound so strange.

"Faye, I just saw the video."

"Oh." My heart drops. "Yeah. I'm sorry." I don't even know why I'm apologizing.

"I thought you set him up with Shana for that fake dating thing?"

"I did. I guess it didn't work."

My knees are about to give out, so I sit heavily on the couch.

"I guess not." He takes an audible breath.

Is this it? Am I about to get fired? Cora puts away the ice cream and slides closer to me.

"Well, I just want you to know that I know you tried. I've been dealing with hockey players for many years now, and if there's one thing I've learned, it's that they rarely listen when you tell them to do something." He laughs. "Which is frustrating, seeing as that's my job."

I laugh politely. "I think it's still ok. Just him having a female friend probably makes people view him differently."

"Yeah, I wouldn't worry about that if I were you."

My heart jumps into my throat.

"Why not? It's my job."

"Listen, I know you take your job seriously, and I just wanted to let you know that this doesn't reflect badly on you. Liam is stubborn and once he gets something into his head, it's pretty much game over.

You just put Liam out of your mind, and we'll move on with the rest of the team. I know we're in for a slower period right now, but we're still looking forward to what you can do."

"Of course." I relax at his words. "I already have some plans to keep things going over the summer."

"Somehow, I knew you would. I'm sure we'll have an opportunity to discuss things in the following week or so. Right now there's a lot going on, but I'll reach out to book a meeting."

"Sounds good."

"Great. Bye now."

"Bye." I hang up the phone and exhale as I look at Cora.

"Well?" she asks.

"My job is safe. At least for now. He told me not to worry about it."

"I knew it would be fine."

I frown, something about the call didn't feel right. But as my nerves calm down, I can't think of what it was. I still feel like my brain is scrambled from everything that's happened since the Lions lost the game.

The doorbell rings.

"Are you expecting someone?" I ask. Cora shakes her head. I get up and shake out my hands as I go to open the door.

My heart stops at the sight of an enormous bouquet of white roses.

"I couldn't get ahold of any Iceberg roses," Liam says.

"What?" I blink at the flowers. Then my eyes drift up to his face. He looks nervous. He's breathing rapidly, and he's blinking too much.

"I left the team."

"You left the team?"

He nods. "Can I come in?"

I stand there, hesitating. Mostly because my heart is beating so fast I'm worried it's going to explode my chest. He wants to come in. I know what all the words mean. But I don't know what he's saying.

"Yes," Cora shouts. She comes storming out of the living room, grabbing her boots. "Come in, Liam." She jumps on one foot as she pulls a boot on. "The flowers look lovely." She grabs her jacket and puts it on while pushing her way past Liam, nudging him inside in the process. I've never seen her get ready so quickly. Not even when there was a fire at her parents' house a while back. "I'm hanging out with Carlos tonight. Have fun."

With a hand on Liam's back, she forces him forward so she can close the door after herself.

The door shuts, and it's just me and Liam and a giant bouquet of white roses.

Chapter 57 – Quitting for her

Faye

"Did you…" I clear my throat, avoiding his eyes. "Did you really quit the team?"

He nods. "I did."

"Why? The season isn't over yet. You have the charity game with Rivers and…" I desperately try to remember their schedule. "And there's still more hockey to play."

"The guys understand. I already talked with them. I told them what's going on and they told me to go for it."

"Go for what?"

He pushes the bouquet toward me. "These are for you."

I forget how to breathe. I reach out and take the flowers. "Thank you. They're beautiful."

"Good. I mean, I'm glad you like them."

They smell so good. Calming. "I don't know if we have a vase big enough for them." To have something to do, I take the flowers to the kitchen.

"So, I don't know if you saw, but Shana made a video."

I put the flowers on the small table and look through our cupboards.

"I saw," I say slowly.

"Yeah, so what did you think about that?"

I open every door and drawer in the small kitchen. We have nothing that could work as a vase. I stare at a small pot, contemplating how useful it would be, but it's too short by far.

"What do I think of the video?" I'm stalling, but what does he want me to say? He brought me flowers. Does that mean I'm the one

Shana was talking about? Or is it just an excuse for messing up my work plans?

"Yeah, if you saw it."

I take a deep breath. That was a mistake. He's standing in the doorway to the kitchen, close enough that his woodsy vanilla scent fills my nostrils. "Well, I'm not mad. I guess if you didn't want to be with Shana, that's not something I can force."

"Ok." He sounds like he wants more.

"And I spoke to Coach. He says my job is safe."

"Good. That's really good. But what about the rest?"

I resist the urge to ask him what rest. I watched the video too many times. I know exactly what he means.

"She said... that you're in love with someone." I toy with one of the stems of the roses. There are no thorns.

"Yes."

He moves forward, and I finally allow myself to look up at him.

"Did you..." My palms are getting sweaty. "Did you mean me?"

"Yes." His voice is husky, but he still looks nervous.

"Oh." My insides flutter and tingle. Then what he said earlier hits me. "You quit the team?" I furrow my brow.

"Yes."

"For... me?"

"Yes."

"Oh." Everything is spinning and I try to make sense of it all.

"Faye?" He sounds breathless.

"Yes?"

"You still haven't told me what you think."

"Are you sure you want to quit the team? You love hockey. And you have your teammates, and..."

He steps forward so close I can breathe him in. "Fuck hockey, Faye. Tell me you feel the same." His hands are on my waist.

I nod.

"Thank fuck." The relief in his voice is almost painful as he leans in to kiss me.

His lips are soft and demanding, desperate. I wrap my arms around his neck and answer his kiss. It's been way too long since I tasted him. He holds me tight and kisses me as if I'm much needed oxygen.

"Liam?" I murmur against his lips.

"Yeah?" He buries his face against my neck.

"Did you really quit hockey for me?"

He nods. "You drive me crazy, Roses." He inhales deeply. "I can't get you out of my mind. I tried to forget about you. I tried not to be in love with you, but I couldn't."

"Liam." I kiss his cheek. He gave up hockey for me.

"I'm really glad you set me up with Shana, though. She's a good friend. I was up most of the night talking to her and after you and Cora left on that motorcycle, I gathered the team and spoke to them."

"What did you say?" The nerves are back now. Does everyone know what we've been up to?

"I told them that I suck at picking women. They agreed. And I talked about how I've been trying not to get into another relationship. I explained that everything with Shana was fake. That's when I told her to upload the video. And then I told them how I can't get you out of my mind."

"Did you..." I steel myself for the answer. "Did you tell them we've been sleeping together?"

He shakes his head. "No. I wouldn't do that. But I asked them what I should do. I told them that I need you, and that I'm terrified. But they all told me to go for it."

"You asked them about me? What if they would have said no?"

"I would have done it anyway."

"You still would have quit hockey for me? Even if they had told you not to?"

"Yes. But I had to talk to them first. Because they're my team, you know."

I nod. I do know. I've seen the bond they all have and I know what the Lions mean to each and every one of them.

"I never wanted you to quit hockey. What happens if one day you start resenting me for it?"

He shakes his head and holds me tighter. "I lost out on like four games. I was always going to quit hockey. You just sped things up a bit. But here's the thing." He leans back so he can look me in the eyes. "I can't stop thinking about you. When you broke it off, it was worse than any torture I can imagine. It was a million times worse than losing the most important game. You still haven't actually told me how you feel, but if there's one chance in a million that it could ever be us, please give me a chance."

I drop my hands from his neck and put them around his torso instead, then I lean my cheek against his chest.

"I missed you so much. I only ended it because I was falling for you. Because you started to mean too much to me."

"So you'll go out on a real date with me?"

I smile. "In front of people?"

"Yes, no more sneaking around."

I nod. "Yeah, I'll go on a date with you."

"I can't wait." He starts to pull away.

"Liam?"

"Yeah?"

"I don't want to wait until our date."

Our eyes meet, and it takes a couple of seconds for his to darken as he understands what I'm saying.

"I'm going to make you scream my name."

I smile and take his hand. "Come on, then."

Chapter 58 – Intense and sweaty

Faye

I close the door to my room and can barely breathe.

Liam is here again. His presence fills the space, and I'm full of anticipation. I've missed him. I've missed his hands on my body, his breath in my ear as he takes me. The feeling of him between my legs.

He stands right in front of me and raises a hand to my cheek.

"I'm sorry it took me so long to realize what was going on."

"You said that you don't want to do relationships."

He lowers his mouth until I can feel his warmth against my lips.

"I was a fucking idiot. I thought, because my previous relationships turned out to be... bad, the next one would too." His lips flutter against mine.

I twist uncomfortably as his hand caresses my cheek.

"Cora may have looked into you." I feel kind of bad I never told him.

He straightens a little. "She did?"

I nod.

His eyes narrow. "What did she find out?"

"Well, she met Eve, and told me she was... a bitch. Her exact words were that she's a genuine evil bitch."

He tilts his head. "I'd like to say she's wrong. But I don't know that I can."

I take a shaky breath. "And she went to Rivers and found out what Kaitlynn did."

He nods. "Right, so now you know exactly what a loser I am when it comes to picking girlfriends."

He turns away and his shoulders slump.

"Well... You.... You also picked me." I walk up to him and touch his arm. As I lean forward, I see a small smile on his face.

"I guess I did. Although I really tried not to." He turns and grabs my waist. "Fuck, but I tried to stay away from you. I guess all it took was one night, and I was lost."

"Too bad I can't remember a thing we did that night."

"It doesn't matter. We'll have plenty of nights to make up for it."

I smile and pull at his t-shirt. "How about we start right now?"

He smiles back and kisses me. "Your wish is my command."

Within a few seconds, his shirt is on the floor and his pants aren't far behind. I grab my own shirt and he gasps as I pull it over my head.

"I'm going to worship these tits." His hands cover my bra and it's my time to gasp. I back up until I hit the wall.

One thumb sneaks its way under the bra and strokes over my nipple, making it instantly hard. He leans in and kisses the soft skin. I grab his head and entangle my fingers in his hair. He pulls down the bra and his mouth kisses a trail toward my nipple.

I hold on as my knees go weak and my heartbeat races. His tongue carefully circles my nipple before he takes it in his mouth.

"Liam," I groan and arch against the wall to present myself to him.

"Mmm." His mouth is full, but his hands make their way to my pants. He sucks and teases and before I know it, I'm stepping out of my pants.

He pulls at my underwear, breaking them in the process. I don't give a fuck as he slides a finger between my lips. I gasp. Then he stands up and breathes heavily. His hands are on either side of my head, leaning against the wall.

"Faye, I need you." He sounds desperate and there's a light sheen of sweat on his forehead.

I nod. "I need you too." My core is aching to be filled.

He shakes his head. "No, you don't understand." His arms shake. "I'm struggling so bad to not take you right this second. I've never neglected foreplay before."

I smile at his discomfort, then I reach forward and take his cock in my hand. His entire body shivers and he closes his eyes. I pull him closer and lift my leg so I can wrap it around his hip.

"Liam," I whisper into his ear as I line him up. "I don't need any more foreplay. Fuck me. Now."

I've barely said the words before he plunges into me. Deep and hard. I cry out and throw my head back. It's intense. It's a wave of pleasure. And he's mine.

He groans into my ear as he presses me into the wall. I grab the back of his shoulders and hold him as tightly as I can. My lips lock on his neck and I mark him. He's mine and the entire fucking world will know.

"Faye." He's shaking, and for a moment, I think he already came. Then he starts to move. Long, slow movements that relish in our closeness.

"Liam."

"You're so fucking perfect."

He thrusts into me again and again.

"Fuck, yes," I say and grab his face in my hands. I kiss him and ease his lips open with my tongue. His tongue greets mine and we explore frantically as the pace picks up. He lifts me up and drops me on the bed.

"Spread your legs for me."

I feel empty and needy and ready to do anything for him. I don't even feel embarrassed when his eyes study my open pussy and he smirks. "So fucking perfect."

Then he's on top of me, filling me up once again. There's no slowness this time. He is frenzied as he fucks me and I need it all.

The orgasm builds and builds until he opens his eyes.

"I'm close," I whisper. "Keep going."

He does as I ask. Sweat shining on his brow. "Say my name, Faye. Scream my name as you come on my cock."

I gasp and try to catch my breath under his hectic movements.

"Liam. Liam." I clutch at his shoulders as something releases inside me and pleasure washes over me. "Liam." I'm vaguely aware of being too loud, but it doesn't matter. I say his name once more as he twitches and buries himself deep, prolonging my orgasm.

"Liam," I whisper as he collapses on top of me. His breathing is heavy. He tries to roll off me. I hold on and stop him. "Wait," I say and enjoy the feeling of his body covering mine.

"I'm crushing you," he says, but doesn't move.

"I like it. I like being close to you."

He laughs into my hair and hugs me tightly. Then he rolls over and pulls me on top of him.

"How's that?" he asks.

"Pretty good," I say, and snuggle into him.

His hands trail down my back and one hand reaches my ass. "I like this," he says after a while.

"My ass?"

"Lying here with you. It's my favorite part."

I raise my head and look at him. "But you always left."

His cheeks redden. "I couldn't stay or I would have revealed my feelings."

I blink at him. Still laying on top of him, I rest my chin against my hands. "So you're saying that if I managed to keep you in bed longer, you would have confessed, and we wouldn't have had to go through this not knowing part?"

He places his hands on the sides of my face. "I thought you only wanted sex. You were so professional at the Den."

I shake my head. "No, I wasn't. I was barely keeping it together."

He holds me tight again. "It doesn't matter now. Now, you're mine. And I love you."

My stomach flips. "I love you, too."

I shift to get more comfortable and feel something against my thigh. Smiling to myself, I place my hands on his chest and push off until I'm straddling him.

"You don't mind, do you?" I ask and smile as I reach down and grab his cock.

His smile is beaming. "You can do whatever you want with me."

So I do.

Chapter 59 – No more playing

Liam

I still can't believe my luck.

I'm sitting in the stands watching a hockey game instead of playing, and I couldn't be happier. Faye keeps giving me worried glances, and I wish I could relay to her how utterly, ridiculously happy I am with her.

I know she's worried I'll regret quitting the team, but honestly, I don't. Not even a bit.

"You know, I knew you guys would end up together." Morgan is sitting with us, looking smug. "I told Lily you would."

"No, you didn't." Faye laughs.

"Tell them, Lily. Didn't I predict this would happen?"

Lily nods. "She did. I remember. It was just after you started working here."

I frown.

Faye gapes at Morgan. "How did you know?"

Morgan grins. "Because I saw you that first night. You were both drunk as fuck, but there was something there."

Faye goes pale. "You saw us?"

Morgan rolls her eyes. "You walked right past me. I was downstairs, getting something to eat, when you burst in, laughing and kissing."

"Sorry about that," I say, trying desperately to remember that first night.

"Yeah, I was a bit worried you were going to keep me up all night. Turns out, you didn't."

Faye leans forward. "What do you mean?"

"You," she points to me, "pretty much tore her clothes off on the stairs. I waited a while before going back up. I got her clothes and figured I'd at least leave them outside of your door so she could find them in the morning."

I clear my throat. "Sorry about that."

"My clothes weren't outside the door," Faye says. "I got dressed in the room."

"Yeah," Morgan continues. "Because when I got up there, the door was still open."

My insides freeze and I stare at Faye. What did we do? "We left the door open?"

Morgan nods. "And you were both in bed when I noticed. Sleeping."

I relax.

"Wait, what?" Faye says.

"Yup, as far as I know, nothing happened that night. You got undressed, cuddled in bed, and fell asleep."

"What do you mean, cuddled?" I ask suspiciously.

"I should have taken a picture," Morgan sighs. "If it wasn't such a breach of privacy, I would have. You looked adorable. All entangled in each other and cutesy."

"Wait." I squeeze Faye's hand. "Are you saying that we didn't have sex that first night?"

"You most definitely did not," Morgan says. "At least not when I saw you. You fell asleep so quickly, there was no time, and you were both wearing underwear. Thank god. I just left her clothes in the room and closed the door. Then I went to sleep."

I look at Faye, and she looks astonished. Our eyes meet and she slowly smiles. I do as well.

"Our whole relationship started because of something that never happened," she says.

"I guess so," I say. "Thank fuck it did." I pull her closer and put my arm around her shoulders.

I'm vaguely aware of someone taking our photo. I don't care. I lean in and kiss her, showing the whole world that she's mine.

"You know there's going to be headlines, right?" Faye asks.

I nod. "Washed up hockey star chooses love."

She shakes her head. "You're not washed up."

"I don't care. I'm ready to start a new chapter in my life."

The crowd around us goes wild. The Lions scored and are now in the lead.

"I like it in the stands," I say. "I get to spend more time with you." I move to kiss her again, but she keeps it to just a quick peck.

"I still work here, you know." She says and gives me a stern look.

"I'll behave." I remove my arm from her shoulders and turn my attention to the game.

A huge smile takes over my face as she grabs hold of my hand.

My eyes find Coach. He's staring straight at us. I nod in greeting and feel nervous. What if he's figured it out? What if he knows that we broke the rules? Would he fire her? He can't do that anymore, right? I quit.

His mouth curls into a knowing smile and I wonder how much he's been aware of. Why does he look like he knows exactly what's going on here? There is no way he could know about us. Absolutely not.

He gives me a small salute before returning his attention to the game. I'll be fucked. The bastard knew. Smiling, I lift Faye's hand to my lips. As long as her job is safe, nothing else matters. All I want is for my girl to be happy.

"I love you," I whisper to her.

Her smile is all I need to know we'll be very happy together.

"I love you, too."

I'm the luckiest man in the world.

Thank you so much for reading Just One Pucking Night!

Have you read all the books in the UNI Lions series?

Just a Pucking Prank

Just a Pucking Grumpy Goalie

Just a Pucking Kiss

Just Pucking Money

Just One Pucking Night

If you want early access to more UNI Lions books please visit reamstories.com/sofiamkay[1] where you can also find exclusive short stories.

Have a wonderful day!

Milton Keynes UK
Ingram Content Group UK Ltd.
UKHW042000291124
451915UK00004B/349

9 798230 573104